D1296702

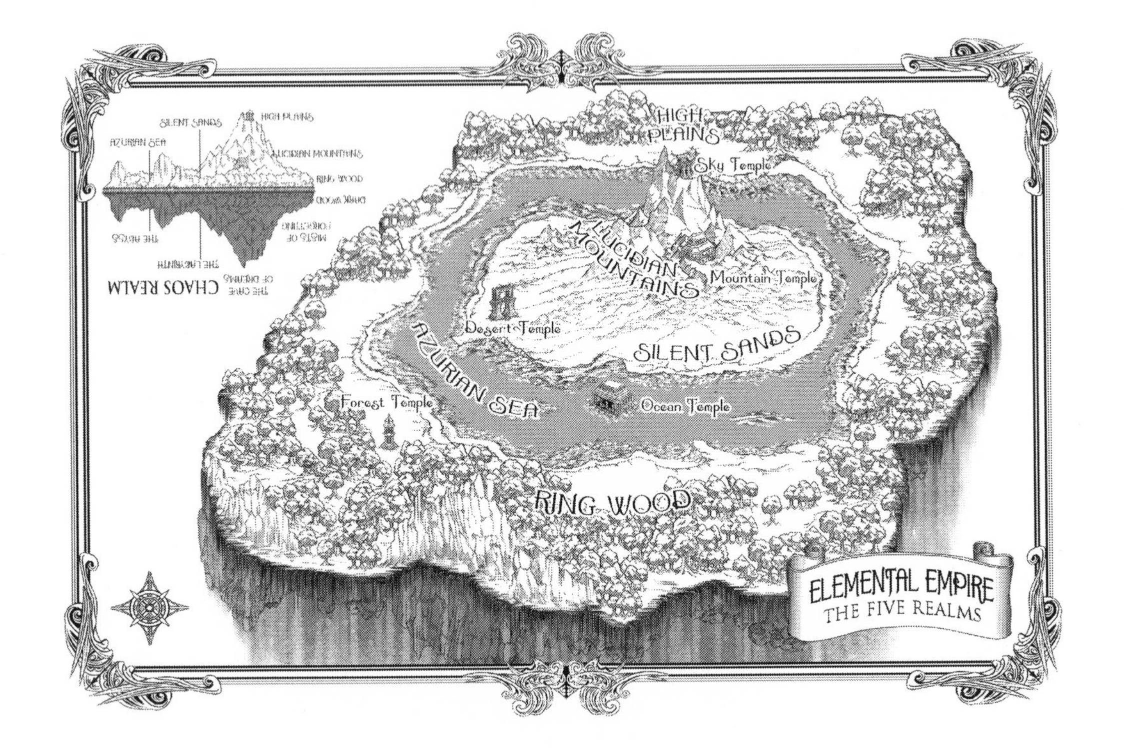
ELEMENTAL EMPIRE
THE FIVE REALMS
HIGH PLAINS
Sky Temple
LUCIDIAN MOUNTAINS
Mountain Temple
Desert Temple
SILENT SANDS
AZURIAN SEA
Ocean Temple
Forest Temple
RING WOOD
SILENT SANDS
HIGH PLAINS
AZURIAN SEA
LUCIDIAN MOUNTAINS
RING WOOD
DARK WOOD
MISTS OF FORGETTING
THE ABYSS
THE LABYRINTH
THE CAVE OF DREAMS
CHAOS REALM

Elemental Empire

Peter North

Peter North

This is a work of fiction. Names, characters, places, and incidents either are the product of the author's imagination or are used fictitiously. Any resemblance to actual persons, living or dead, events, or locales is entirely coincidental.

First e-book edition May 2022

First paperback edition May 2022

Cover design by Andrew Dobell — www.creativeedgestudios.co.uk

ISBN 978-1-990306-10-5 (paperback)

www.peternorthauthor.com

Contents

Chapter 1

I opened the back door of the restaurant to the dirt parking lot out back and swore under my breath. I knew I shouldn't have agreed to pick up the extra shift. The dull-gray sky I'd driven under to get here had darkened to the ripe, purple-black color of a fresh bruise. Wind stirred the tangy ozonized air into little dust devils that spun across the empty lot and flung bits of gravel and sticks at my truck, leaving marks on the freshly washed black paint.

A few fat drops splattered onto the dusty ground, creating clots of mud I had to dodge around as I ran to the vehicle. Figures. I had even shelled out an extra fifteen bucks for the premium wax and polish. I might as well have lit some sage, done a rain dance, and begged for the clouds to piss on me.

I groaned. Why had I taken the shift?

It's not like I needed the work. I'd taken a leave of absence from my consulting business in the city in order to give my mom a hand at home. I'd told my clients she was recovering from a health scare. They'd been very understanding.

I felt a little guilty about lying to them.

In truth, Mom had been drinking. A lot. It was me who was scared, and there was no sign that she was recovering. If anything she was getting worse. I had more than enough money saved up to float me for months if I needed to. But I couldn't stand hanging around my childhood home—glorious pile of trailer park junk that it was—while she drank herself into a stupor and cried herself to sleep. I had never been great at relaxing in the first place, but that was enough to drive anyone insane.

Getting a job had seemed like the perfect solution. I could be "home" without having to be in the house. Maybe I'd even catch up with some of the people I'd gone to school with and brag up my big-city success. Great idea, right?

Too bad the only help-wanted ad I'd been able to find was one for Finger Lickin' Chicken. Story of my life.

The fact that I actually took the job just shows how bad the situation at home really was.

I fumbled my keys out of the hideous pleated pants of the uniform, which probably hadn't been updated since Nirvana was an up-and-coming new band, unlocked the door, and slid onto the cracked leather bench seat of my truck. I'd spent the better part of my salary last year restoring the old International Scout's engine, drive-train, and body, but I hadn't gotten to the interior yet.

I cranked the ignition and listened with satisfaction to the throaty rumble of the restored engine.

Who said money couldn't buy happiness?

That happiness was short-lived as a sour smell drifted into my nostrils. I wrinkled my nose.

The reek of deep-fryer grease and "secret spices" mix—which was basically just salt and pepper and MSG—oozed out of my pores and filled the cab of the truck. The damp air pulled out all the musty-old-upholstery smells a forty-year-old vehicle could hang onto and mingled with the *eau de fast-food* from my uniform to give off the pungent trailer-trash vibe I was desperate to avoid.

This was a nightmare.

I was barely going to have time to get home, shower, and change before I had to pick up Jessika. Now I was going to have to stop at the gas station to grab an air freshener for the truck, too.

As if on cue, my phone buzzed from where I'd thrown it on the passenger seat.

Then I grabbed the phone, put the truck in gear, and checked my messages while I pulled out of the parking lot onto the optimistically named Regal Street. There was the text from Jessika and one from my mom. Mom probably wanted me to swing by the liquor store and grab her another box of Sour Grapes Pinot Grigio. Forget that. I opened Jessika's instead.

It said: Oh no! Rain! We'll have to make new plans!

Shit. I hadn't even considered that. We'd been planning to play a couple of rounds of mini-golf and see a movie. Not exactly a high-class affair, but this was Evergreen Hills—home of dirt roads, oil rigs, and rusty pick-up trucks—not Denver. It was the best I could come up with on short notice.

To be honest, when I'd run into Jessika at the grocery store last weekend I hadn't expected to ask her out. And I sure as hell hadn't expected her to say yes.

Everything about this situation felt like a flashback to some pre-pubescent wet dream, right down to the ache in my groin at seeing her profile pic on my phone.

I had been dreaming of a date with Jessika "It's-not-Jessica-it's-Jeh-SEEK-ah" Lambert since seventh grade. Even back then I'd thought her name was laughably pretentious for a kid from Evergreen Hills. But Jessika's wavy auburn hair, milky white skin, and crystal blue eyes had a way of making me forget about it. That and the fact that she was the first girl in our grade to need a real bra, so she could have been called Steve for all I cared. By the time we hit high school, her curves were the stuff of locker room legend.

Not that it mattered. Until last weekend I'd have put money on Jessika never even knowing my name. She came from one of the wealthiest families in this pissant town and I'd never been anything but a skinny trailer-park reject. We might as well have lived on two different planets. And now...

I stared at her image on my screen from the corner of my eye. It had been taken at the beach, the kind of profile pic girls obsess over to give just the right impression of their lifestyle-of-choice. Jessika was wearing a retro, pin-up style bathing suit that pretended to be modest while the cut accentuated her curves in ways that made my mind wander. Her rich reddish-brown hair was pulled up in a messy bun, pouty red lips posed for the camera, and mounds of creamy cleavage spilled out of the top of the suit and begged me to bury my face into—

Shit, I almost missed my turn.

The road had turned into a greasy mud slick in the downpour and I slid around the corner like a rally driver. So much for impressing Jessika with the shiny new bodywork on the old Scout. Guess I was going for the mud-drag look, instead.

I sent a quick text back to Jessika: *Yeah, too bad. Any suggestions?*

The rain came down in sheets now, buffeted by howling winds, and despite the best efforts of my windshield wipers, I could barely see the sign to Pine Ridge. The "mobile home park," as my mother liked to call it, was, if possible, even dumpier than when I'd left. I'd offered to set her up with an apartment in the city, or to buy her a nicer townhouse in the new development on the east side of Evergreen Hills, but she'd refused. That was the home my father had bought for her and that's where she was staying.

Never mind that we hadn't seen the asshole since I was in diapers.

I glanced back at my phone again, my chest tight. I felt like a nervous teenager getting ready for his first date. Somehow, despite the fact that I'd moved to Denver, started my own business, made a bunch of money, and dated dozens of beautiful women in the past eight years, being in Evergreen Hills made me feel like that same skinny loser I had been in high school. Waiting for Jessika's reply made my palms sweat against the steering wheel.

To distract myself, I decided I might as well check the message from my mom. I could honestly say that it was too late to go get her more booze if I was going to make it to my date on time. The red notification on my message app glared at me accusingly. I sighed and opened it.

It read: I'm so sorry.

Great. Way to be cryptic, Mom. She was probably in one of her morose drunks where she blamed herself for everything from my father leaving to not being able to keep her roses alive through the winter. Sometimes she'd call me when I was in the city and cry over the phone about how she'd ruined my life. That made me feel worse than anything. No matter how well I did for myself, for some reason, in her mind I was 'ruined.' Some people just wanted to be unhappy.

My phone buzzed. Jessika said: *I have a couple of ideas...*

The blood rushed out of my head so fast I saw spots before my eyes. Sure, I had some ideas about how to spend a raining evening with a red-headed bombshell, too. What were the chances she was thinking the same thing? Christ, she knew how to yank a guy's chain. I threw the phone back on the passenger seat and tugged my pants into a more comfortable position.

The trees in the wooded area surrounding the trailer park were bent nearly sideways in the wind and gusts of rain drenched my windshield like someone was dumping buckets on me from the roof of the truck. Screw mini-golf and movies. This was definitely the kind of night I'd rather spend getting to know Jessika Lambert a little more intimately.

I slowed down as I crossed over the cattle guard at the entrance to Pine Ridge, not because I was worried about the truck, but because Oli Jenkins, the park superintendent, would give me hell if I so much as made the gate rattle. Normally, I'd punch the gas and roar past his unit just to piss him off. When I'd gotten home from work yesterday, I'd hammered down as I hit the cattle guard and Old Oli had come tearing out of the double-wide, plaid bathrobe flapping behind him, shaking his quad footed cane at me like a poleaxe, and screaming "Logan Greenwood, this is the last time!"

I snickered as I snuck past his trailer. The blue-white glow of his television flickered through the slatted blinds and I imagined the scare I might give him if I blasted the horn right outside his living room window. I didn't have time to play games with the old man tonight, though, even if he'd been giving me a hard time since I was a kid.

I would never understand why Mom insisted on staying in Pine Ridge. She never said so, but I had a feeling that my father had set her up pretty well before he took off. Despite not having a job, she always had enough money for pad fees and bills, groceries, and booze. As a kid, she'd paid for team registrations and sports equipment, online classes for anything that struck my fancy. But she refused to leave the dilapidated old trailer we'd been living in for my entire twenty-eight years of existence. If she'd been able to afford to move us out of Pine Ridge, and refused to do it, maybe in a way she *had* ruined my life.

Maybe, if we'd lived in a nicer part of town, Jessika would have noticed me back then. Instead, I'd gone through school as a nobody. The rich kids thought I was a poor kid and the poor kids thought I was weird.

The better part of my pre-teen and teenage years had been a lonely, living hell.

I'm so sorry.

I gritted my teeth as I steered around the corner onto the narrow road between the last row of trailers in the park. The trees whipped back and forth behind the faded gray siding of our unit. Mom's garden—mostly weeds these days—was being flattened by the wind and rain. Puddles formed around the concrete foundation of the cracked basement the trailer sat on. I'd have to check to make sure we didn't have any leaks.

Forget it. I pushed the thought out of my head. I had a date with the girl of my dreams. I'd deal with my drunk mother and leaky basements tomorrow. The tires crunched on gravel as I turned onto the driveway. My phone buzzed again from the passenger seat. I reached for it with a tightness in my chest.

Jessika texted: *How about we stay in tonight? My place.*

A notification for a photo message came through immediately after. My throat went dry.

When someone called out my name in the produce section of Bigway Foods last Saturday, and I looked up to see Jessika's sparkling blue eyes staring at me, I completely froze. It took me half a minute to remember that I had grown six inches, gained thirty pounds of muscle, and built a six-figure business since the last time I'd seen this girl. For an instant, I became that skinny, pimple-faced runt again, and the words I wanted to say stuck in my throat.

It was with an almost inhuman feat of willpower that I shook off that moment and remembered who

I was now, not who I was back then, and gave her the smile I reserved for clients with deep pockets. She melted like vanilla ice-cream. Before long, we were chatting like old friends. I managed to avoid mentioning that I was staying with my mom at the trailer park and that I'd taken a part time job at Finger Lickin' Chicken. She gushed about how she'd heard I was back in Evergreen Hills and that she'd been hoping to run into me.

At first, I'd been confused. I didn't keep personal social media accounts. Then I realized she'd probably followed my Greenwood Consulting page. Money talks, and it had always been the language Jessika Lambert understood best. I'd known there was a buzz when I made Denver's Entrepreneur of the Year Award a couple of months ago. I'd secretly hoped the news would make it back to Evergreen Hills, and maybe make a few people jealous.

Petty? Sure. But I had years of social invisibility to make up for and I still craved the approval of the people who'd failed to acknowledge me as a kid.

The look in Jessika's eyes when I'd asked her out had felt even better than holding that award and cashing the reward check. Yeah, maybe I needed to spend some of that extra money on therapy. So sue me. Every high school loser wants to have their rising phoenix moment, rebirth from the ashes, blah, blah, blah.

Now, pulling into the driveway of my mother's run down mobile home, I was staring, open-mouthed, at my own rising phoenix moment.

The photo was of Jessika in a thin white tank top and tiny pajama shorts. Her hair fell loose around her pale shoulders and she had a cute pair of over-sized, thick-rimmed glasses on, like she was ready to relax for the evening. She had twisted her torso to give me a glimpse of both her front and back. The lace at the bottom of her shorts barely covered her ass cheeks. The tank top stretched tight across her breasts, as round and firm as a couple of melons. Through the thin fabric of the shirt, I could see the pink shadow of areolas and the hard points of her nipples straining to be released from their gauzy prison.

"Fuck." The word slipped out of my mouth like a moan.

Another message said: *Don't be late!*

There was a crunch as I clipped the mailbox with the corner of the Scout's front bumper. I dropped the phone and slammed on the brakes, slapping the steering wheel with both hands. I swore again, louder this time. "Fuck!"

I turned off the truck, picked the phone up off the floor, kicked the door open, and stumbled out into the rain to assess the damage. With the darkening sky, water gusting into my face, and the dim glow of the porch light, it was impossible to see anything. I kicked the driver's side tire in frustration and stomped up to the house.

I couldn't decide if this was the best day of my life, or the worst.

If Jessika's photo wasn't just an evil tease and she actually had something fun planned for us tonight, I'd have to go with 'best.' If she was playing with me and I just put a dent my new bumper for nothing I was going to be seriously pissed.

Did that make me shallow? An asshole? Desperate? Maybe. Then again, Jessika hadn't been interested in me until I'd become one of Colorado's youngest self-made millionaires, so what did that make her? I'd been with women as beautiful as Jessika before, but this was a conquest I'd been dreaming of since before I could summon a boner. I wasn't going to let a little thing like pride get in my way.

Lightning flashed across the sky and a crack of thunder rattled the windows of the old trailer. I pulled the storm door out of the way and leaned on the door into the kitchen. The wood of the door was old and rotting up from the bottom, but I hadn't been able to convince Mom to let me fix it. It was like she couldn't even see the world she lived in anymore, she was so stuck inside her head.

From the living room, someone on the TV was rambling on about English gardens. Whenever she was really depressed, for some reason Mom's self-punishment of choice was HGTV. From the kitchen I could see her feet up on the couch, wrapped in a quilted blanket. She was probably asleep.

I tossed my jacket on the back of one of the dining room chairs and tip-toed down the hallway toward the bathroom. The old trailer creaked and groaned as the winds picked up outside. I showered as quickly as I could. If the weather was going to get much worse, I wanted to hurry. That and the half-naked babe had told me not to be late, and I wasn't the kind of man who argued with half-naked babes, even if they did only like me for my money. If it was good enough for actors, musicians, and politicians, it was good enough for me.

I inspected my chin in the foggy mirror and decided I'd go for rugged stubble over a clean shave to match my mud-spattered truck. I was in Evergreen Hills, after all. I didn't have to look like a clean-cut businessman here. Maybe, if my date with Jessika went well, I'd invite her to go camping with me next weekend. I hadn't been out on the land in far too long. What was that joke about sex while camping?

It was fucking in tents. Ha.

Good job, Logan. I shook my head. You're about to meet up with your scantily clad high school crush and you're thinking about camping. Definitely time to spend on some therapy.

I splashed a little aftershave on my throat, just for effect, wrapped a towel around my waist and headed for my bedroom.

Or as I liked to call it "The Shrine to Logan's Misspent Youth."

My mother had kept my room exactly as I'd left it when I moved out. The walls, instead of being covered with posters of hot girls, motorcycles, or heavy metal bands, were plastered in Certificates of Achievement for every extra credit course or online class I'd ever completed. I had medals for all the sports I'd attempted over the years. Participation medals for the team sports where I was a VIP bench warmer, naturally. But I'd also collected some golds and silvers in solo events like archery and fencing. The bib number from my first Iron Man Triathlon hung over the twin sized bed that still had my favorite comforter on it, patterned after the elvish runes created by the grandfather of modern fantasy, J.R.R. Tolkien. Floor-to-ceiling bookshelves filled the far wall, stuffed with every Sci-Fi and Fantasy series I had room for. And on the bedside table, there was a photo of me, as a toddler, with my mother and my father holding me and smiling happily as if nothing in the world could tear their little family apart.

I still felt more at home in this room than I did in my fashionably minimalist luxury condo in downtown Denver. No matter how much I tried to distance myself from the person I was in the past, I knew the person I'd become was nothing more than a shell, a suit of armour I wore to protect that nerdy, friendless kid from the realities of the world.

I sat down on the edge of the bed and picked up the photo of me and my parents. Tears stung my eyes. I cursed and wiped them away with the back of my hand. But I didn't put the photo down. Another flash of lightning illuminated my walls and thunder rumbled overhead like the old gods were angry.

My mother had been so beautiful, with an ephemeral quality to her that would have been more at home in Middle Earth than in Pine Ridge trailer park. My father was a handsome man, too. Wise, understanding eyes, a strong jaw, just the hint of a smile playing at the corner of his mouth like there was some joke only he knew about.

Well, the joke was on us. He left three months after that photo was taken, and he never came back. This room was evidence of an entire childhood spent trying to make up for whatever was lacking in me that had made him leave. I strove so hard to be good at everything I did. Not just good, but the best. And yet every victory I'd ever won had been hollow. It had never been enough for me. Because the person whose approval I was so desperate for wasn't here, and he wasn't coming back.

How's that for needing therapy? Pathetic.

I yanked the towel out from under me and dried my hair. Then I reached for the duffle bag containing all the clothes and toiletries I'd brought from the city and pulled out a pair of gray hiking pants and a plain black t-shirt. No need to overdress if I planned on getting undressed as soon as I got to Jessika's place. Though some of the magic of my upcoming date seemed to have washed away in this fit of melancholy. Would this conquest be just another hollow victory?

Christ, I was as bad as my mother.

I slipped on a pair of trail runners, pulled a lightweight jacket out of my closet, and I headed to the living room to say goodbye to Mom.

The air had a strange, charged feeling to it, as if static was building up before the next lightning strike. I hoped we weren't about to get hit by a tornado. Everyone knows trailer parks are tornado magnets. Maybe I should tell Mom to go sleep it off in the leaky basement, just in case.

"Mom?" I called out, just as another rumble of thunder came to a tooth-rattling crescendo above the roof. "I'm going out. Are you gonna be okay with the storm?"

She didn't answer. The TV nattered on about roses. A surge of electricity made the lightbulbs in the hallway and the kitchen flare brighter. The bulb over my head burst with a pop and the lights went out. The television went silent.

Fantastic. Just what I needed. Anything else the universe wanted to throw my way?

I muttered to myself as I got my phone out and turned on the flashlight app. I banged my shin on the coffee table before I got the stupid thing working.

Mom was still asleep on the couch. Passed out, more likely. Dead to the world, with a blanket wrapped up around her shoulders and an empty wine glass next to her hand where it had slipped out from under the cover and dangled on the floor.

"Mom?" I said again.

A chill crept up my spine. The air in the room seemed to buzz and hum like the TV was still getting juice but all its circuits had been fried. What the hell was going on here?

Dead to the world, I thought again. My stomach dropped. I fell to my knees next to the couch and put my hand against her cheek.

It was cold.

I'm so sorry...

I heard her voice, like she was whispering in my ear from somewhere very far away. All thoughts of my date with Jessika evaporated.

Dead. My mother was dead. My throat tightened and I screamed out for someone, anyone.

But no one could have heard me over the storm.

My fingers tingled where they touched the cold, marble flesh of my mother's face. I pulled my hand away and bright, golden sparks jumped from her skin to my fingertips.

"What the hell?—" More golden sparks exploded from the surface of her skin, swirling in a whirlwind around her body. I stumbled backward, and tripped over the coffee table. My phone clattered to the floor and the flashlight disappeared into the cheap vinyl floorboards.

It was as if the golden sparks were dissolving my mother's body, like she was breaking apart into tiny flecks of glowing light and floating away. I reached out my hands to touch her again, to grasp her, and hold her here with me.

The tingling intensified, and I stared in horror as my own fingers began to break into bits of glittering gold. The sparks whipped around us both like a miniature version of the storm raging outside.

My body jolted with electrical energy and the sparks twisted in a frenzy around us. My mother's body had all but disappeared.

Before my eyes, my own body faded until it was a transparent, glittering ghost of itself.

And when the last spark of light disappeared, the world I knew disappeared with it.

Chapter 2

When I awoke, it was night. Cool dew soaked through my T-shirt and chilled my skin, but the night air felt warm and humid, almost tropical. I lay on my back, staring up at a deep blue sky full of stars like pin-pricks in a piece of thin fabric. Swirls of colored clouds wove between the clusters of stars the way I'd only seen in photographs of the Milky Way taken with a long exposure. The moon hung directly above me like a spotlight, full and bright, echoed on each side by opposing crescents. I blinked my eyes, trying to bring it into focus.

I must have hit my head or something, because the triple vision didn't go away. Fireflies danced into view and swirled around my head like they were urging me to get up. They reminded me of something, but I couldn't quite put my finger on what it was.

I groaned and tried to roll onto my side. What had happened? Where was I?

I remembered leaving the restaurant and the storm whipping up as I drove home. I remembered getting ready for my date with Jessika.

Shit. She was going to be pissed if I stood her up.

An image of an auburn-haired beauty in barely-there pajamas rose in my mind.

Had I been there? Had we been drinking? Maybe that was why I couldn't remember.

I wasn't much of a drinker. Never had much taste for it after watching Mom wash herself away with the stuff.

Mom...

Something about her. She was in trouble... She was—

My heart smashed like a hammer against my ribcage. Panic cloyed in my chest, but I couldn't remember anything.

I pushed myself onto my knees and stood slowly, in case I did have some kind of head injury. I felt around my skull, probing tentatively with my fingers.

Nothing hurt.

I turned in a slow circle, taking in my surroundings. Trees loomed above me like a circle of sentinels. I stood in the center of a clearing, surrounded by a dark forest. The grass beneath my feet was lush, like a carpet of green velvet. Little white flowers grew in clumps here and there, their tiny faces pointed up at the moon.

Moonlight streamed down on the clearing in pale, white beams, so bright that I could see moths and other nocturnal insects fluttering around in them. I stared up at the moon again and blinked. I shook my head and tried again.

Nope.

There were three moons. One large and full, and two similarly sized moons on either side, in waxing and waning phases as if the bigger, closer moon were casting a shadow on them.

I must be dreaming, I thought. That would explain why I couldn't remember how I got here. It would explain the vague sense of unreality that permeated this place. The alternative was that I'd gone insane, which... well, if that was the case, there was no sense worrying about it.

The trees at the edge of the clearing weren't like the trees I knew in Colorado. These were massive, ancient-looking giants that would have taken ten of me to link arms around. The circle of sky above was so small that it was a miracle I'd woken up when the moon was directly above. If it was moving at a similar rate of speed to Earth's moon, that meant I only had an hour or two before it dipped below the treeline and I was plunged into darkness.

Whether I was dreaming or mad, that was an infuriating little detail for my mind to have invented. I didn't want to be stranded in the middle of a strange forest with nothing but the light of fireflies to guide me. I felt around my pockets for my phone, but I knew it wasn't there. I'd dropped it somewhere, I remembered. But where?

Inside the clearing, a ring of large gray stones had been placed about halfway toward the centre. With a start, I realized I stood directly in the middle of it, like the hub on an enormous wheel.

More fireflies flickered between the trees and floated toward me, like they were drawn to my presence. I'd gathered a thick cloud of them, shining with a soft bioluminescent glow. They seemed agitated, swarming around me as if to get my attention.

The cloud developed a kind of tail with a trail of fireflies leading from the stone circle and into the trees.

A narrow dirt path lay beneath them. I had a strong sense that they wanted me to follow them.

Why not? I didn't have anything better to do. If my brain was feeding me this hallucination, maybe I had to see it through before I'd be able to wake up again. Then I'd...

What?

My sense of the real world was fading. It was like trying to remember a dream. The longer you're awake the harder it becomes to pin down the details. Except I was sure this must be a dream and it was reality that I was losing touch with.

Okay, then. Follow the fireflies. Made as much sense as anything else. Maybe I'd find the Mad Hatter and be invited to a tea party.

When I stepped out of circle of stones—*summoning circle*, my mind supplied—the fireflies buzzed around me excitedly. The trail of their light thickened into a clear path for me to follow which, I was relieved to see, was supplemented by an actual path on the ground. That gave me some confidence that if my insect escort decided to bail on me for some reason, I'd at least be able to find my way back to the... summoning circle?

Weird. But okay, who was I to argue with my own brain.

I followed the path out of the clearing and into the thick, black murk of the forest. Branches creaked above me in a breeze too high-up to feel. Moths fluttered past my face, drawn to the light of the fireflies. Somewhere in the distance, an owl hooted, a low, mournful cry that made the hairs on the back of my neck stand on end.

I was no stranger to the outdoors. I'd been exploring the forests behind Pine Ridge for my entire life, and I'd graduated to hiking and back-packing in the Rockies. I'd never felt more alive and at one with myself and the world as when I was in the forest.

I stopped dead in my tracks.

Why could I remember that, but not what I'd been doing immediately before I'd come here? I probed my conscious mind for other memories, but nothing revealed itself. I just knew I felt at home here, and that I'd always felt at home in the woods.

Still, I wished I had a weapon of some sort. I didn't want to run into a mountain lion or a bear or anything when I was out here alone. Some food would be good, too. It was warm enough that shelter wasn't too high on my list of immediate concerns, but if I was going to be stuck here for a while that was something I'd have to think about, too.

My ears strained against the ambient noise of the forest. I breathed as shallowly as I could, trying to hear if anything else was moving between the trees nearby. Wind sighed through the leaves far above, and the branches creaked as they rubbed against one another in the wind. The fireflies made faint fluttering noises and little clicks when they ran into each other. But other than the owl, there were no other signs of animal life around me.

I stepped lightly on the path, balancing my weight on the balls of my feet and moving forward in silence. In a forest this size, it would be unlikely that

I was truly alone. That meant there was a very real possibility that I was being watched. Perhaps even followed. Whatever might be out there I hoped it wasn't too much bigger than me.

A branch snapped somewhere in the darkness to my left. I tensed and dropped instinctively into a crouch. Blood pounded in my ears making it harder for me to hear. The movement seemed to rush toward me from the darkness beyond the path. My eyes darted around for something I could use to defend myself. A rock, a stick, anything...

A huge shape burst out of the trees and onto the trail in front of me, scattering the fireflies like bioluminescent confetti. My eyes took in the tawny hide and rippling muscles and massive antlers before my brain processed what I was seeing. A bull elk stood before me, bigger than any I'd ever seen before. Its orb-like brown eyes stared down at me disdainfully, as if I was the one who had disturbed it. The rack on its head must have stretched four feet above it. The tines scraped the bottom branches of the giant trees next to the trail.

The beast lowered its head and fear seized my chest. If it charged, I was a dead man. The thing must have weighed a thousand pounds. It would hit like a steam roller with spikes. I didn't want to leave the path but I edged closer to the trees hoping I'd be able to dodge behind one if I had to.

It stretched its forelegs out in front of it and dipped its head further so that I could see every prong of its antlers and the top of its regal skull. It seemed to be... bowing to me? Maybe this was something male elk did during the rut to challenge a competitor? I didn't know. I didn't even know what month the rut occurred in, or if the months I knew translated in this strange new world. But when the elk didn't attack, I relaxed slightly.

"Easy there, big guy," I said, keeping my voice low and calm. "I don't want any trouble."

The big bull gave a final bow, then stood slowly back up to its full height, like it was acknowledging my words. It blinked at me with its huge round eyes. Then it nodded once, and strode regally into the forest on the other side of the path. I watched as it was enveloped by the darkness once more. I stared after it until its footsteps faded into the undergrowth.

"I don't care what they say about lions," I said to the fireflies. "That there was the king of beasts."

The bugs whirled around me like a glowing tornado before stretching themselves out to illuminate the path once more. I shrugged and carried on. The encounter had been weird, but so was everything else about this place.

The farther along the path I went, the deeper and darker the woods around me became. A damp chill replaced the warm, humid air of the clearing. Goosebumps prickled the flesh of my arms. I wished I'd bothered to put on a jacket before getting sucked into an alternate universe or fantasy dreamscape or whatever this was.

Long pale tendrils of moss dangled from the limbs of the trees overhead. They tugged at my hair and tickled my cheeks as I passed. Perhaps I was imagining it, but it seemed like even the fireflies huddled closer to me now. Eerie clicking noises came from the darkness above and rustling sounds that didn't belong to the trees. I had an apprehensive feeling like something up there was watching me, waiting to pounce.

I swallowed my nerves and carried on. I didn't have much choice. If I was going to get out of this place, the only way to go seemed to be right through the middle. I picked up a fallen branch that lay across the path and hefted it to test its weight. It was heavy and dense, and if I had to clobber something with it, I figured it would at least leave a couple of lumps before it broke. I felt a bit better with it gripped in my hand and I picked up the pace.

After a time—I didn't know how long; I fell into a kind of trance—I came to another clearing. There was no summoning circle here. Only a greasy black pond which rippled in the moonlight as if something lurked just below the surface. I was grateful that my firefly guides steered me well away from the shores of the little lake and whatever lived in it. But I was getting the sense that the forest was becoming darker and weirder the farther along this path I went, and I wondered why the fireflies wanted me to come this way at all.

Then again, maybe I had been an idiot to think the fireflies were leading me anywhere. Maybe they weren't fireflies at all, but miniature will-o-the-wisps luring me to my doom.

A shriek cut through the silence, a sound like metal being twisted and torn. Garbled voices rose from somewhere on the other side of the pond. I hid behind a large tree trunk and peered into the blackness. A warm yellow glow bounced through the trees like a giant firefly. It took me a moment to realize it was a lantern, held aloft on a long pole being carried by a low, broad, lumpy shape that could have been a boulder if it wasn't moving so quickly. A small group of the creatures—whatever they were, they didn't seem to be human—marched through the underbrush, mowing down shrubs and saplings as they plowed ahead. In the midst of the group, the lantern-light caught on something that blazed with a deep, coppery glow. I squinted my eyes and focussed on the shining object.

My breath caught in my throat.

A long braid of auburn hair dangled from something strung between two of the lumpy creatures. I held my breath as they approached and hoped to whatever gods looked over a place like this that it wasn't what I thought it was.

I sidled around the other side of the tree as the troop broke out of the woods and onto the path, about ten yards ahead of me. My firefly entourage dissipated into the trees and many of their lights went out. A couple buzzed and flickered around my head and landed on the tree I was hiding behind. They blinked at me, somehow reassuringly, and then extinguished their lights too.

"I told you it were dis way," one of the shapes grumbled. "You never listen to noffin' I say."

The low, broad-shouldered creatures each wore mottled cloaks of gray and brown that looked like they'd been stitched together out of the hides of rodents. There were two of them, each carrying the end of a long pole. A pale, fleshy shape was strung between them.

The creature in the back carried the lantern pole tucked under one arm so that it shone its light down on their captive. The creature snarled at its companion and said, "That's because most of what you say stinks worse than the shit I took this morning, you bone-headed—"

"Enough!" A voice like crushed gravel hissed out of the darkness. A tall black-robed shape materialized at the edge of the path, hovering just outside the light of the swaying lantern like a spectre. "We will make camp here. Ready the prisoner for questioning."

"Here, my lord?" The lump with the lamp swivelled its head around on its thick rounded shoulders, turning my way. I flinched back, but it looked right through me. The thing had gray, warty flesh and a bulbous nose. Two yellowed tusks jutted from its lower jaw. The one on its right had been broken off, leaving a jagged stump. Large toad-like eyes swiveled in its head, but in the light of the lantern, I could see they were milky with cataracts.

Troll...

The word rose, unbidden, from the depths of my consciousness. Whatever it was, the thing didn't seem to be able to see more than a couple of feet in front of its face. Perhaps why it had been at the back of the group while its friend led the way. It grumbled, "What you want to stop here for?"

The black figure snarled like a rabid wolf. A glint of sharp teeth shone out of the darkness of its oversized hood. "I don't pay you to ask questions. Do as I say."

"Dat's right, Grimstone." The other troll snorted up a gob of mucus and spat onto the path. It grinned over its shoulder at its companion. "You know da rules. He who haff da biggest teeff... uh... makes 'em."

"Shaddap, Flint," the one called Brimstone said. It propped the lantern against a tree and dropped its end of the pole onto the path. The prisoner whimpered. My eyes were drawn away from the monstrous creatures to their poor victim.

I choked back a scream of rage.

A woman, long and lithe with pale white limbs, hung limply from the pole. Her wrists and ankles had been tied tightly with thin, ropey vines that cut into her skin, leaving raw, red flesh at the edges of her bindings. The thick braid of her auburn hair dragged in the dirt. Then the other troll dropped its end of the pole and the woman cried out again. It was the same twisted cry of pain I'd heard earlier.

A wave of anger, hot and urgent, coursed through my veins.

Flint stomped over and kicked her in the spine. She whimpered. The troll spat another gob on the path next to her head. "Quiet yous. Don't want you bringin' the Arachana down on our pretty little 'eads, now do we?"

"Never mind that, you fool." The tall, black shape growled menacingly. "She'll be screaming well into the night once I get my claws into her. Now build me a fire."

The troll, Flint, grumbled to itself. "I hates fire."

I sank into the shadows as the two trolls lumbered around the path, collecting deadfall for their campfire. Or was it meant to be a pyre? I shuddered at the thought. I didn't know who she was, or who her captors were, but there was no way I was going to stand by and watch them torture a helpless woman.

I gripped the heavy branch I'd picked up in my hand and wondered if it would be strong enough to knock out a troll. The fireflies began to buzz and flicker around my head as if sensing my thoughts. I couldn't tell if they were warning me against the plan or encouraging me.

It didn't matter. I already knew what I had to do.

If this was a dream and I died, I'd probably just wake up in my bed—or wherever I'd passed out—and carry on with my normal life. If it wasn't, and I really had been sucked into some kind of parallel world full of sentient insects, trolls, and cloaked monsters... Well, I still had to take a stand. When it came to violence, bullying, and abuse, apathy and avoidance of conflict were just as bad as aggression.

That was probably still true even if the assholes had tusks and teeth like steak knives, although somewhat harder to rally oneself to rise against.

I swallowed hard and crept off the path into the shadows. Slowly I inched my way closer to where the trolls were working, careful to stay out of the light of the lantern. The forbidding figure in the black cloak hovered on the other side of the action, its invisible eyes seemingly pinned on the captive woman.

I took another step and almost snagged my foot on the root of a tree when a couple of fireflies flew into my face and battered themselves against me. I stopped and waved them away.

"What is wrong with you?" I mouthed at them. I had no reason to believe they could read lips, but I felt I had to say something.

Once they had my attention, the tiny glowing lights zipped deeper into the woods and hovered above a dark shape in the undergrowth. I glanced back at the trolls and figured I had a bit of time for a detour, and so far, the lightning bugs hadn't steered me wrong.

Unless we counted leading me into a confrontation with a trio of monsters straight out of an epic fantasy novel. But I was going to give them the benefit of the doubt and assume I was meant to rescue the damsel in distress. As far as fantasy themes went, that one was pretty much never on the list of "optional side quests."

I stumbled ahead, managing to keep the noise to a minimum, until I saw what the fireflies wanted me to find. An ancient, rotted stump rose from the groundcover like a decayed giant's tooth. The stump was uncomfortably close to the greasy black pond I'd avoided on my way up the path. The surface bubbled and frothed as I approached as if it could sense my proximity. Keeping half an eye on the roiling black waters, I inspected the stump. The two fireflies danced excitedly around it, whirling in circles around the center.

A beam of moonlight filtered through the trees and illuminated something hidden inside the rotted tree. A glint of silver made my heart beat faster. I'd wished I had a weapon. Was it possible that the fireflies had found one for me?

I passed the roughshod club to my left hand and, taking a deep breath, reached into the stump with my right. Tentatively, I explored the hollow with my fingers until they touched something. I grabbed and tugged. The object slid out of the old stump as smoothly as a sharp axe through green wood.

I held up my find.

A long, thin blade glinted in my hand, its silver length gleaming in the white light of the three moons. It seemed to absorb the moonlight, growing in intensity until the entire shaft blazed like a beacon. My eyes widened in surprise. I glanced over my shoulder to make sure the trolls and their sadistic leader hadn't noticed the luminous sword.

No sound of alarm came from the camp. The lumpy shadows of the trolls continued to lurch back and forth in the glow of the lantern as they carried branches and logs for the fire. I couldn't see the ominous, black-robed creature, but if they hadn't seen me, it likely still lurked in the shadows, hungrily eyeing its prize.

Satisfied that I was safe, I turned back to inspect the blade.

The metal was lightweight and razor sharp. The hilt fit snugly in the palm of my hand, so perfectly it was almost like it had been moulded for my exact grip. How could that be? Was I destined to carry this weapon? Had it been made for me?

I shrugged. It was a magical, glowing sword. More likely, it shifted its shape to suit whoever wielded it. Nothing could surprise me at this point.

A wet, gurgling noise drew my gaze away from the blade and back to the pond. The surface was bubbling like a cauldron of boiling pitch. My firefly buddies buzzed in my ears and I swatted them away. I backed up, keeping an eye on the water. Whatever was in there, I didn't want to have anything to do with it.

Too bad it didn't feel the same way.

A writhing tentacle exploded out of the pond and whipped toward me like a rope snapping under tension. I screamed in terror and fell backward onto my ass, slashing at the thing like a madman with my glowing sword.

The blade cut through the meaty appendage with a wet *snick*. The remaining section whipped back and forth above the water, spraying droplets of dark purple blood across the clearing. The severed piece coiled around my ankle like a boa constrictor. I whacked at it with my club, trying not to break my shin in the process. Another tentacle burst out of the murky sludge and shot toward me with lightning speed.

Screw that.

I scrambled backward on my hands and feet like a crab, swiping at the thing with my club or my sword depending on which direction it came from. When I was out of reach of the thing, I stumbled to my feet. I backed up, staring at the lake and dragging the remains of the first tentacle through the bushes. A dozen writhing limbs twisted in the moonlight like some kind of obscene swamp squid.

I breathed a sigh of relief when I broke through the undergrowth and onto the safety of the path.

That is, until I realized where I'd come out of the thicket.

A fire blazed in the middle of the path and two goggle-eyed trolls stared at me with their mouths hanging open. Grimstone blinked its milky eyes in confusion, its broken tusk jumping up and down as it tried to form a suitable word. Flint turned its yellow, toad-like gaze on me and grinned. The shifting form of their mysterious leader hovered on the other side of the campfire like a wraith.

Well, that could have gone better. Not exactly the entrance I'd planned to make. I sighed. Oh well. At least I'd wanted to fight these bastards, unlike the creature from the black lagoon.

I hopped on my right foot and speared the last of the slimy purple tentacle on the tip of my sword.

"Calamari, anyone?" I asked, and flung the thing into Flint's face.

The camp erupted into chaos.

Chapter 3

The troll, Flint, bellowed in surprise and whipped its thick, gray arms around in circles. Its fist connected with the back of Grimstone's head and one of the creature's dull, sightless eyes burst out from its skull with a wet pop. The blind troll fell to its hands and knees, grasping desperately at the ground for the missing eyeball. I jumped back, lifting my club into a guarding stance and letting my sword hang loose at my side. I kept my gaze locked on Flint.

Behind them both, the pale limbs of the woman writhed against the ropes binding her to the pole. Her scant clothing had been torn to shreds by the beasts and a deep purple bruise was spreading across the bare flesh of her back where Flint had kicked her. Rage bubbled up inside my chest and burned the back of my throat like bile. I gripped the hilt of the sword tightly. It wasn't gleaming like moonlight anymore, but it hummed in my fingers, like it was looking forward to the fight.

You and me both, I thought grimly.

Flint crouched low and clenched its hands into massive fists. Its mouth spread into an evil grin, its yellowed tusks gnashing in anticipation. “A visitor. I do like visitors. Don’t I, Grimstone?”

“You knocked me bleedin’ peeper right out me ’ead!” Grimstone blinked its remaining eyeball at the ground, sniffing with wide-slit nostrils. It patted the earthy path gingerly. “I oughtta—argh!”

Grimstone’s searching hands found a burning log. The troll lurched backward, screaming and shaking its burning hand, its single eye rolling in its socket with pain. Flint advanced.

The creatures collided and Flint toppled ass-over-end into the flames. A shriek like metal dragging across granite echoed through the forest. The burning troll rolled around on the ground. Tendrils of fire licked up its flesh hungrily and the motley cloak burst into flame. Angry red boils blistered up on its gray flesh everywhere the fire touched it. The troll squealed as its hideous body twitched helplessly.

My lips curled into a cruel smile. If this was a dream, it was turning into a good one. Ever since I was a kid, I’d gotten pent-up aggression out in my sleep, living the life of a hero, if only in dreamland. I knew exactly what to do. My muscles tensed in expectation.

I lunged at Grimstone, swinging the club up and through the troll’s huge, broken-tusked jaw. There was a loud crack, and the troll’s jaw snapped sideways. Its remaining eye rolled backward in its head and it crumpled to a heap next to the woman. It landed with a thud that shook leaves out of the trees.

I felt it in my bones, as if the thing was made of solid stone. The woman had rolled deftly to the side. A handy thing, since I think squishing damsels-in-distress with warty-assed trolls was frowned upon in the Hero Handbook. I noticed she already had one wrist free of her bindings. She might be in distress, but she wasn't completely helpless.

I strode toward the prone body of the unconscious troll. Standing above it, I raised the sword in one hand and drove the razor-sharp point down. I felt a moment of panic as I thrust toward the creature's ribcage with the blade. What if the troll really was made of stone? What its flesh destroyed my only real weapon? But the moment the point connected with Grimstone's gray hide, a burst of light blazed from the sword and the troll exploded in a barrage of heavy, rocklike flesh. I stumbled backward, momentarily stunned.

Then I shook my head and dropped to my knees beside the woman.

"Let me help you," I said, reaching for the vines that imprisoned her ankles.

With her free hand, she touched my wrist. A tingle of energy coursed between us, making my heart skip a beat. She gazed up at me with eyes the color of new spring growth and said, "No. I will be fine. Deal with the other two."

The burned troll still rolled on the ground in agony as the fire did most of the work for me. But where was their black-cloaked leader? It must have slipped away into the darkness when I was distracted by the trolls.

I nodded brusquely to the woman and pushed myself back up to my feet. I held the club like a staff in my left hand and the sword in my right. Black troll blood dripped along the length of the blade, and the sword buzzed eagerly, egging me on toward my next kill.

As I approached the shrieking, still burning troll, I scanned the trees for the hooded figure. It was nowhere to be seen.

I stood over Flint and considered what the most painful way to dispatch it might be. But I could think of nothing worse than the red, blistered flesh the burns had already left across its body. I could just wait for the fire to kill it. The flames licked across its body as if the creature was covered in some kind of flammable oil. Its shrieks bubbled in its chest, growing weaker by the second. I wanted it to suffer after what it had done to the woman.

But I wanted to speak with her more. I slid the blade across its gurgling throat and watched with satisfaction as black blood spilled out on the ground, hissing as it quenched the flames.

With the second troll dead and the mysterious cloaked figure fled, I spun eagerly back to free the auburn-haired beauty.

The woman had managed to get the rest of her bindings undone. Raw red welts burned into the pale flesh of her wrists and ankles. Her long, lean body was now stretched upright. Bruises and lacerations covered her skin, exposed by the tears in her clothing. Her toes dangled inches from the trampled earth path.

But as I stepped toward her, I realized I'd made a terrible mistake.

The black-cloaked figure stood behind her, one of its arms wrapped around the front of her body. A hand, covered in dark, matted fur gripped her throat. Vicious black claws pierced into her moon-white skin. A droplet of blood ran over her clavicle and between her breasts. She clawed at the creature's hairy arm, her green eyes flashing desperately as it tightened its grip on her throat.

My shoulders tensed and the hairs on the back of my neck stood on end as I stared into the black depths of that hood. A flash of something wet and white reflected in the light of the firelight. I pointed my sword at the figure, gripping hard to hide the trembling of my hand.

"Let her go," I said, pushing my voice up from my belly like they taught in business elocution classes. If you want to be powerful, you have to sound powerful. If you want to be respected, you have to command respect. "Or I'll—"

"You'll what?" The thing snarled. Long blade-like teeth glinted from the darkness of the cloak. "Cry over her broken, bleeding body after I tear out her throat and feast on her insides?"

The woman writhed in the monster's grasp. Her pale cheeks flushed red and then purple as she struggled.

My throat went dry. I didn't have anything to say to that. I couldn't approach without risking the creature hurting her even more. I swallowed and opened my mouth to say... what?

For the first time since awaking in this strange new world, I felt true terror. What if this wasn't a dream? What if I hadn't taken things seriously enough and now the woman was going to die?

The woman's green eyes pierced me with a gaze that burned straight through my chest. She dragged at the creature's forearm and gave herself just enough room to suck in some air. It came out in a burst as she rasped two words at me. "The staff!"

Then she let go of her captor's arm and stretched her hands toward me. Without pausing to think about the strange request, I threw the club-like brand toward her grasping fingers. The beast roared and pulled her back, but it wasn't fast enough.

She snatched the club out of the air, and the moment the wood touched her fingers it burst with a glittering green light. The top of the branch swelled into a gnarled knot of wood wrapped around an emerald green stone. She twirled the staff—which is exactly what it had transformed into—in her hands, whipping up a magical whirlwind of energy. The beast dropped her to the path, howling angrily. It crouched low to the ground, using its arms like an extra set of legs as it prowled toward her like a wild animal about to pounce.

The woman squeezed the staff with both white-knuckled hands, and her auburn hair whirled around her in an invisible vortex. The torn shoulder of her tunic—I assumed that's what it had been before her captors had destroyed it—slipped down, exposing her left breast. Yet she no longer looked vulnerable. With the magical weapon in her hands, she exuded raw power, the kind I had only dreamt of obtaining. Though she faced down the demonic creature in black, I took a step back as well.

Her voice rushed from her chest like the violent rustling of leaves in a storm, an insistent hiss. "Be gone, beast. You will not have me tonight."

Crouched on all fours, the monster couldn't hide its true form any longer. The black cowl pulled back to reveal a long, pointed muzzle covered in dark fur. Black lips rippled over dull pink gums and long white teeth. It snarled and backed away, hackles rising beneath its cloak.

It backed straight into the tip of my sword.

The blade hissed as it nicked into the flesh of the werewolf's exposed haunch. The beast yelped like a kicked dog, and whirled its face toward me. Its eyes blazed like molten metal in the darkness. My sword glowed with the blue-white light of the moon. The woman advanced with her staff held aloft, and a green haze of effervescent air swirled over her head. The werewolf snapped at me, its long white teeth flashing dangerously. I jumped back and brandished the blade again.

Its burning eyes darted between me and the mysteriously powerful woman. Then it turned tail and ran into the depths of the forest beyond the path. We stood motionless, listening to the creature crash away through the bushes, until we were sure it was truly gone.

The woman lowered her staff and leaned upon it like a walking stick. Before my eyes, the staff shrank back down until it resembled nothing more than a club-shaped stick. Her lips parted in a languorous smile as her green eyes travelled up and down my body.

I shifted my feet uncomfortably.

"Greetings, stranger." Her voice was low and sweet, like the whisper of a summer breeze through fresh green leaves. I shivered at the sound of it. She licked her lips and winced. A crack bisected her plump bottom lip. She said, "Thank you for your assistance."

"Thank *you*," I said, struggling to return her appraising gaze. "That was some trick you just performed."

"Too bad I couldn't have performed it a little earlier." She laughed lightly. "I might have saved myself some trouble."

Questions swirled around my brain like the magical winds she had summoned. Who was this woman? Was she some kind of witch? I fumbled with the hilt of my sword, trying to find a comfortable way to hold it now that I wasn't fighting. I said, "Why didn't you? I mean... before you were..."

Her green eyes flashed with amusement. "How did I let myself get caught by a couple of trolls and a mangy mutt, you mean?"

"Well, I—" I stammered, searching for the right words, trying not to stick my foot any deeper into my mouth. "You don't seem like the bumbling around looking for trouble type. I should know."

At her full height, the woman stood about as tall as my shoulder, but her lithe, muscular body made her appear taller. The way she held herself, she could probably look down her nose at a giant. She was the kind of woman I would have avoided back home. The details were hazy, but I knew that much. This was no bar fly, no ambitious gold-digger. In another world, she would have made me feel nervous and insecure. But here, I felt drawn to her. I had a strong desire to prove myself to be her equal.

The woman smiled. Loose tendrils of auburn hair escaped her thick braid and fell around her face, glinting with coppery highlights in the light of the fire.

"What is your name, stranger?" she said. "And how did you come by such a blade?"

"My name is Logan," I said. "Logan Greenwood."

Her green eyes widened.

"Loghann Grenwyld?" she said, pronouncing it with a foreign inflection that didn't seem to touch her other words. "I haven't heard that name in many years."

"No," I said. "It's Logan Greenwood."

I sounded it out as clearly as I could.

She nodded and said, "And the blade?"

I explained to her about the fireflies and the old stump, and she listened with rapt attention, a smile playing at the corners of her beautiful lips. And because I wanted her to keep listening to me like that, I told her the rest of my story. How I'd awoken in this strange place, the summoning circle, and the firefly-lit path. She nodded slowly, and the smile dissolved into a far-away expression. For a moment. the woman was lost in thought, and the two of us stood in silence.

While she was distracted, I took the opportunity to stare. She wore the tattered remains of what seemed to be a fine leather tunic and leggings, though most of the lower half had been stripped away and the top hung in rags that barely covered her chest and stomach. The back of my throat tightened as I counted the bruises and cuts on her skin, and my heart beat faster. I wished I'd found her earlier and saved her from the abuse the trolls and the wolf-man had subjected her to.

I also noticed other unusual marks on her pale white skin. Hair-thin veins, like fine marbling, criss-crossed her limbs and torso in a green just the same color as her eyes. They reminded me of the veins in leaves that you could only see when you held them up to the light. The streaks of blood on her throat, where the werewolf had pierced her with its claws, were green too. In the heat of the moment, I hadn't realized that before.

"Stranger still," she said after a time, like she was speaking to herself. Then, "Well, Loghann, it seems Fate has brought us together. Together we shall stay, if you don't have any objections. I owe you a life bond and will remain with you until it is repaid."

I blinked slowly. "A life bond?"

"You saved my life," she said, bowing her head toward me not unlike the bull elk had done. "It belongs to you, now. Unless I settle the debt by returning the favor."

I swallowed. "I don't even know your name."

"I am called Ruhail," she said. "By others of your kind. My other names you would be unable to pronounce."

"My kind?"

"Yes," she said. "There are others like you here in this forest. Would you like me to take you to them?"

What was that supposed to mean? Other travellers from a parallel world? Other dreamers? Maybe she meant other humans, though she looked human enough to me. I said, "Sure, I guess."

She waved an elegant, long-fingered hand, and a glittering green mist descended upon the troll's fire, extinguishing it and casting us into the pitch black shadows of the forest. One by one, the fireflies turned their lights back on and hovered around us like drunken revellers. They no longer formed a path in any direction. I supposed Ruhail knew her way through the woods.

Above, high branches creaked in the wind. The still air surrounding us on the forest floor filled with the eerie clicking noises I'd heard earlier.

And they were getting louder.

"That is good." She smiled again and strode along on the path in the direction I had come from. "The Arachana are stirring. It would be best to be far away from here before they decide they are hungry."

In surrounding shadows, the bushes rustled. The sound of things scraping against the trunks of the trees overhead sent a chill down my spine. Milky white tendrils of silk spooled down from the branches above and pooled on the path around us.

Ruhail beckoned me with a finger, and I followed her down the path. In the darkness, my sword pulsed with a faint, glowing light.

"Keep your blade ready," she said. "We may not be done fighting just yet."

Chapter 4

Ruhail led the way along the path in silence. She gripped the disguised staff tightly and watched the treetops with her bright green eyes. Even with the rustling in the bushes and the clicking overhead, she remained calm. I managed to do the same, though I had a sneaking suspicion tickling the back of my mind that the Arachana were probably enormous man-eating spiders. I kept my weight balanced as I walked, and my sword arm ready.

The sounds dissipated.

"We have been spared," Ruhail said. "We are safe now."

"That's a relief," I said, relaxing my guard somewhat. "They won't follow us? Whatever they are..."

"Not outside Arachana territory." She stopped on the path and leaned her staff against the trunk of one of the enormous trees. Fireflies danced around her face, and by their light, I could see her wounds were already beginning to heal. She said, "Though, if you ever find your way to this area of the forest again, I would not expect them to be so generous. The spider-folk are not known for their mercy."

"In that case, I hope very much that I can avoid it," I said with a nervous laugh. My gaze darted back to the black forest behind us. The air had lost its chill, and the warm, almost tropical feel had returned. Knowing these woods were filled with trolls, werewolves, and giant arachnids made it feel somewhat less inviting than I had first imagined, but here the comforting familiarity of the trees soothed my fears.

Ruhail untied her long, auburn hair, and ran her pale fingers through its tendrils. I watched as she re-braided the strands with methodical precision. Every time she lifted her arms, I caught a glimpse of her naked breasts beneath the tattered leather. She stared back at me as if she knew exactly what I was thinking, but she didn't move to cover herself. When she was finished, she said, "We will make camp in the summoning circle and continue our journey to the forest temple in the morning."

The thought of sleeping next to this strange, gorgeous woman made my stomach muscles tighten. I cleared my throat and said, "Forest temple?"

"That is where the rest of your people are," she said. "And it happens to be where I need to go as well."

"I thought you were bound to me," I teased. "What if I don't want to see my people?"

She sighed and picked up her staff again. "There are some bonds which supersede even a life bond. I would be forced to complete my task before committing myself to you. Do you wish to part ways? It would not take me long to find you again."

"No," I said. "I don't want to leave you just yet. There are things I need to know about this place before I go stumbling around in the bushes again."

"You are wiser than many of your kind." Her lip curled in amusement, and she turned to lead the way back toward the circle. I caught myself staring at her ass. A soft crease of skin had been exposed where the fabric covering her rounded bottom had been torn. The fabric that remained was stretched so tight I could see every movement of her muscles as she walked. I stood there, mesmerized by the swaying motion of her hips. She stopped and spoke over her shoulder. "Aren't you coming?"

Gods, yes, I thought. But I said, "Yeah. Sorry. I was just thinking."

"What about?" she said coyly. If I wasn't imagining things, she swung her hips a little more than she needed to. The soft green glow of the fireflies added to the exotic atmosphere so that almost anything seemed possible.

But I hadn't been lying. There were things I needed to know before I allowed myself to get distracted.

"I'll tell you," I said, staying a step behind her so that I could still partake of her teasing strides. "If you'll tell me about this task of yours that almost got you killed."

She whirled around with one hand on her hip and the other clutching the staff. Her eyes blazed a darker green, like the murky depths of an ancient lake. She said, "What makes you think I'm at liberty to speak of it?"

"Are you forbidden to?"

She clenched her jaw and stalked farther along the path. "There are some I may trust. Spirits of the forest, those whose intentions are pure and incorruptible."

"Not people like me?" I said, calling after her.

Silence hung in the growing space between us.

I hurried to keep up with her, annoyed at myself for angering her but not really understanding what I'd done wrong. "You keep saying that. 'People like you' and 'your kind.' What am I exactly?"

She huffed over her shoulder at me. "If you do not know what you are, it is hardly my place to tell you."

I reached for her hand. My fingers brushed up against the raw red skin of her wrist, healing, but still tender. She sucked in a sharp breath.

"I'm sorry," I said, withdrawing my touch. "I didn't mean to hurt you."

"I'm fine," she said, and her shoulders softened as she turned toward me. Her eyes searched mine as if trying to read my intentions.

"May I ask you another question?" I asked.

She nodded cautiously. Behind her, I saw the clearing with the summoning stones, still awash in pale moonlight but not as brazenly as before.

"You can't tell me what I am," I said. "But what are you?"

"You really don't know?" she said. "That isn't why you rescued me?"

I shook my head. "I rescued you because I was afraid those creatures were going to kill you."

"They would have," she said, looking away. "Eventually."

"Tell me," I said, cupping her chin with my hand and forcing her to look into my eyes. "Whatever you are able to tell me, I want to know."

She closed her eyes and leaned against me, her body shuddered against my chest. When she looked up there was longing there, but it was tinged with an anger I didn't understand. I drew back. She flinched away from me as if she was ashamed.

She took a deep breath and stood taller, leaning on the staff. Then she turned away from me.

"Let us make camp," she said, with cold iron in her voice. "Then we will talk."

As she strode toward the summoning circle, the fireflies went with her, leaving me alone in the darkness of the woods. What the hell was that all about? Talk about mixed messages. First she's all business, then she's flirting, next she's... whatever that was. *She must still be in shock from her ordeal,* I thought. *I should back off and let her tell me about it when she's ready.*

And what if she started wiggling her ass in my direction again? Was I going to be able to hold onto my resolve? Back off. Ha. If she kept up the seductress routine I was going to have to find a place to *jack* off. Hopefully the fireflies wouldn't tell on me.

"Hurry up," Ruhail called from the clearing. "And bring some wood."

I readjusted my pants. I had wood all right. I snorted to myself. "Uhh, yeah," I called back. "Sure."

By the thin light of the moon, I scoured the bushes for deadfall and dragged a few good-sized branches into the center of the circle. I sat on the pine-needle strewn ground and started to break the thinner branches into kindling. Ruhail arranged them in a small cone-shaped stack and stuffed some dry leaves inside. Then, with her hands on either side of the tinder she closed her eyes and mouthed a silent verse of poem or prayer.

Green flames rose from the middle of the pile, and she smiled as if she was greeting an old friend. As I'd promised myself, I didn't ask her any more questions. I simply passed her some larger sticks to add to the flames. When we ran out of kindling, I stood and hunted for larger dried logs. The fireflies seemed to understand what I was doing and helped guide me.

When I returned she stood and offered a small green parcel to me. It sat in her palms and I realized it was a large leaf wrapped around something.

"What's this?" I asked, taking it from her gently. Something warm and sticky oozed out of the parcel and onto my fingers.

"Eat it quickly," she said. "It's best when it's warm."

I shrugged my shoulders and lifted the food to my mouth.

She stopped me with a laugh. "Not the leaf. Your stomach would not thank you for that. Open it."

I felt my face flush and was glad of the darkness. How was I supposed to know? I had the feeling that she was testing me, somehow. The sparkle in her eyes said that, although I hadn't been able to figure out how to eat the food, I'd passed the test. I opened the leaves to reveal a large slab of white... something... covered in what looked like honey. I picked it up with my fingers and bit off a piece.

It was warm and firm and the honey had a floral tang to it. The texture was a bit like sponge cake, but denser. As soon as I swallowed the first bite, my stomach grumbled, and I realized just how hungry I'd been. I said, "It's delicious. What is it?"

She laughed and shook her head. "You really aren't from around here, are you?"

"Didn't you believe me?" I asked around another mouthful of the stuff. "I mean, I know it sounds a bit far-fetched that I just woke up here and somehow wandered into you. But it's the truth."

"I am beginning to believe it is, Loghann Grenwyld."

"That's not my name," I said, settling back down onto the ground. Ruhail had also found us some springy moss to use for pillows, and I leaned against a clump of it. I looked up at her. "Though it seems to suit this place a bit better than Logan Greenwood. Loghann Grenwyld. It sounds old and powerful, like this forest."

"You don't even know for whom you've been named?" Her eyes widened. "And that sword, its's... It's a wonderful coincidence if that's all that it is."

I ate the last piece of the honey cake, tossed the leaf into the fire, and licked my fingers. I said, "I don't know what to tell you."

She sat on the other side of the fire from me, and the green flames danced over her features, casting an unearthly glow over her face. She really did look like some kind of witch. But I bit my tongue rather than asking her outright.

Ruhail had a stack of the same large leaves next to her. She picked up one at a time, turning them around in her pale hands, and worked at something in her lap. I watched her in silence, thinking I could outlast her stubbornness. After a time, I realized she was making something to wear. I rested my head on the moss and observed her deft fingers pulling a fine thread through the leaves.

"If you ask me again, I will tell you," she said.

"You've had a change of heart?" I asked.

She didn't answer immediately, staring at the leaves in her lap. Then, almost bashfully, she held the finished product up against her chest and said, "What do you think?"

I shrugged. It looked like leaves to me. I said, "Try it on."

Her eyes flashed at me over the green flames.

"Here?" she said.

I closed my eyes. "I won't watch."

I heard her breathe out softly, the way I sometimes did when I was trying to keep calm. But she didn't seem angry anymore, just nervous. The idea of this woman who had fought off a werewolf with a magic staff being nervous about getting naked was kind of cute. I pressed my lips together so that I didn't smile. I didn't want her thinking I was laughing at her.

Then I realized that I had no idea what those beasts had done to her, and being naked might very well be terrifying. The mirth died in my throat. The logs in the fire crackled gently, and warmth from the flames flickered against my skin. But inside, I felt suddenly cold and angry.

"Well?" she said. "What do you think?"

I opened my eyes slowly and let the vision of her wash away the ugly images in my mind. In a feat more miraculous than transforming the clubbed branch into a magical staff, Ruhail had transformed the leaves into a short, ragged-edged tunic or dress. She put her arms up and spun around for me. A large leaf cupped each of her high, firm breasts and seemed to press them together to form a deep valley of pale white cleavage. Her back was mostly bare, and her braid hung in a thick rope all the way down to her tailbone. The bruise left by the troll had already faded to almost nothing. The dress hugged her curves, cinching in at her waist, and barely covered her plump, muscular bottom. If she bent over, I didn't think the material would be long enough to cover her—

"You don't like it."

Her voice stopped my train of thought like a rockslide across the tracks. I said, "What?"

"I don't understand you at all," she said, stomping a bare foot against the soft dirt floor.

"I'm starting to feel the same way." I rubbed my face with my hands. "The dress is beautiful. I'm very impressed."

"Aren't you attracted to me?" she asked.

I laughed. "Of course I am."

"Well," she drew out the word and looked at me like I was some kind of idiot. "I am bound to you. All you have to do is tell me what you want me to do, and I must do it."

My throat felt thick. "You want me to command you to sleep with me?"

She breathed in sharply. "No, but—"

"But if I did," I said. "You would have to."

She pressed her soft pink lips together and nodded. I have to admit the idea gave me a thrill. I'd played games like that with lovers in the past.

Yes, Master... whatever you say, Master... But the way Ruhail's shoulders tensed, and her arms wrapped around her belly protectively, kind of took the fun out of it for me.

"Do you want to sleep with me?" I asked. I felt I already knew her answer, despite her earlier flirtations, and a pang of regret stabbed my chest that I didn't have the nerve to simply command her to take the little green dress off whether she wanted it or not.

"If that is your plan," she said, "I'd rather you got it over with."

From the moment I'd laid eyes on her, I'd had a feeling a woman like her was out of my league, even if this was my fantasy world. I sighed. "But do you *want* to?"

She shook her head back and forth, slowly, as if she didn't understand the question. "I am under a life bond to you. What I want doesn't matter."

"It matters to me," I said, studying her in the flickering green light. Above the flames of the campfire the fireflies danced like huge sparks. I clapped my hands together and made a tossing motion, like I was throwing something away. "So that settles that."

"You aren't going to make me?" she asked in a small voice.

"No!" The word came out a little louder than I intended it to, and Ruhail jumped. I said, "Sorry. No. Now can we please talk about something else?"

"Like what?"

"Anything." I sighed and searched the stars for inspiration. "What was in that food you made me?"

"Breadshrooms and honey," she said, coming to sit a little closer to me. "There's a hive on the far side of the clearing, and breadshrooms grow under all the big red-barked trees."

I laughed. "A mushroom? If you'd told me that ahead of time I never would have eaten it."

"They're abundant in the forest and very nutritious," she said, a little defensively. "You said you liked it."

"I did!" I laughed and tried to reassure her. "I didn't think I liked mushrooms. I guess I was wrong."

She stared at my face intently. "You are very strange."

"Says the girl who turns sticks into enchanted weapons and summons green fire out of thin air."

"I'm a dryad." She crossed her arms petulantly over her chest, squeezing her breasts together in the process. "That's perfectly normal dryad magic."

I tried not to stare at her cleavage and let my mind process the word. It was like bubbles trying to rise through honey. "A dryad? Like a... tree spirit?"

"We serve the Spirit of the Forest," she said. "We are her corporeal vessels."

"I don't know what that means," I said. "You are alive, though, aren't you? You're not like... the ghost of a tree or something?"

She wrinkled her forehead at me. "Of course. Corporeal vessels have living flesh."

"This is the weirdest dream I have ever had."

"You think this is a dream?"

"I don't know what I think," I said, closing my eyes so I wasn't tempted to keep staring at her. "But you're pretty cute for a tree."

She made a disgusted noise in the back of her throat, and I grinned to myself. She said, "Didn't you have something else you wanted to ask me?"

"You know what I want to know," I said. "You are the one who didn't want to tell me."

"I said—" She snapped a twig between her fingers and I could feel her eyes burning a hole in the side of my head. "—that if you asked me again I would tell you."

"You mean if I command you to," I said, cracking an eyelid to watch her expression.

She huffed.

"Forget it," I said. "I'm not playing that game. Tell me what you want to tell me, but I'm not going to force you to do anything."

"Fine," she said, her voice as sharp as a snap from a sapling whip. "Then I won't tell you. Some bonds—"

"Supersede others," I said. "Yeah, I remember. Don't worry about it. I'll figure out what I need to know as I go."

"As long as you don't get yourself killed first."

Without opening my eyes again, I said, "Do you have information that might keep me from getting killed?"

"I suppose you'll never know."

"That'll be on your conscience then," I said. "You could tell me if you wanted to."

There was a sound like teeth grinding. "You are an infuriating man."

"You are a beautiful and equally infuriation woman," I said. "Do you know what I think?"

"No," she snapped. "And I don't want to."

I rolled onto my side and pushed myself up onto my hands and knees. I took one crawling step toward her. She flinched back from me.

"I think you want me to command you to tell me your secrets," I said, inching my way closer to her. "I think you want me to tell you to strip off that sexy little green dress."

I was close enough to feel her breath on my cheek now, and I leaned in so that she could feel my lips moving as I spoke. "You want me to tell you to do all kinds of nasty, dirty, terrible things."

She trembled. "Why would I want that?"

"Because," I said, drawing back and leaning on my heels, "you want to be angry at me. You want to hate me. But why you want that, I *don't* know."

Her eyes blazed, and a deep pink flush rose across her high-cheekboned face. "I haven't been life-bonded in three hundred years."

"Three hundred—" I blinked. "How old *are* you?"

She ignored me. "At first, I was grateful for your help, grateful that I escaped Drakkus's general without revealing what I know. But..." She heaved a great sigh and tears spilled from her bright green eyes. "My freedom is my pride, and you've taken it from me. I want to hate you."

"Do you?" I asked.

She turned away from me and wiped her tears away. "I'm sorry, you haven't done anything to deserve the way I feel about you."

"If this life bond is so bad," I said. "We'll break it. That's not why I helped you. I'm not trying to manipulate you. It's done, I release you."

The green flames of the fire made her face ethereally beautiful, the kind of beauty I'd only experienced in the rawest of nature—old growth forests, canyons formed over millennia, the bare cliff faces of ancient mountains—and suddenly I could believe that she was hundreds, maybe thousands of years old.

"It is not that simple," she said. "It is the price I pay for my long life, and for the honour of serving the Spirit of the Forest. I am bonded to you by deeper magic than I have. Until I have repaid my debt, my life is yours."

"What exactly does that mean?" I said. "Beyond the fact that you have to do what I tell you to do."

I was ashamed to admit that knowing I had that power over her was arousing, even if I never intended to use it.

"If I fail to protect you..." she said, "If you are killed, I shall die with you."

And that was the buzz kill.

"Shit," I said, imaging the horror a near-immortal being must feel at being tied to the life of a mere human. "No wonder you hate me. I'm so sorry."

"It's not your fault," she said. "I realize that now."

"I promise you," I said. "I will not use the bond power against you. And I will do everything I can to set you free—"

"You will put yourself in harm's way so that I may rescue you?" she sounded dubious.

"Wouldn't be the stupidest thing I've ever done," I said. My real life memories were hazy, but I was pretty sure that was true. The words *'Hold my beer'* floated up from some dark region of my subconscious mind. I shook away a chill. Then inspiration struck.

"Oh, I know!" I crawled back over to my mossy pillow and felt around for my sword. I lifted it up to my throat and pressed the gleaming silver tip beneath my chin. "Save me from myself. I'll slit my throat if you don't stop me."

She reached out with her long, pale fingers and touched my hand. She said, "Do not joke about such things. It won't work if you don't really mean to."

I closed my eyes and tried to convince myself to press the blade in farther. My hand trembled. Sweat broke out on my forehead.

Then I let the sword clatter to the ground. "I can't do it."

She smiled at me then and took my face in her hands. She said, "I'm glad."

Then she lowered her soft, pink lips to mine and kissed me gently.

I froze, unsure if I should kiss her back or try to touch her. I didn't want to ruin the moment.

When she leaned back she said, "Loghann Grenwyld, I will tell you my story."

Chapter 5

We lay next to one another beside the campfire, our shoulders almost touching. I rested my hands on my belly and felt my breaths rise and fall with the rhythm of her voice. I didn't speak much.

Not that I didn't have questions. I had a million. But I didn't know where to start. Whatever this place was, wherever I had ended up, I was beginning to realize that it was far too complex for me to have invented in a dream. It was too cohesive to be a hallucination.

Which meant somehow, in some way I had no way to understand, I was actually in another world.

So I kept my mouth shut as much as I could. [Spoiler: I've never been good at keeping my mouth shut.] And I listened, trying to put as many pieces together as I could before asking questions. I wanted to make sure that, when she was finished, I asked the *right* questions.

The more I listened, the more I knew my life—and hers—depended on it.

"I wasn't entirely truthful with you before," she began. "When you asked if I was forbidden to speak to you, I implied that I was. The bonds of my duty are such that I may divulge my orders only to those who serve the Spirit of the Forest, those who are pure and incorruptible."

"I remember," I said.

"That part is true," she said. "But I had already received a sign from the forest—two, in fact—that you were one I could trust. I was just too angry to acknowledge it. The first was that you carried my staff. I lost it trying to outmaneuver Drakkus's general in the Dark Woods. Though you found it on the path, I am certain that is not where I dropped it. Even if I had, the glamor magic on it should have hidden it completely from you. When I am carrying it, it appears as knotted walking stick. When I am not, it should be invisible. You found it, however, and you brought it to me. The Forest Spirit would not have allowed this unless it trusted you deeply."

"So you can't just turn any old piece of wood into a magic wand?"

She continued earnestly. "My staff is made from the root of the Heart of the Forest, the oldest tree from which all others spring. No mere stick could be so powerful."

"What about an average-sized stick wielded with unbridled enthusiasm?" I slid my gaze toward her to see if she cracked a smile. Just because I was stuck in a parallel universe didn't mean dick jokes had to stop being funny.

"No," she said. "It has to be the right kind of wood. Dryad magic would destroy a lesser tool."

Nope. Not even a twitch of the lip.

"Duly noted," I said, biting my tongue. "So the forest allowed me to find the staff. What was the second sign?"

She turned her head and gazed at me incredulously with her impossibly green eyes. "You really have to ask?"

"Give me a break," I said. "I can't be pretty *and* clever. That just wouldn't be fair to the other boys."

She snorted indelicately. Then her eyes widened, and she covered her mouth with her a pale, green-veined hand. She blushed and turned her head away. Through her fingers, she said, "Take a guess."

I pretended to think about it for a while, making the occasional pained noise. She giggled behind her hand and watched me.

"Well," I said, listing off on my fingers, "I woke up in the summoning circle which is—I believe—a sacred space. The fireflies have my back. The Big Daddy of Elks didn't spear me with its ridiculously oversized antlers. I somehow stumbled upon you in your hour of need. And... drumroll, please... I pulled a magical sword out of a rotten stump like some kind of hillbilly Excalibur. I'm going to take magic sword for two hundred dollars, Alex."

She blinked at me, slowly, then glared at me from under her thick auburn eyelashes. "You're making fun of me."

"I'm not." I rolled onto my side and curled my arm under my head. "I'm really not from here, all of this is beyond strange to me, and I have no context for what is unusual and what is not. Is it the sword?"

She sighed and leaned back, crossing her arms behind her head and staring up at the stars. I couldn't help but notice the hard points of her nipples forcing their way up from beneath the skin-tight leaf costume. I imagined peeling the leaves off, one by one, to expose the firm white flesh underneath. It was like she had been sculpted from exotic marble with veins of crystalline green.

"Many things are possible in the Ring Wood," she said. "But the magic we wield here is all connected to the Heart and Spirit of the Forest, green magic, connected to the life force of all things. It heals, it strengthens, it speeds growth. In some rare cases, it can even bring the recently dead back to life—though the Spirit frowns on this. The opposite is also true. Green magic can weaken and decay, wither the flesh from bones, and it can take life away. Both types of magic are necessary for the health of the forest."

"There needs to be balance," I said, tearing my eyes away from her before she noticed me staring. "It's an ecosystem."

"Precisely," she said. "There can be no life without death, no death without life, they feed on one another in a continuous cycle. Life and death, light and dark, order and chaos. These are the alignments that magical forces can take. There are those who practice light magic and dark magic in each realm—and occasionally neutral parties—but always, balance is the key to our survival. In the Ring Wood, there are areas where darkness thrives, like the Dark Woods which is home to goblins and trolls, werebeasts and witches. The temple is for nymphs, dryads, gnomes, and elves, and other order-minded creatures. We don't get along, exactly, but we co-exist. At least, we did."

"It isn't normal for them to attack you?" I asked. "The trolls and the werewolf?"

Ruhail shook her head and curled onto her side to face me. She drew her knees up like a child who was afraid of the dark. But she was no child, and by the look in her eyes, the darkness she had seen was far beyond anything I could imagine.

"The balance has been shifting," she said. "In all the realms, across the Empire, chaos is stirring."

"Why?" I asked. "What has changed?"

"Illdrian, Lord of Order and Emperor of the Realms, is old and dying," she said, tears glimmering in her eyes. "And there is no one to take the throne. His only son, and heir to the Empire, has been missing for nearly two-hundred years. Illdrian has waited patiently for his return; he has remained adamant that his son is safe and that he would be called back in time to be handed the scepter of power. But his time is running out. As long-lived as the elves are, even they cannot cheat death forever, and the heads of the other royal families are growing restless for him to name a new heir."

"Why doesn't he?"

"He refuses." Her voice cracked. "Illdrian is sure his son will return. There are some who believe he's been taken by the sickness which sometimes infects the minds of the ancient races, a madness caused by time. And Drakkus, Lord of Chaos and the Underworld, knows of the dissent. He is gathering his forces, his generals stir discontent amongst the dark magic users, and the balance is shifting farther and farther away from order and light and life. If Illdrian does not name an heir soon, the Empire will enter another Dark Age."

"What happened to his son?" I asked. "Was he on a quest?"

Ruhail shook her head sadly. "No. He was but a babe when he disappeared, taken by the emperor's first consort, the child's mother. Illdrian claims that he sent them away because of a prophecy that foretold the boy's doom. But no one else ever heard the prophecy, and most believe it is a story he concocted to save himself from the shame of his wife's betrayal. It is a tragic tale, and it will be more so if Illdrian does not make a decision soon."

"And what do you think?" I said. "Is the emperor mad? Or is his son out there somewhere, biding his time?"

"I don't know," she said. "I'm not sure any of us ever will."

"You know, it hardly seems fair," I said. "I've been transported to a magical world, just like something out of my favorite stories as a child. It should be a dream come true. Instead, this dream world is on the brink of destruction."

"Would you like to know something funny?"

"Sure," I said. "We could use something to lighten the mood."

"First," she said. "How old are you?"

"You didn't answer that question when I asked you," I said petulantly. I was feeling a bit out of sorts about this news of impending doom.

"I'm 3057 years old," she said. "In this incarnation."

My eyes bugged out of my head as I stared at her. "I'm sorry... that's just—wow. Okay. You know, I really don't want to answer this question now. I'm embarrassed."

"You can't be that much older than me," she said.

I choked on a laugh. "No. No, I can't. I'm a human. I'd be dead. I'm twenty-eight. Years, not centuries."

She sat bolt upright and whirled on me as if I was making fun of her. "Human?"

"Last time I checked," I said. "Yeah. What did you think?"

"And you're twenty-eight *years* old."

"Yes."

"There has not been a human in this realm for eons," she said. "Not since the last Dark Age."

I pursed my lips and frowned. "We didn't cause it did we? Because we're kind of fucking up the world I live in, too. You might be better off without us."

"Would you like to know Emperor Illdrian's family name?"

"Uhh," I said. "Is that part of the joke?"

"He is of the Grenwyld clan."

My mouth began to feel dry and fuzzy. "Like you called me."

"And his missing son," she said, "was named Loghann."

"Loghann Grenwyld." The muscles in my chest clenched. "And Logan Greenwood. That is kind of funny. If only I was a couple hundred years older, I could have been Emperor."

"It gets better," she said. "That is not just any traveller's sword you pulled from the tree stump, Loghann."

"Please stop calling me that," I said. "It's starting to creep me out."

"That is one of the ancient clan weapons," she said. "They are not rare, exactly. Each clan has many. But they may only be wielded by one of the family blood. Do you know which clan forged the blade you carry, Loghann?"

I rubbed my hands over my face. "You're not going to make me guess again, are you?"

"It is a sword of Grenwyld," she confirmed with a satisfied smirk. "See the trifecta of intertwined leaves on the pommel? That is the family crest. You *are* Loghann Grenwyld."

I pushed myself up into a sitting position and turned to face her. The green flames had burned down to a bed of eerily glowing embers, and their warmth spilled out across the clearing. Yet goose-bumps prickled across my arms.

"I can't be," I said. "I'm not even from this world, for one thing. And I'm not old enough, for another. Or even the right species, for that matter."

"You might not be Emperor Illdrian's son," she said. The green light of the flames seemed to glow inside her, making the fine leaf-like veins along her skin shine. "That would be too uncanny. But whatever is going on here, I am certain of one thing. The Spirit of the Forest believes you are fit to take his place. The Ring Wood has chosen you as the heir of this realm."

"What was that illness you talked about earlier?" I said. "The kind that plagues the ancient races? Dryads fit the bill, don't they?"

"I am not mad."

"Well, if you talk like that around anyone else, they're going to think you are," I said.

Her eyes grew wide. "We cannot tell anyone. Your life would be in danger. It is my job to protect you, and I—"

"Okay, cool," I said. "Glad we're on the same page. How about you start calling me Logan, then. Just in case."

"Good idea," she said. Then she tested it out, slowly. "Low-Gun Green Wood."

"Now are you going to tell me about your super-secret mission?" I said, yawning despite myself. "Or are we going to sleep? I need at least forty-eight hours to process this."

"My mission," she whispered to herself, nodding her head into the shadows. "Yes, it's all connected. Of course! You were meant to save me, and I am meant to be your protector."

"I saved you," I said. "Remember? I get to be the protector."

She waved my words away like they were nonsense.

"I carry a message from the emperor to the priestess of the Forest," she said. "It reveals the identity of a member of one of the rival family clans whom the emperor's spies believe to be corrupted by Drakkus, Lord of Chaos."

I blinked in surprise. "Can creatures of order by corrupted by chaos? Or vice versa?"

"It is rare." Her voice was a thin as tissue paper, barely audible over the crackling of the coals. "It goes against our very nature. Eventually, a betrayal of that kind will destroy the traitor. Throughout history, if enough power is offered in return, there have been instances of chaos corrupting even the purest of ordered souls."

I breathed out in a long sigh. "Okay, so if wolf-boy and the trolls wanted to stop you from delivering this message, why didn't they just kill you? I'm glad they didn't, obviously, but it seems like that would have been easier. They must know who the traitor is already."

"A dryad cannot be killed so easily," she said. "Not within the Ring Wood. But if they could torture me into divulging the message—encoded or not—then the emperor's bond would have severed my link to the Spirit of the Forest."

Bile burned the back of my throat. "I'm starting to think this Drakkus guy needs a good ass-kicking."

She sat up again, leaning over me with her long red hair dangling in my lap. "You'll do it, then?"

"Sure," I said. "If I ever meet the guy. I mean, I'll try. I'm not exactly the Terminator, if you know what I mean."

She shook her head. "No."

"I'm just a normal guy," I said. "No matter what this weird coincidence with my name is. But I'll fight for you, just like I did against your captors."

She smiled at me, her face bathed in the strange green light. On some level, I knew what I was agreeing to do was completely insane. The Lord of Chaos? Really? What was I going to do against an army of dark magic wielding minions of destruction? But the way she looked at me, I almost believed I could do it.

"Will you come to the High Plains with me?" she said. "We must make the claim of the Forest. The Spirits of the Realm have just as much claim as the Elven clans, they just prefer to stay out of politics. This is an emergency, though. We must make the claim. I know Emperor Illdrian will choose you."

"Let's play it by ear," I said. "First you have to deliver your message to the priestess. Maybe she'll have other plans for you. For us."

Ruhail nodded. Then she smiled gently. And giggled. Suddenly she was laughing with the musical lilting sound of birds chirping in the trees. I couldn't help smiling, too.

"Yes," she said. "The priestess will have plans."

When we finally settled in for the night, the dryad was still smiling. It didn't occur to me to ask, then, what she found so funny.

Chapter 6

We awoke early and trekked through countless miles of untouched wilderness. If I hadn't been travelling with a dryad, I'd have been worried that we were lost. Okay, in the back of my mind, I was still a little concerned that Ruhail was a nut job and that there was a good chance I was going to end up tied to a tree and fed to the Arachana. As I walked along behind her, admiring the way her legs disappeared into the jagged edge of the leaf dress, I figured there were probably worse ways to go.

It was slow going for me, though. I struggled to keep my sword held aloft, so it didn't drag through the bushes. I wished it had come with a scabbard.

Ruhail had removed the glamor magic from her staff. It no longer appeared as a walking stick or a club, but a long, gnarled magical artifact that Gandalf would have been proud to carry. The green stone at the top glowed with an internal light which, although the fireflies had abandoned us in the daylight hours, was bright enough to light the way in the darkest groves of the forest.

If I lagged behind too much, Ruhail would turn around and thump her staff on the ground. The auburn-haired beauty frowned, but I couldn't help smiling. Every time she thumped the staff her breasts jiggled and bounced enough that I had become convinced the only thing holding the damned dress on was magic. It sure as hell wasn't physics.

I tested this theory as often as I could get away with, which might also have been part of the reason I was afraid she might sacrifice me to the spider-folk.

"Would you please hurry?" she snapped after I'd tested her one too many times. "We will be lucky to reach the temple before sundown at this pace."

"Isn't there a path we could follow?" I asked, trying not to grin too widely and give my game away. "You move through the underbrush as if it's not even there, but I feel like I'm dragging half the forest behind me."

"Maybe you really are a human," she muttered under her breath. "You're certainly not like any kind of elf I've ever met."

"The view is pretty good back here, though," I said. "You can't blame a guy for lingering to appreciate the beauty of nature."

She scoffed. "This is no time for sightseeing."

How could a three-thousand-year-old immortal being be so clueless about innuendo? It was kind of cute. Then again, she was busy worrying about the end of days. Maybe once she'd delivered her message she'd relax a little. Or maybe I was the one who needed to readjust my priorities. If I was expected to go to war against the Lord of Chaos, I should probably keep my head in the game.

"Are you hungry?" she asked suddenly. "Maybe you're hungry. I'll find some food and then maybe you'll have energy to walk faster."

She dropped to her hands and knees in front of a huge red-barked tree and began rummaging around in a hole beneath its knotted roots. She certainly wasn't helping the cause if she wanted to me focus on the mission. The dress barely covered her shapely ass. She reached a long arm deep under the earth until her breasts pressed against the ground and her dress pulled up higher. Just high enough that I could see she hadn't had had enough leaves left to make herself any panties.

The blood rushed away from my head so quickly I saw black spots in front of my eyes.

When my vision cleared, she was standing in front of me with a thick slab of breadshroom in her hands. She said, "Here. Eat this. It's not quite as good without honey, but it will help." A look of concern played across her features. "Are you okay?"

I cleared my throat. "Just a bit lightheaded," I said. "Maybe I am hungry."

I took the proffered food in one hand and dropped the other casually in front of the bulge between my legs. I cursed myself for wearing these thin hiking pants.

"I'm sorry," she said earnestly. "I forgot how often mortals need to eat. Stay here. I'll see what else I can find."

"No," I started to say. "It's all right—"

But she was already gone, dancing off between the trees like a glimmer of sunlight from above the canopy. I groaned and tried to think unsexy thoughts. I tried to remember the last time I'd gotten laid. It couldn't have been that long. I had memories of lots of different women floating around in my head. But they were all hazy and half-remembered, like something that had happened in a dream. It might as well have been a hundred years as far as my body seemed to be concerned.

By the time Ruhail came bounding out of the bushes, I had more or less gotten the pants situation under control. She returned carrying handfuls of fresh berries and a slab of honeycomb. I sat down on a log to eat, holding the breadshroom in another one of the plate-sized leaves. She drizzled the cake-like mushroom with honey, and I awkwardly shoveled alternating mouthfuls of berries and breadshroom into my face like I hadn't eaten in a week. I guess I really had been hungry, I'd just been too distracted to notice.

"Sorry, I'm hogging it all," I said, offering her the leaf with the remaining mushroom on it. "Do you want some?"

She shook her head and smiled at me. "Dryads and nymphs don't eat food like other species. We are more like the trees, feeding on the air and the sunshine and the nourishment of the soil."

Ruhail dug her toes into the thick mossy carpet of the forest floor. For the first time, I realized she was barefoot.

"Do you eat through your toes?" I wrinkled my nose. "Like roots?"

She laughed her lilting laugh. "No. It's more like... I feed off the energy of the trees. When I travel away from the Heart of the Forest, I have to spend more time in the sun and be careful to drink enough water, or my magic will weaken. But here, all I have to do is breathe."

I looked her up and down.

"So if you don't eat food, do you still have to—" I raised my eyebrows. "You know... heed the call of nature?"

She stared at me for a moment in confusion. Then her eyes grew wide and she turned away from me, her fair cheeks blushing fuchsia. "That's a very personal question..."

I interrupted her. "Because I do. How far away is this temple?"

"Oh!" She breathed a sigh of relief, but her cheeks burned as red as coals. "Uh, not too far. Can you... can you hold it? If not, there are some kinds of leaves that work well for... for cleanup. And there are some that you must avoid at all costs. I can show you—"

"I was kidding," I said. "I just like to see you blush."

She covered her face with her hands and stomped back to where she'd leaned her staff against the big red-barked tree. "You are incorrigible."

"I will need to go eventually, though. You might as well show me about those leaves."

Her green eyes flashed at me as she glared over her shoulder. "Figure it out yourself. Then we'll see who's blushing."

Oops. I might have over-played my hand that time.

Note to self, dryads are a bit prudish. I grimaced and hoped someone at the temple would be kind enough to steer me away from anything that might leave blisters...

Ruhail didn't speak to me for the rest of the journey, even though I repeatedly tried to apologize for my childish behavior. I tried to impress upon her the fact that I was barely an infant when compared to her advanced years. For some reason, I don't think that helped my cause. Were all women this touchy? I tried to remember. I was missing the strangest bits and pieces of my memory.

In any case, I had no warning when we broke out of the forest and into an enormous grotto. After grinding through the humid trees, getting slapped in the face by bushes that the dryad pushed through ahead of me, and the developing need to actually use the facilities I had made light of earlier, I was completely unprepared for the sight before me.

My breath caught in my throat as I stepped out of the trees into the cathedral-like clearing. Towering trees made arches above a gray stone temple, carved with intricate knot-work designs. Thick roots, like enormous vines, poured over the stone walls both supporting and seeming to imprison the ancient structure. I stared, open-mouthed, as I realized the arches were not made by many trees, but one single, massive tree whose trunk was woven together as if from hundreds of smaller ones. Pale pink and purple flowers bloomed in its branches, floating through the air and filling the grotto with a sweet, heavenly scent.

Behind the temple a sheer rock face rose up so high into the sky that it disappeared into a thick white mist. Bits of blue sky peeked through the clouds and mist that clung to the mountains. A thin cascade of water poured down from somewhere on the top of the mountain, filling a pool at the base of the rock wall and flowing into a burbling stream that surrounded the temple like a moat.

Intricate living bridges criss-crossed the stream. Their filigreed trusses and towers appeared to have been coaxed to grow in a lacy pattern rather than being carved by hand. They, too, were covered in the delicate flowers.

"It's stunning," I said, my voice tight. "It doesn't seem real."

"Well, it is real," Ruhail huffed. But she sounded slightly mollified. "This is the Heart of the Forest."

"And the priestess is inside the temple?"

"Yes," the dryad said firmly. "We will need to arrange an audience through her advisor, Voron Blackthorne."

I stepped forward eagerly, but Ruhail touched my arm. "Let me go first. Voron is very protective of the priestess. He can be difficult to reason with. It may be best for me to introduce you."

"Sure," I said. "Whatever you think is best. Just... remember, it's Logan."

"Low-Gun," she nodded. "I remember."

I shrugged. Close enough. She led the way down a grassy knoll toward the central bridge across the stream. Then she stopped suddenly and spun around. "Wait."

She ran back up the hill toward the trees and lifted her staff. A blaze of green light cast a halo around her figure as she worked on something at the edge of the forest. Before long, she was running back down the hill toward me with a long reddish-brown object in her hands.

"Here," she said, thrusting it into my chest. "For your sword."

I held it up. The object turned out to be a scabbard made from the same wood as the giant species of tree that dominated the Ring Wood. But it wasn't carved. It was like the wood had been coaxed to grow in the right shape, just the way the bridges seemed to have been.

"Thank you," I said. A vine-like strap affixed to each side of the scabbard which Ruhail helped me to slide over my chest. The sword hung on my back, nestled between my shoulder blades, with the pommel peeking up over my right shoulder. "Nice trick. I should have asked you to make me something like this the back when I was tangled in the bushes."

"I'm sorry I didn't think of it," she said. Her bright green eyes became suddenly serious. "The priestess's advisor is a high-ranking member of the Blackthorne family clan, the leading clan of the forest realms. He is not a kind or personable man by any means, but he is an extremely competent political strategist. There is a chance that, if he sees you carry one of the Grenwyld clan swords, he will see you as a threat. I've made a wrap for your pommel that will hide the crest as well."

She stood behind me and I could feel her tugging as she disguised the sword. When she finished, I said, "How do I look?"

"Like a traveller," she said, "who wears strange clothing."

I looked down at my black T-shirt and gray hiking pants, then at her skimpy leaf-dress. "Thanks," I said. "I think."

She marched ahead once more, and I followed her the rest of the way down the hill. The burbling stream and ornate bridge looked like something out of a movie or video game, too perfect to be real. I ran my fingers over the branches that twisted themselves into the lacy pattern of the trusses and admired the craftsmanship—magical or otherwise—that could produce something so beautiful.

The thought of this place being destroyed by trolls and ogres made my stomach tie in knots. As an outsider, I didn't really know how I could help. But my resolve to try strengthened with every minute I spent with Ruhail and this amazing place.

Just as we stepped off the bridge, before we had even approached the front gate of the temple, two armed guards materialized out of nowhere and crossed their spears over our path. The guards were tall and lean, and wore matching golden armour. Their spears were adorned with green gem stones similar to the one in Ruhail's staff. The stones in all three weapons glowed in proximity to one another.

"Greetings, dryad," said the first guard in a low, melodic kind of voice. Light brown hair tied in thin braids spilled over his shoulders. His lips pulled down into a frown as he gazed over her shoulder at me. "Who are you travelling with today? He is not a member of this temple."

"Greetings," Ruhail said. "This man is a friend. I am under life bond to him. Where he goes, I go. Where I go, he too, must come. I have an important message for Priestess Kalia from Emperor Illdrian. I humbly request access to the temple on both our behalves."

"I am sorry to hear of your servitude, dryad," the second guard said. Her voice was much softer than the other guard's, though I detected a hint of derision in her tone. Pointed elven ears protruded from beneath her long blond hair. The gleam in her blue eyes was formidable as she inspected me. She curled her thin pink lips scornfully. "Especially to such a one as this. You may enter the temple, but do not expect Voron to allow this vagabond in the presence of the priestess."

"As you say," Ruhail said, bowing low before the guards. She motioned for me to do the same. I narrowed my eyes at the hostile elf, but I followed the dryad's lead. It wasn't going to do me any good to make enemies this early in the game. Even in the fiction fantasy worlds I knew of, elves had a reputation for haughtiness.

The elf guards lifted their spears and stood aside for us to pass. The instant we crossed the threshold from the bridge into the temple gate, they vanished once more.

Ruhail blew out a breath between pursed lips. "Of course it would have to be Iymbryl. She's probably whispering in Voron's ear as we speak, twisting him against us and grovelling for his favor."

"Is that the blonde?" I said. "She didn't seem to like me much."

"Iymbryl doesn't like anyone without power enough to be useful to her," Ruhail said. "She's ambitious to a fault, and she has had eyes on Voron ever since it was announced that he is Blackthorne's imperial candidate."

We passed through a vine-covered archway and into the shadowy reaches of the temple. Ruhail reached up and plucked a pale pink blossom from one of the vines, lifting it to breathe in its sweet scent. Cool air greeted us inside the building, along with the rich, earthy scent of moss and damp stone. The temple opened into a large entryway, ringed with more arched doorways, leading off toward passages unknown.

"To be the next Emperor?" I asked.

In the middle of the entry, there was a pedestal with a small statue of a naked woman laying upon a bed of leaves. Vines wrapped around her bare limbs and spread her legs wide as if in offering to those who entered the temple. My heart beat faster against my ribs as I wondered what kind of woman this priestess was.

"Yes," Ruhail said. She knelt before the statue and placed the flower she had picked between the woman's legs, as if she were worried about her modesty. "That is, should Illdrian choose his successor from one of the other clans. Priestess Kalia would be Voron's first wife, of course, but Iymbryl fancies herself first consort." She looked up at me, her eyes twinkling. She whispered, "I've heard she already performs the duties of consort to him, though it is forbidden for temple guards to have intimate relations."

"Naughty little elf," I teased. "I knew she was a bad one."

With Ruhail kneeling in front of me, I couldn't help wondering if I'd ever be able to convince her to perform intimate duties on me. My thought didn't escape the dryad's attention. She glanced away from my obvious arousal and stood.

"This way," she said and hurried down a corridor to the left. The passage was lit with sconces that burned with an eerie golden glow, though no flames were visible to me. At the end of the corridor, a heavy wooden door with a large black knocker-ring in its centre stood ajar. A barely audible grunting noise came from the other side of the door.

Ruhail's eyes grew wide, and she looked over her shoulder at me with a high blush in her cheeks. "You see? They are at it right now!"

Laughter bubbled up inside my chest as I realized what we were hearing. Old Voron was giving that snooty elf a good pounding. I wondered if she liked it or if she was just doing what it took to climb the political ladder. Apparently the "sleep your way to the top" kind of woman existed in this world, too. I kind of wished I could see the look on her face.

"What do we do?" I whispered. "If we interrupt before they're finished, Voron's going to be even less friendly to our cause."

Ruhail pushed me back down the hallway toward the entrance, then said loudly, "This is the great Temple of the Forest, home of the priestess Kalia. Before we meet with her, we must beg an audience with her most esteemed advisor, the honorable Voron Blackthorne."

I laughed silently and followed her lead, stomping heavily to echo along the corridor. "To be advisor to someone as important as the priestess, Voron must be a highly respected member of the Blackthorne clan. I am so honored to be able to meet him."

"You should feel honored," Ruhail said, her green eyes flashing in the golden light of the sconces as we approached the door. "You are far too lowly a person to normally be granted permission to speak with the priestess or her advisor. It is only by your life bond to me that you should be allowed to enter this temple at all."

I mimed a hurt expression at her, but I said, "I am but a worm. In the presence of such greatness, I truly know my place in the world."

She rolled her eyes at me, but had to bite her lip to stop from smiling. As we approached the oak door, it swung suddenly inward. A tall, rail thin elf with sallow skin and long black hair stood in the doorway, frowning severely. He wore long robes of deep, forest green, and stitched with golden threads. The finery should have made him look impressive, but instead it contrasted against his sickly appearance to make him look older and more tired. The deep circles beneath his eyes, and his jutting cheekbones, gave his face a skull-like appearance.

He glowered at Ruhail like she was lower than the dirt on his shoes. His fine, dark eyebrows arched cruelly above dull gray eyes. He said, "What is it, dryad? I do not recall sending a summons for you."

Behind him, the blond elf, Iymbryl, hastened to fasten the waistband of her golden chain-mail skirt. Her blue eyes shot icy daggers at me over the advisor's shoulder when she saw me staring at her.

"F-forgive our intrusion," Ruhail said. She stammered a little for effect. "But I carry a message for the priestess from the High Plains, from the emperor himself."

The elven man's gray eyes fell upon me and his thin lips curled as if he smelled something foul. "And this is?"

"A traveller," she said. "His name is Low-Gun. We are bound by a life bond, and so I had no choice but to bring him here. A thousand apologies, your greatness."

The elf's right arm was concealed behind the edge of the door and he seemed to grip something tightly. I noticed the green stone on Ruhail's staff begin to glow slightly. I tensed, wondering if he was about to attack with a hidden weapon or magic spell.

"We have had word from the emperor already." He sneered at Ruhail, and his eyes flashed dangerously. "From another source. It warned of a traitor in our midst. What reason do I have to believe a word you say? Dark forces gather in the Ring Wood since the last blood moon. The Lord of Chaos grows stronger. Surely he is strong enough now to corrupt a foolish dryad." His gaze shot to me. "Or a lowly traveller such as this."

The blond elf turned her head toward us and her eyes darted around in fear. Was she the traitor? Maybe that's why she was so eager to claw her way to the top of the temple. Or was she worried that she'd be blamed for allowing us into the temple? I couldn't tell. I kept my eyes on her.

"Please, sir," Ruhail begged. This time I didn't think she was acting. "I can prove it. I only need to speak to the priestess, and she will know that what I say is true."

The door slammed against the wall and Ruhail jumped backward, colliding with my chest. The dark elf's sallow complexion grew deathly pale. In his right hand, he gripped a staff of gnarled black wood with a massive red stone glowing in the burl at the top.

"So that you may assassinate her?" Voron Blackthorne bellowed. His eyes blazed, and Ruhail slumped to her knees as if in pain, her own staff clattering to the floor. "Over my dead body."

Suddenly the blond elf was behind him with her golden spear pointed at my throat, and her blue eyes burning with vindicated rage. I raised my hands quickly, afraid that if I made a wrong move one of them might hurt Ruhail. They clearly saw her as the greater threat.

"Iymbryl, seize these saboteurs." The advisor's voice became a hiss like that of a snake warning from the grass. "Throw them in the dungeon. I will ask the priestess how she wishes to dispose of them."

"Yes, Master," Iymbryl said in a simpering tone, so different from the way she'd addressed us at the gate. "Your desire is my command."

Voron whirled around in a flurry of dark green fabric and strode toward the desk on the far side of the room. He walked with a limp, leaning on his staff like an old man with a cane. On his desk, a massive tome lay open, its pages fluttering as if in a breeze, but there were no windows in the advisor's study. He slammed the book shut and scowled at the guard. "What are you waiting for? Throw them in the dungeon."

"You heard Master Blackthorne," the blond elf said. She gave me a sharp poke with the tip of her spear. I backed up a step. Ruhail struggled to her feet. I bent to retrieve her staff and wrapped an arm around her waist to help hold her up. Her face was ghostly pale and her lively green eyes seemed dull and confused. The guard said, "Let's go. Walk ahead of me and do as I say. Don't try anything clever."

"If either of them attempts to escape," Voron called from the safety of his desk. "Kill them."

Ruhail and I stumbled backward and Iymbryl grinned sadistically. "It would be my pleasure."

As the elf guard stepped into the corridor with us, the huge wooden door slammed closed behind her as if it had been pushed by a sudden wind.

The echo rattled along the stone walls and floors like a death knell.

Chapter 7

The blond elf marched us down endless corridors until we came to a spiral staircase. She forced us down the stairs, and we descended for what seemed like hours into the cold, damp, darkness below the temple. Eventually, we came to a heavy wooden door with black-barred windows which the elf-guard opened with a large brass key.

When she was distracted, I raised my eyebrows at Ruhail and looked at the guard. I was pretty sure we could take her. But the dryad shook her head sharply and glared at me. I shrugged. I guessed she was still hoping to see the priestess once Voron Blackthorne was done being a drama queen.

Iymbryl snapped to attention as the door swung inward, and she swivelled her spear around to point against my throat like she knew what I'd been thinking. We stood almost eye-to-eye. I raised my hands in the air again and smiled as charmingly as I could. The blond elf glowered. Her chest heaved and fell. The golden, filigreed armor pressed her breasts together enticingly.

Up this close, I could see the bulge of skin pressing against the decorative chest piece—I mean, it had to be decorative, right? No way was armor full of holes going to be tactically advantageous—and I wondered if the male guard-elf had been wearing the same ridiculous outfit. I hadn't really noticed when we'd first been stopped by the guards. I'd been so distracted by the unreal quality of everything else that the scantily clad elf woman had managed to escape my attention. It was standard fare for fantasy games and graphic novels, so it's like my brain had just glossed over that little detail.

But here, in the low light offered by the wall sconces, shadows danced across her fair skin and fell into the crevice of flesh between her breasts. A blush rose across her chest. The smell of sex rose up off her skin like a heat-wave, and I remembered that we'd interrupted her little office triste with the advisor.

Had Voron left her wanting? He didn't seem like the "ladies first" type. A sudden, animalistic urge to take the blond elf for myself drove all the blood in my body to my groin.

Iymbryl brought me back to reality with a sharp poke from her spear to my chest.

"Move," she said, and her icy blue eyes flashed angrily over me. Her gaze lingered on the evidence of my wandering thoughts.

As I turned to follow Ruhail deeper into the dungeon, a flash of pink caught my attention between the ornate swirls of Iymbryl's armor. She was completely naked under the skimpy golden cage.

Fuck. That didn't help the situation in my pants.

What the hell was wrong with me? I was being marched into a prison cell, possibly to my doom, and all I could think about was boning the snotty little elf who put me there. For fuck's sake, she had offered to kill me not long ago!

Then there was the barely covered dryad glaring over her shoulder at me like she, too, knew exactly what I was thinking and now hated me.

This stupid fantasy universe was turning into the most sexually antagonizing experience of my adult life. At least, as far as my foggy memory went.

The elf jabbed me in the back with the tip of her spear and directed Ruhail and me into the final cell in a row of empty cells. She scowled as I walked past her into the dark room and then slammed the door behind us with a clang.

On the other side of the door, I heard her fumbling with the keys. They fell to the floor, and she cursed loudly. Then they jangled again and the lock clicked home. At least I had the satisfaction of knowing she had been as flustered as I was by our encounter. I pressed my ear against the door and listened to her stalk down the corridor, muttering to herself.

When I turned around, Ruhail stood in the middle of the dark room with one hand gripping her staff and the other planted firmly on her hip. A look of blazing fury burned on her pretty features.

"You're attracted to her?" she said.

"Is it that obvious?" I said. Though the straining fabric of my pants told me it probably was.

"*Her*?" she shrieked, slamming the butt of the staff against the stone floor of the cell. "She's despicable!"

"Yeah," I said. "Maybe. But she sure fills out that skimpy armor nicely. It's even sexier in real life than I imagined."

She made a disgusted noise in the back of her throat and turned her back on me. A swirling green mist formed around the top of the staff and, for a moment, I thought she was going to blast me. Then little lights, like fireflies, danced around the room, filling the space with a soft, green light.

"Hey," I said. "What do you care? You're not interested, remember?"

She gave me a baleful glare over her pale, white shoulder.

Then I realized something. "Hey, she left us our weapons! I don't think my sword will be much good unless they decide to march us to the gallows, and we want to go down swinging. But maybe you can magic us out of this place!"

The cell seemed ancient. The stones that made up the walls and ceilings were cracked and crumbling. Thick, vine-like tree-roots protruded from the walls and grew straight through to pierce the floor. A cluster of them in one corner made a kind of throne-shaped chair. The floating green lights illuminated a pile of dirty hay or grass that was probably meant to be a bed.

Ruhail touched the tree roots with her hand and then her forehead. She closed her eyes as if she were listening to something. Then she said, "No. Voron cannot mean to keep us here. He simply likes to be in charge. As soon as he speaks with the priestess he will come for us."

"You don't think he really believes you are the traitor?" I asked.

"He must have been rattled by the message he received," the dryad said. "I did not know the emperor sent more than one envoy. But it is a good thing. I was nearly caught, after all. Had I failed, the priestess would be completely vulnerable. Perhaps the priestess has not yet told Voron who the traitor is, and he is doing his best to protect her."

"Doing his best to protect himself, more like," I muttered, and I stomped over toward the knot of roots and sat down in the seat-like divot. I pulled my sword and sheath over my shoulder and rested it on the floor beside me. "There's nothing altruistic about his motivations. He only wants to protect the priestess because he thinks her power will be his when the emperor passes the crown, or whatever, to him."

The dryad raised her eyebrows at me skeptically.

"For someone who knows nothing of this world," Ruhail said, "you certainly talk like you know a lot."

She flipped her auburn braid over her shoulder and leaned against the damp stone wall.

"Call it a hunch," I said. "I've known guys like him before, in my world. As different as this place is from my home, some kinds of assholes are a universal constant."

"Voron Blackthorne is not a pleasant man," she said. "But this is all just for show. It must be, unless he's growing senile. It would be impossible to trap a dryad in this cell. These are roots belonging to the Heart of the Forest. My magic is stronger here than anywhere else in this realm. Only a fool or a madman would think he could imprison me in the forest temple."

I sat up straighter. "So you *can* magic us out of here?"

"Myself, yes," she said. "Not you. Until I know what they mean to do with you, I'm staying here. It wouldn't do me much good to escape if Voron decides to behead you as soon as I'm gone, now would it?"

"This makes no sense," I said. "Why bother with this charade then?"

Ruhail shrugged. "To save face in front of his lover? To impress upon you his supreme importance? To buy himself enough time to try to shift the priestess's opinion? Who knows...?"

She slid down the wall until she was in a seated position on the floor. She held the staff across her lap and leaned her head back against the stone.

Concern washed over me suddenly.

"Are you feeling all right?" I said, "You look pale."

She shook her head. "Tired, I suppose. Whatever that magic was he used on me has left me feeling drained. I'll recover in time."

A strange sound, like the slithering of snakes echoed through the chamber. Ruhail sat up, cocking her head to the side to listen. A smattering of dust fell from the roof and I wondered if the whole place was in danger of caving in. What was that noise? My seat trembled and the roots of the makeshift chair stirred beneath me.

I leapt to my feet with a start and watched with dread as the chair disappeared. The roots parted until a narrow opening was visible, revealing a cavernous black hole beyond. I stared inside, and three pairs of yellow eyes stared back at me.

I screamed and stumbled backward, pointing at the hole. "What the hell is that?"

Ruhail turned reluctantly until she was looking at the roots and the eyes hiding inside them. She groaned. "Oh no, this is the last thing we need."

"What is it?" I asked, my heart hammering in my chest. "Trolls? Goblins?"

A chorus of giggling came from beyond the roots. Ruhail sighed and said, "Worse. Nymphs."

As if she had called them by name, three creatures came crawling out of the tree roots on hands and feet. They scampered around me in a semi-circle, and then stood up, blinking their lively yellow eyes at me.

I couldn't believe what I was seeing.

They were women, of a sort. Though about three-quarters the average size. I had seen paintings of nymphs before, in the single Art History course I'd taken in university. They were usually depicted as slight, almost child-like creatures, as slender and sexless as saplings. Though for some reason men were always falling in love with them. I'd never understood that.

These nymphs, on the other hand, hadn't gotten the memo about the sapling-look. They were slight in their bodies, but rather than being sexless, these women looked like they'd been designed by a mad plastic surgeon. Someone who'd become numb to the beauty of average women and sought to pump everything up to the *n*th degree. Massively rounded breasts, tiny waists, and plump heart shaped hips filled my vision as the nymphs surged forward.

"Hello," said the first, a curly-haired brunette with pink flowers pasted over her nipples and between her legs, and nothing much else on. "Who are you?

Did that big mean dryad think she could keep you all to yourself?"

"Uhh," I said, the ache in my groin springing back with a vengeance. "I'm Logan. Who are you?"

The nymphs pushed me back toward the tree roots, which had re-formed into a chair, and forced me to sit down.

"Ugh," Ruhail said. She crawled over to the grass mattress. "I'm going to sleep. Wake me when you're finished."

"Finished with what?" I asked, feeling heat rise in my neck and face as the nymphs ran their hands over my body.

"You seem stressed," said a nymph with a black pixie cut that emphasised her huge yellow eyes. She wore a dress made out of a fine mesh that seemed to be woven from spider silk. Her dark nipples were clearly visible on her heavy, swaying breasts as she climbed into my lap and pushed my shoulders back. "We can help with that."

"Ruhail?" I said. "What am I supposed to do here?"

"I'm sure you'll think of something," she snapped, and rolled over on the mattress so she didn't have to watch.

The third nymph, with impossibly long strawberry-blond hair, waved her hands toward the chair. Vines wrapped over my chest and around my arms, binding me to the roots. Something twined over my ankles and thighs as well. I craned my neck to see what was happening but the black-haired nymph giggled and blocked my view by pressing her breasts into my face. I was pinned down. It was completely impossible to move. I could barely breathe around the bulging flesh that swelled to cover my mouth and nose.

I struggled to turn my head to the side and suck in a lungful of air when the black-haired nymph giggled and grabbed my face between her hands. She said, "We want to play. Can we play with you?"

"That depends what you mean by play," I said, gasping through fish lips as she squeezed my cheeks together. "I kind of like being able to breathe."

With a flick of her wrist, the nymph disappeared and then re-appeared behind her friends. The strawberry-blond and the curly haired brunette crouched before me on the ground. The blond crept forward until she was positioned between my knees, and she slid her small hands along the insides of my thighs.

The sudden touch after hours of pent up sexual tension sent shockwaves straight to my brain. She dragged her fingers languorously over the thin fabric of my hiking pants, which hid nothing of my excitement. The clear shape of my engorged cock was visible for all of them to see. I struggled against my bindings, but I couldn't even sit up, let alone cover myself. The nymph scratched her fingernails lightly over the fabric covering my tightening balls, and sent a zing of vibration up my spine. I groaned in spite of myself.

"He likes to be able to breathe," the blond nymph said. "I'd like to take his breath away."

She pulled at the button that held my pants closed, and it popped open easily under the pressure. Then she slid her hands inside the top of my boxers and pulled the elastic down. The nymphs giggled in appreciation as my erection sprang up out of its prison and bounced in the blonde's face. She licked her fat lips, her yellow eyes darting up and down the length of me, hungrily. Then she cupped my balls with her hand and shocked me by sucking them into her mouth, rolling her hot little tongue around my sac like she was licking a jawbreaker candy.

The muscles in my stomach clamped down, and the ache in my groin became maddening. The other two nymphs watched eagerly as she teased me. The brunette slipped her fingers beneath the little pink petals hiding her sex, stroking herself as she watched. Her yellow eyes jumped from the blond to me. She said, "Can I help?"

She seemed to be asking my permission, not her friend's. I nodded, and opened my mouth to scream, "Yes, for the love of the gods, help me!"

At that moment, I felt like if I didn't get release soon, I was literally going to explode and take everyone in the room with me.

But all that came out of my mouth was another groan as the blond applied more pressure to my most sensitive bits. I strained against vines until they dug into my skin. If I'd gotten free, I don't know if I would have smacked the blond nymph or fucked her, but I wanted to make her pay for what she was doing to me now.

The brunette caught my drift, though. She pulled the flower pasties off her cartoonishly large breasts, exposing hard pink nipples, and leaned over my lap. The weight of her breasts pressed on my thigh, and the pressure of those nipples right though the thin material of my pants, as she bent her lips over the head of my cock and lowered her mouth onto me.

"Oh, fuck, yes," I groaned. The tightness at the back of her throat wrapped around my shaft, and she lifted her head up and down again to thrust the tip deeper. I wished I could get my hands free so I could push her head all the way down. The thought almost put me over the edge. The brunette bounced her curly head over my cock and her breasts slapped my thigh. As she did this, the blond nymph's head bobbed up and down as she continued to suck on my balls. Suddenly, I didn't hate her quite so much anymore.

"What about me?" The black haired nymph stomped her foot. "I want to play, too."

The brunette got on her knees next to the chair, letting her heavy breasts spill over my lap. Then she squeezed my erection between them by pressing on both sides.

She said, "I'll hold him for you."

The nymph slid her tits up and down my spit-slick cock, slowly and squeezing hard. When the black-haired nymph bent over my other side and swirled her little pink tongue over the tip it was like sensory overload. My heartbeat pounded in my head, and my eyes tried desperately to take in the sight of the three miniature porn stars as they fawned over me. It was the stuff of my most depraved fantasies come to life. Okay, not my *most* depraved, but it was painfully fucking hot.

Then I noticed Ruhail on the other side of the room. She wasn't pretending to sleep anymore. Her eyes were glued to the action, and her hand slipped between her thighs as she watched. So much for not being interested. I was going to have to have a talk with the sexy little dryad once we had some privacy. Despite the horny trio of nymphs bouncing and rubbing on me, it was Ruhail that made the blood surge through my groin. I strained against the vines that held me as the pressure built in side my balls and my breaths came in sharp, panting gasps.

I was so close it hurt.

Suddenly, there was a noise in the corridor outside of the cell, and the three nymphs froze. One of them snapped her fingers, and all three disappeared into a puff of sparkling green smoke. The vines holding me onto the chair disappeared with them.

The door swung open and Iymbryl stalked inside the room. She held the door open with one hand and her spear in the other, and she opened her mouth to say something.

She stopped and stared, open-mouthed at me, where I sat—just a guy in a tree-chair with his massive throbbing boner out on display for all to see. It pulsed with my heartbeat.

Eventually, she tore her gaze away and said, "The priestess will see you now, traveller. Please make yourself decent."

Enough blood managed to reroute itself to my brain that I understood her, slowly. Then I cursed and rolled out of the chair, trying to stuff my fading erection back into my pants with whatever dignity I could scrounge up. There wasn't much.

After zipping up my pants, I swung my scabbard over my shoulder and took a deep breath. I turned to face the guard.

"Sorry," I said. "I'm ready now."

Ruhail stood, brushed the grass off her dress, and pulled a long strand out of her thick auburn braid. She said, "Thank you, Iymbryl."

"Not you, dryad," the blond elf-guard snapped. "You stay here. Voron and the priestess wish to see the traveller alone."

Ruhail paled. She turned her green eyes to me in shock. I knew what she was thinking. If Voron Blackthorne had evil intentions for me, she would be unable to help. But if she attempted to escape the cell in order to save me, he would have her killed.

I paused on my way out and touched Ruhail's pale shoulder with my hand. Her skin was hot beneath my fingers. I said, "It will be okay. I'll talk to them on your behalf."

As she gazed up at me, she seemed to remember the scene she had just witnessed, and her cheeks burned a deep shade of red. She looked at the ground and whispered, "If you need me, the trees will tell me. Be safe, Low-Gun."

I summoned my courage and gave the dryad's shoulder a reassuring squeeze. The elf-guard made an impatient sound as I stepped toward the door of the cell. She sneered as I walked past, and even more than ever, I longed for a chance to teach the snotty blond elf a lesson. But that would have to wait.

I had a meeting with a Priestess.

Chapter 8

Iymbryl forced me back into the corridor at the tip of her spear, and we began to retrace our steps back up to the main floor of the temple.

"You have really bad timing," I said over my shoulder. "Did you know that?"

She prodded me between the shoulder blades with a sharp jab and hissed between her teeth. "Shut up, you deviant. I don't know why the priestess wants to see you at all."

"Who are you calling a deviant?" I snorted as we entered the long stairwell. My laughter echoed up into the darkness above us. "Last time we met you were the one getting dressed in a hurry. Or have you forgotten?"

She sucked in a sharp breath. Then she grabbed me by the back of the shirt and slammed me against the stone wall of the staircase. She braced the spear across my chest and held me there, her face inches from mine. The heat of her breath brushed against my cheek, and my relentlessly teased body flushed at her closeness. She said, "How much did you see?"

"Easy now," I said, soothingly. "Not enough to get myself killed over. Just enough to get curious. What do you see in that guy?"

"It is none of your business what I do with whom, or why." Her voice trembled slightly. "Just as it is none of my business why you choose to pleasure yourself while there is a perfectly foolish dryad there to service you."

Her eyes widened as if she'd made a sudden realization. She backed away from me, swinging the spear around to point at my throat.

"You like being watched, don't you?" she said. "You were probably hoping I would walk in on you, too. I should have let Master Blackthorne come for you himself, like he wanted to."

"Master Blackthorne?" I swallowed, and my Adam's apple pressed against the spearhead. "Does he make you call him that?"

Her pupils dilated in the dim light of the stairwell. I couldn't tell if she was aroused or angry. Either way might end up being a problem for me if Voron had already staked his claim, but I couldn't help asking. She didn't answer me.

She grabbed the sleeve of my shoulder and pushed me roughly back up the stairs. "Keep moving."

We walked in silence for a while, the tension between us thick enough to swim through. My heart hammered with the aerobic exertion, and the blood throbbed through my body. Every nerve felt alive. My skin tingled.

I thought I might be able to overpower the elf-guard if I wanted to make an escape. I was bigger than her, but she seemed to be skilled with the spear and she had magic I didn't know the limits of. Besides, what would happen to Ruhail if the visitor she had vouched for attacked a temple guard? She said she could escape the cell, but despite her claims, there was no denying that she had been weakened by Voron's spell. What if she wasn't strong enough to get out?

And it hadn't escaped my attention that the elf-guard had allowed me to remain armed. Maybe Ruhail was right, and all of this was some kind of ruse put on by Voron in order to demonstrate his power. I slowed my pace and decided to probe for answers.

"Why *did* you come for me yourself?" I asked.

The blond elf jabbed me again with her spear as an answer.

"Why do Voron and the priestess want to see me?" I continued. "Ruhail is the one with the message."

"It is beyond me." Her voice was stiff and tinged with bitterness. "I simply follow orders."

I managed to keep any snide comments about what kind of orders she might like to follow to myself. I assumed her bitterness came from Voron's relationship to the priestess, jealousy perhaps. That information might come in handy later on. I decided it would be a good idea to stop antagonizing the elf-guard, as much as I wanted to get under her skin. If Voron wasn't treating her right, or if she was jealous of the priestess, I might be able to get her on our side if we needed an ally in the temple.

That is, assuming the spark of attraction I'd felt early was mutual and that she wasn't planning to gut me at the first opportunity. And assuming that she was not, in fact, the traitor whom Ruhail had come to warn the priestess of.

The fact that she hadn't found an excuse to maim me yet was encouraging, though.

At the top of the staircase, Iymbryl guided me—not quite gently—through another corridor, this one covered in hanging vines and sweet-scented flowers. Dust motes danced in the beams of soft, yellow light spilling through cracks in the stone walls. The air smelled of dust, moss, flowers, and fresh water. I inhaled deeply and sighed.

"It's beautiful here," I said.

"Of course it is," Iymbryl said from behind me. "And you are fortunate to live to see it, outsider."

"I'm grateful," I said. It was true, despite the fact that I was seeing it as a prisoner.

She didn't reply. She simply prodded me again, and we stepped out into a lush, inner courtyard that hadn't been visible from outside the temple.

Flowers of every shape and color grew intertwined with vines and shrubbery, climbing up the narrow, towering trunks of white-barked trees with trembling spring-green leaves. At the centre of the courtyard, a fountain gushed and burbled, sending up a misty spray that hovered gently between the greenery. Behind the fountain, a wide, stone staircase rose toward a pillared balcony. Its gray slab steps were cracked and falling apart in places, seemingly held together by the moss, roots, and vines that tore them apart.

It was a place of delicate balance, I thought. Like the balance between good and evil, of order and chaos, that Ruhail had spoken of.

At the insistence of Iymbryl's spear, I climbed the crumbling staircase and was surprised by how solid it felt beneath my feet.

As we neared the top, I saw that the stone pillars on the balcony held up a roof over an open gazebo-style pavilion. Lush vines hung like drapery from the rafters, encompassing the space in a velvety quiet from the sound of the birds and fountain outside. Light trickled in between the vines like golden spears cutting through the air. A path—like a bolt of purple silk, unrolled across the floor—led from the top of the staircase to a small, raised dais at the back of the pavilion.

On the dais sat the most beautiful woman I had ever seen.

Even in this world full of sexy dryads, pornographic nymphs, and clandestine elven booty calls, she was on a pedestal above the rest.

Her skin was warm and sun-kissed brown. Waves of yellow hair, like spun gold, washed over her naked shoulders and small, covered breasts. She wore a sheer, glittering purple cloth wrapped around her chest and cinched at her waist with a thin golden cord. The fabric spread across her lap and pooled between her legs where she knelt upon the dais with her eyes closed and her hands held out before her like she was awaiting a gift. There was something about her that seemed untouchably perfect and pure.

Then there was Voron Blackthorne, hovering just behind her shoulder like a black spot of mildew on a perfect painting. He whispered something in her ear. His gaze oozed across her skin as he spoke, possessively, like he sought to claim her body with his eyes. When he looked up at me, he smiled with thin, curling lips, gloating over his prize.

"Here he is, Priestess," the sallow-skinned elf said, like he was identifying a particularly repugnant sort of insect. "The vagabond."

The woman on the dais opened her eyes, and I was startled to see that her irises were a bright, clear purple, like polished amethyst. Dark lashes seemed to weigh her eyelids down and she gazed at me, dreamily, as if awaking from a long sleep.

She smiled at me with soft, inviting lips. "Come closer, traveller," she said. "Let me look at you."

Iymbryl shoved me forward.

Voron snorted and tossed his greasy black hair. "There is not much to look at, Priestess. A dirty wanderer, here to sully your temple. We should cast him out immediately."

Her purple-eyed gaze flicked up at him in amusement, though I thought I caught a hint of irritation in the twitch of her gentle pink lips. She said, "Thank you, Voron. You have made yourself clear. I would see him for myself, if you don't mind."

The advisor narrowed his eyes and frowned, but he kept his mouth shut.

"It is an honor to meet you, Priestess," I said. I knelt, and bowed my head respectfully. To be honest, I over did it a little, just to make Voron look bad. "I apologize for my intrusion."

Up close, she appeared quite young, though she spoke with authority. Her face held the fullness of youth, and her curves were soft and plump and unweathered by age, and there was a guilelessness in her gaze that spoke of a kind of innocence the other women I'd met in this place did not have.

"Why have you come here, traveller?" she asked

"Only to accompany a friend, Priestess," I said, trying to remember how one was supposed to speak to royalty. "The dryad, Ruhail, brings evil tidings from the emperor. She languishes in your dungeon as we speak, her message unheeded."

I'm afraid my years of reading fantasy novels and playing role-playing games had given me a flair for the dramatic, but the priestess didn't seem to notice. She rubbed the fabric of her sheer purple wrap between her fingers and cocked her head to the side, like she was trying to see beyond the words I said.

"We have already received the message from the emperor," Voron Blackthorne snarled from behind the priestess. His hand tightened on the gnarled black staff, and the red stone glowed ominously. "I delivered it to the priestess myself."

I raised my eyebrows at the elven advisor. "Is that so? Interesting. I understand the message Ruhail carries has been magically encrypted by the emperor, so that only the priestess may hear its contents—"

"Liar!" The black-haired advisor slammed his staff into the stone floor, the sound echoing across the pavilion. "You only seek to sow doubt in the heart of the priestess, to feed her the untruths of the dark ones."

I doubted that the priestess had seen very much of the world beyond her temple, of the trolls and werewolves that prowled her realm. Was she so innocent that she could not see she was being manipulated by this pompous elf? I wondered how seriously the priestess took the threat of the Lord of Chaos. Was it real to her? Or was Drakkus simply a scary story that Voron Blackthorne whispered in her ear when he wanted to get his way?

"You don't have to believe me," I said. "Ruhail can prove it. You only need to speak to her."

"Do not listen to this creature, Priestess," the advisor pressed. His dull gray eyes darkened beneath his sharp black eyebrows as he glared at me. "We should never have let this filth inside the temple."

"I asked you to be quiet, Voron," the priestess said. "Allow me to judge this man for myself. Or don't you trust me?"

She smiled up at him benignly, but there was an edge to her words that said he had pushed too far. The advisor's jaw opened and closed. Finally he stuttered, "I-I only urge caution, my lady."

She turned back to me, her amethyst eyes flashing. "I am in a difficult position, traveller. My advisor says that he has received the message from the emperor and that he has passed the identity of the traitor to me. Now that traitor claims to bring a message from the emperor. My advisor was appointed by the emperor, and I have no reason to distrust him. But if what you say is true, and that the dryad's message has been magically encrypted... Well, I have to admit that I am curious, if nothing else. What do you propose?"

"Only that you speak with Ruhail," I said. "I know nothing of the contents of her message, and neither does she. She may only deliver it to you."

"Is there danger to me in meeting with the dryad, Voron?" The priestess pinned her advisor with a steely gaze. She said, "Speak truthfully."

Voron's jaw worked in circles without any words coming out. The red stone atop his staff glowed flared as if he were trying to cast a spell of some kind, but his magic was blocked by something more powerful. Finally, he croaked out, "No, my lady."

"It's settled then," she said. "Iymbryl, fetch the dryad. Voron, leave us. I wish to speak with the traveller alone."

Voron's hand lashed out, and he gripped the priestess's shoulder with thin, yellowed fingers. "Kalia, no. I cannot allow—"

"You overstep your place, Voron Blackthorne." The priestess pulled her arm away, but he held fast. "Unhand me!"

"Kalia," he begged. Desperation cloyed at the edges of his words and cold fury burned in his eyes. "You must not be alone with this man. He will defile you. He will—"

Rage boiled inside my chest at the sight of Voron's claw-like fingers digging into the priestess's soft skin. Without thinking about it, I reached behind my back and pulled my sword from its sheath. I whipped the blade over my shoulder and pointed it at the advisor's throat. Behind me, Iymbryl made a choking sound and I felt the point of her spear against my spine. But I refused to stand down.

"Let go of the lady," I said.

"Treachery!" Voron Blackthorne shouted with a strangled cry. "Why has this vermin been allowed to enter the temple with a weapon on his back? Iymbryl, you have doomed us all!"

"You did not say to take his sword," the elf-guard said. "You said—"

"Are we in the habit of leaving our prisoners armed, you fool?" the advisor snarled. "I suppose the dryad has been left in her cell with her staff as well?"

Iymbryl's silence spoke volumes.

"Get your greasy fingers off the priestess, elf," I said. "And I will lay my sword at her feet. Would that satisfy you?"

"Go, Iymbryl," Voron said, his staff blazed like a burning ember. "Make sure she is where you left her, and this time, you will take her staff."

"Yes, Master," the guard said in a trembling voice. I felt the tip of her spear and her presence behind me disappear. But I did not take my eyes off the sallow elf.

"How about it, Voron?" I said. "A truce?"

He curled his lip at me and said, "You first."

I glanced at the priestess, who watched me carefully. She smiled slightly and dipped her head. Voron did not seem to see the movement, focussed on my blade as he was. Trusting the priestess to handle herself, I lay my sword at her feet.

The advisor grinned triumphantly and released the woman's arm. He lifted his staff and the red stone burst into a flaming vermillion blaze. The look on his eyes was like that of a vengeful god about to smite a defiant mortal.

But before he could cast his spell, or blast me with his staff, or whatever he intended to do, the priestess raised a hand, and the red light snuffed out. She said, "Voron, bring me the Book of Elders."

"But Priestess," he said, "I cannot leave you alone with this—"

"I have heard your protests," she replied coolly. "I appreciate you concern, but you need not treat me as a child. I can protect myself within my own temple, Voron. Do not defy me again."

Her golden hair floated around her shoulders like it was charged with electrical energy, and the air filled with a buzzing tension. The elf-advisor's staff remained dull and lifeless in his hands, and a faint sheen of sweat had broken out across his sallow forehead. His eyes jumped to me, where I stood a respectful distance from the priestess. His lips pulled into a frown, and the gray of his eyes deepened until they seemed like the dead black eyes of a shark. Around the edges of his dilated pupils, a strange light glowed as hot as molten rock beneath a crust of blackened earth.

Then he blinked, and the light was gone. Voron said, "As you wish, Kalia."

And he disappeared.

I swallowed, staring at the space where he had been, with a thickness at the back of my throat. Priestess Kalia's face remained impassive as she gazed upon me with her purple eyes. It seemed she was waiting for me to speak. So I said, "Can they all do that? Elves, I mean."

The corners of her lips quirked up and she lifted a perfectly shaped eyebrow. "You speak as if you do not think I am one of them," she said. "Nor yourself."

"I am just a man," I said, staring up at her in awe. "But even I can see that you are something far greater and more powerful than Voron Blackthorne."

"A fact that Voron forgets from time to time." Her lips parted, and a musical laugh trilled through the stillness. "I usually let him."

"Why?"

She slipped a long, tanned leg off the dais, and ran a bare toe along the length of the sword I had laid at her feet.

I swallowed hard.

She said, "What did you say your name was, traveller?"

"Logan," I said. "Logan Greenwood."

She licked her lips and cocked her head at me. "Interesting. Do you know anything about this sword, by chance?"

"Only what Ruhail told me," I said. "I found it in a stump in the forest. She seemed to think Voron wouldn't like it."

"Your friend the dryad sounds like a clever creature," she said. "Tell me, is she very beautiful?"

I was tempted to flatter. *Nothing compared to you, Priestess*. But I had the sense that she heard enough of that kind of empty praise from Voron and the others who hung around for her power. I said, "Yes. She is very beautiful."

"Is she like me?" The priestess dropped another leg to the floor. The fabric that pooled between them stretched tight and lifted slightly. I had to tear my eyes away from the apex of her thighs so I could look her in the eye.

"You are beautiful, too," I said. "But it is different. Ruhail has an earthy, natural kind of beauty to her. One longs to touch her. You... you are untouchable."

"Do you know why I seem untouchable to you, Logan?" the priestess asked. She spread her legs farther apart and rested her hands between her thighs, pressing the sheer purple fabric down to hide anything I might have glimpsed there. "It is because I am untouched."

"Untouched?"

"I represent the virgin forest," she said. "I was promised to the next Emperor before I was even born, and I have been saved for him. Each realm gives a priestess to the emperor once a new one has taken the scepter, and the Ring Wood—the Realm of Life—always provides the first wife. I am powerful here, in my temple, and my power rests in my purity. When the new Emperor takes me, my power will become his."

My muscles tensed at the idea of Voron Blackthorne being the first to touch this perfect woman. How horrible it must be for her to have this fate looming over her head. I said, "Don't you get to keep anything for yourself?"

"Oh yes," she said. "The power of each realm always resides within the priestess wives of the emperor. It is not lessened by sharing. And by having the power of each realm, the emperor becomes a symbol of unity, the most powerful person in all the realms."

"Forgive me," I said, closing my eyes and bowing my head before her. "But I shudder to think of Voron Blackthorne as the next Emperor."

I could feel her watching me, and I looked up again.

The priestess's eyes twinkled, and she smiled. "It will be as it was meant to be."

I took a deep breath and gazed at her like I was drinking fresh water after a long thirst. She seemed to glow from within with a kind of ethereal golden light. She could have been hundreds of years old, for all I knew, but to me she looked barely eighteen, young and fresh and full of life. I couldn't bear the thought of Voron's hands on her.

"I am not from this place," I said, bile rising in the back of my throat. "And I do not presume to know better than your Emperor. But it would be a crime against nature for one as perfect as you to give yourself to a man like that."

"It is kind of you to worry," she said. "But I have no such qualms. When Voron returns with the Book of Elders, I will show you why."

I gritted my teeth and nodded. What else could I do? This was her world, her rules, and as much as I hated it, it was her life.

"All the same," I said, not quite able to let it go. "If you change your mind, I would help you. I mean, if you wanted to escape or something."

Her purple eyes rode up and down my face and body in a way that I swear I could physically feel, and I froze there, pinned beneath the power of that look. I had no choice but to return her gaze, and in my mind, I was pulling off the sheer purple fabric to expose her small, ripe breasts. The air between us crackled like static.

"Thank you, Logan Greenwood," she said. "I will remember that. Pick up your sword."

I knelt to take the blade from its place at her feet, careful not to touch her bare toes. I wasn't sure, but I had a feeling that touching the untouchable Priestess was probably the sort of sin a lowly traveller could be executed for even if her advisor had gotten away with it. I tried not to pay too much attention to the warmth emanating from her naked legs. As I picked up the sword, the hairs on my arms stood on end, as if they were reaching for her.

Ignoring my impulse to touch her, I stumbled backward with the blade in my hands and took a deep breath. I counted to ten in my head as I slid the sword back into its scabbard on my back, trying to collect my thoughts.

The moment I dropped my arms down to my sides, both Iymbryl and Voron appeared on either side of the priestess.

The advisor held a fat book beneath his right arm—the same ancient-looking tome he'd been poring over in his study—and gripped his gnarled black staff with his left. He had a surly expression on his pasty face, and he glowered at me like it was my fault the priestess had sent him away.

Iymbryl, on the other hand, looked like she'd seen a ghost—or whatever the equivalent supernatural creature would be in this world. Her fair skin had a deathly pallor and her long, blond hair was disheveled. Her electric blue eyes were wide and terrified.

"I am sorry, my lady." The elf-guard dropped to her knees before the priestess and sobbed. "I have failed you."

Voron's dull gray eyes darted between the priestess and the prostrated woman. Then his lips curled into a sinister grin. "Where is the prisoner, Iymbryl?"

The blond elf's shoulders shook violently as she tried to speak through her tears.

"She's gone, Master," she cried. "The dryad is gone."

Chapter 9

"Aha!" Voron slammed his staff into the stone floor, his sinister smile growing wider and wider. "There you have it. Proof of her guilt."

"Gone?" I said. "What do you mean she's gone?"

Worry tickled at the back of my mind.

"Obviously, she is the traitor we suspected her to be," Voron said. "Why would she run if she is innocent?"

I glared at the sallow-skinned elf. "Maybe because you kept threatening her."

"Shut your foolish mouth, you vagrant," Voron snarled. His fingers gripped the ancient leather of the book so hard that the tips became white.

I wasn't surprised that Ruhail *could* escape the cell given that she'd had her staff, but she hadn't wanted to. Had something happened to change her mind? Or was something else going on here that I wasn't seeing?

"Iymbryl," I said gently and knelt beside the stricken elf-guard. "Are you certain that she was gone? She could have hidden herself from you somehow. She had her staff."

The blond elf pushed herself up off the stone floor and turned on me like an angry cat. Her bright blue eyes blazed behind a shimmer of tears. She said, "You don't have to remind me."

Voron Blackthorne drove the butt of his staff against the floor. It cracked like thunder, shaking the entire pavilion. The red stone blazed brightly and cast eerie shadows on the elf-guard's face.

Iymbryl flinched and crawled backwards as if she expected him to strike her.

Instinctively, I stepped between the blond elf and the priestess's irate advisor. He pointed the staff at my chest and said, "Move, you fool. Don't think I won't go through you to punish her."

"She hasn't done anything wrong." I stared into his dull gray eyes. Again I saw something flicker beneath the surface of his gaze, but in a flash it was gone. I said, "I was there when you gave your orders. You never said to disarm us."

"You speak of one of the highest ranking guards in the temple," the advisor sneered. "And you think she doesn't know how to handle a prisoner? You insult us both."

"Enough." The priestess rose from her dais, her long, tanned legs unfolding like petals on an exotic flower. The sheer purple wrap spilled from her lap and pooled around her feet. She wore the fabric tied loosely, so that her form made a pale shadow behind its many folds. She held out her hand to Voron. "Give me the book, please."

Voron clutched the book tightly against his chest, his gaze jumping to the priestess. "I will need it back when you are done. My research is—"

"Your research, Voron, is secondary to my needs as the priestess of the forest temple," she said. The long waves of her hair poured over her shoulders like liquid gold. She was so beautiful it was hard to look at her, but her purple eyes flashed dangerously. "The Book of Elders belongs to me. I will give it and take it as I see fit. Do you understand?"

Voron stared at the priestess as if she'd asked him to cut one of his kidneys out with a rusty scalpel. She paid no attention, waiting patiently until he handed it over. His pale fingers trembled and his sallow skin took on a waxy pallor. The priestess accepted the book with both hands, like an offering.

"Thank you," she said. "You may leave us now, Voron."

His sharp, black eyebrows arched all the way up to his greasy hairline. "What? But—"

"I am not concerned about the dryad," the priestess said. "Even if she has turned traitor and sold herself to the Lord of Chaos—"

"She hasn't," I blurted out, loudly and without thinking. Then I cringed that I had interrupted the priestess. I made an apologetic motion with my hand. She smiled slightly and indicated for me to continue. More quietly, I said, "She was nearly killed trying to deliver this message to you."

"That's just what a servant of Drakkus would say." Voron's voice trembled with barely contained rage. The dark circles beneath his eyes seemed to sink deeper into his skull and his eye bulged. "You cannot listen to this man, Kalia. He is a danger to you and to the entire realm."

"Am I so weak, Voron?" The priestess turned her back on him and descended the steps from the dais, coming nearer to me with the enormous book held in her hands as if it weighed nothing at all. "That I would endanger the Ring Wood for the sake of a handsome stranger? You must think me a very incompetent leader, indeed."

"That is not what I meant, my lady," he said in a wheedling tone. "But you are young, yet, and inexperienced in the ways of men. I worry that—"

"You worry needlessly," she said, and she reached down to help Iymbryl off the floor. The guard kept her head lowered and her shoulders slumped, but she allowed the priestess to lift her to her feet. "I am well aware of my duty to the realm. And I am not some helpless babe in the woods, without guile or defenses of my own. But I will keep Iymbryl with me, if it makes you feel better."

The blond elf-guard looked up, confusion glittering with the tears in her blue eyes. Her gaze danced between the priestess and her advisor.

"But she failed you," Voron said, stumbling after the priestess. His leg seemed to be bothering him more than before, and he walked with a pronounced limp, clutching his gnarled black staff as if he might fall without it.

"She has not," Priestess Kalia said. "She has displeased you, which is easy enough to do."

I snorted and covered my mouth with my hand, pretending to cough. Voron's eyes pierced me with a look of hatred so pure I felt it like knives in my chest. The red stone blazed again and I wondered if he was casting some magic against me. But the sensation disappeared after a moment, and the light dimmed. The greasy-haired elf looked more exhausted than evil, then. He said, "I beg your forgiveness, my lady. I have overstepped myself in my desire to protect you."

The priestess smiled up at her advisor, and he seemed to grow a little taller under her gaze.

"Rest easy, Voron," she said. "You work yourself too hard, and you begin to see shadows in even the most unlikely of places. I do not believe the dryad to be a threat. As I was saying, even if she were a servant of the Chaos Lord, she would not be able to harm me in my own temple. I am protected by the Heart and the Spirit of the Forest."

"Of course." Voron ran a bony, sallow-skinned hand over his luxurious green robes as if he was trying to wipe away the embarrassment he'd cause himself. "I will return to my study, Kalia. If you need me, I am but a summons away."

Then he disappeared.

"That's a trick I wouldn't mind learning," I said, mostly to myself.

Though it did make me wonder, if Iymbryl and Voron could disappear and reappear in an instant, why had they each been away from the pavilion so long? Iymbryl may have searched for Ruhail before reluctantly coming back to admit defeat. But Voron should have known exactly where the book was. What else had he been doing while he was gone?

I didn't like the elf, but I did feel a bit sorry for him. I could understand his wanting to protect the priestess. Now that I had met her, I was pretty sure

I'd have been violently over-protective of her too. Especially if I thought she was going to be my wife.

The thought of the mean-tempered and sickly advisor marrying the beautiful Priestess still turned my stomach. I knew such marriages of convenience happened in my world, too, though. It was the kind of thing that people in positions of power had to put up with.

"You would have to become one of my elite guards or staff," the priestess said, "to be allowed the power of magical transport within the temple."

She sauntered along the purple silken path from her dais back toward the entrance of the pavilion, her hips swaying seductively beneath her long golden hair. She carried the ancient book in front of her like it was something precious. Iymbryl fell immediately into position at the priestess's flank, with her spear at the ready. From behind I could appreciate the elf-guard's short gold-mail skirt and the pale skin of her bare thighs before her legs disappeared into the tops of her knee-high boots. Her gait was stiff and nervous, though, as if she wasn't sure why she had been allowed to stay when Voron had been sent away.

I watched the women walk away from me, with my mind half distracted. Then I realized what the priestess had said and my mouth went dry.

"Does that mean Ruhail couldn't have escaped her cell with her staff?" I called after them. "Where is she, then? Has Voron done something with her?"

"Come with me, Logan," the priestess said without turning her head. "I want to show you something, and then we will speak of all the things that are possible in the forest temple. And a few things which are not."

I shrugged my shoulders and followed the women. There wasn't much else I could do until I knew what was going on. For now, I would have to trust that Ruhail could take care of herself.

We descended the stairs into the lush courtyard garden below, with its burbling fountain and twittering birds. Multi-colored butterflies fluttered through the air and around my face. Beams of sunshine broke through the shivering green leaves overhead and warmed my skin. But inside I was cold with fear.

I had promised to speak on Ruhail's behalf. I had believed that I could plead her case to the priestess and have the dryad exonerated of Voron's accusations simply because it was the truth.

But the political situation here was much more complex than I had realized, and now it seemed naïve of me to believe the truth would be enough to set Ruhail free. Not only was Voron willing to lie and manipulate to get his way, the priestess seemed to have her own power game against the advisor, and I didn't know where me or Ruhail fit into any of it.

The priestess and the blond elf-guard slipped behind one of the tall, white-barked trees and seemed to disappear. I placed my hand against the warm, papery trunk of the tree—I wanted to call it a birch, but I didn't know if the name would apply here—and peered around it. A stone archway, not quite as tall as me, was hidden behind a shrub with pink-flowering branches. The branches bounced and swayed gently, as if someone had just passed through. I couldn't see anywhere else the pair might have gone, so I pulled aside the shrub and ducked through the arch.

Inside, the air was cool and damp. Strange lanterns cast a dim yellow glow on the walls, just enough to show that the passage turned into a narrow staircase that disappeared into the darkness above and below. I stood on the platform between flights and listened, trying to hear which way the women had gone. Somewhere below, water dripped into a pool and echoed up the stairwell. Above, there was nothing.

"Hello?" I called out. My voice bounced off the walls, repeating and fading until it receded into silence. "Priestess?"

Still nothing.

Drafts moved through the stairwell forming a strange bubble of swirling air around the platform. The breeze from above felt warmer and dryer, more inviting somehow. The air from below had a dank, cave-like feel, cold and dark, yet... undeniably enticing. If I was playing a video game, I'd be tempted to explore the downward passage, because it was the kind of place that you'd find a hidden chest with treasures, potions, or magical artifacts.

Or there would be a monster.

And this wasn't a game. It was reality—as crazy as that still seemed. If I was going to save Ruhail I didn't have time to fight monsters or hunt for treasures. I'd have to save that for later, if I got the chance.

I took the first steps up, into the warmer, drier air above. As I turned around the first corner of the winding staircase, I ran into a pair of warm, bare thighs. The elf-guard had come down to retrieve me.

Iymbryl squeaked and leaped back up the steps, her gold-mail skirt clinking faintly. She said, "What are you doing, you fool?"

"I didn't know which way you'd gone," I said. My chest hummed with the nearness of the haughty elf. She might be a little uptight, but that didn't stop my body's physical reaction. I stared after her as she climbed back up the steps. The golden skirt glittered in the dim light, and from this angle I could see the rounded edge of her ass cheeks peeking out the bottom of the skirt.

"Hurry up," she said. "The priestess is waiting."

I swallowed hard and cleared my throat. "What's down there?"

She ignored me and kept climbing. Irritation burned my face. Why was she so stuck up? I imagined bending the elf over my lap and lifting up that skirt to give her a good spanking. My breathing sped up as we climbed. I forced myself to stay back a little, so I could maintain my view of her legs disappearing into the skirt. I fantasized about all the ways I would punish the elf if I had the chance.

Eventually we came to a wooden door. Iymbryl pushed it open and a pool of soft, warm light spilled into the staircase. The elf guard stepped aside to let me enter the room. In the light, my arousal was clearly visible, but I didn't have the urge to hide it from the elf. She bit her lip as I passed and kept her eyes lowered. A blush crept across her cheeks. I wondered if she was tempting me on purpose, if she wanted to be punished.

"Close the door, Iymbryl," the priestess said from somewhere deeper in the room. "And come here."

I stepped farther inside to allow the elf to perform her duty and looked around.

Walls of bookshelves surrounded us and an ornate chandelier hung from the ceiling. The scent of dusty old books and leather filled the room. The priestess had arranged herself on an oversized chair upholstered in rich, red velvet. She held the Book of Elders, also oversized, in her lap, so that she looked like a doll some child had set up in a play library. The priestess's sheer purple gown gaped slightly at the neck, and when she leaned forward over the book I could see the tops of her breasts hanging over the pages.

Iymbryl obediently strode over to stand next to the chair and propped her spear up next to her. She stood as still as a statue, her bright blue eyes fixed straight ahead.

"I was worried that you'd gotten lost," the priestess said, sitting up in her chair. She leaned on the armrest and touched Iymbryl's leg with her hand. The guard trembled slightly at her touch but stood still. The priestess's hand slid slowly up the inside of the elf guard's thigh. My pulse throbbed in my temples as I watched. Her hand stopped just before I had a heart attack. She said, "I sent Iymbryl back down to look for you."

"I did lose you." My voice came out sounding parched. "I wasn't sure which way you'd gone on the stairs."

"You must be careful," the priestess said, stroking the pale flesh just below the elf-guard's golden skirt. "There are many dangers in this temple."

"I thought you weren't worried," I said, tearing my gaze away from the priestess's hand to look into her eerie purple eyes. "That's what you told Voron."

"I am not the one who is in danger here," she said. "Tread carefully, and I'm sure you will be safe, too. You haven't been led astray yet."

"Was it a test?" I asked, a certainty settling over me. "The stairwell?"

"You felt it, didn't you?" The purple-eyed maiden smiled, and though she was young and beautiful, there was something ancient and powerful in the look she gave me. "The pull of the darkness, of secrets and treasures and danger? Yet you chose to come to me."

"I chose the path I thought most likely to help me save Ruhail," I said. "Do you have any idea where she could have gone?"

The priestess let her hand fall from the blond elf's thigh and ran her fingers over the edge of the enormous book in her lap. She flipped the pages without looking at them, like an invisible force was guiding her.

"I promised to tell you about the temple, and the things which can and cannot happen here," she said.

I breathed deeply of the comforting scent of old books and watched her flick through the ancient tome. "Yes," I said. "Please. I don't understand this place at all."

She stopped on a page covered in complex drawings done in faded purple ink. From what I could see, the symbols and images had a mystical air, like a prop from a B-grade fantasy movie. Under her fingers, the purple ink began to glow. She said, "Tell me, Logan. Where do you really come from?"

I glanced at Iymbryl, but she continued to stare straight ahead. Her chest rose and fell rapidly, as if she were afraid or maybe anxiously anticipating something. I said, "I will tell you, but it will sound insane."

"You might be surprised," the priestess said. "Listen, Iymbryl. It will be as I told you before the last blood moon."

The elf-guard stiffened and gripped her spear with a white knuckled hand. Her gaze shot to me and then straight ahead again, like an involuntary flinch. As I told my story to the priestess—from the few foggy memories of my old world, to the strange happenings that had occurred since I awoke in the forest—the blond elf became more and more agitated.

The priestess listened with the big book in her lap, and the magical symbols glowed brighter. In the faint purple glow of the book, I could see her fingers slip back between Iymbryl's legs as she began to stroke the inside of elf woman's thigh. Iymbryl trembled under her touch.

I finished my story with our arrival at the temple and let my words trail off as the priestess's fingers slid beyond the edge of Iymbryl's short skirt. The elf's skin had flushed pink everywhere that I could see and her legs shook as the priestess teased between her legs. My voice caught in my throat as I watched, helpless with desire for the two women and unable to do anything about it.

"You see, Iymbryl?" the priestess said. The elf guard closed her eyes, took a shaking inward breath, and nodded her head. The priestess's purple gaze turned to me and she said, "What did you say the dryad called you?"

I cleared my throat and croaked out, "Loghann Grenwyld."

A smile spread across the priestess's face, bright enough to light the darkest night.

"I told you so," she said to the elf. "Now, you know what you have to do."

Iymbryl's eyes shot open. Her spear dropped, so that she held it in both hands, and she took a cautious step toward me as if she were a huntress advancing on an enraged boar.

I took a step backward, my heartbeat thundering in my ears. I cursed the priestess and her teasing. I attempted to process what had gone wrong, but my fuzzy brain only had a fraction of the blood and oxygen it needed to form coherent thoughts. The rest of it throbbed between my legs with a painfully hard and thick erection.

Then the elf let the spear clatter to the floor and took another step toward me. She bit her lip as she approached, staring up at me with her cold blue eyes brimming with resentment and... something else. I couldn't think. When we were face to face, she turned her back on me and leaned forward until her firm, chain-mailed ass pressed against my crotch. I froze there, unable to comprehend what was happening.

Iymbryl lowered herself to her knees, slowly, dragging her ass and back against my rigid cock as she went. Then she crawled forward, exposing everything that I had attempted to catch a glimpse of on the stairwell. She lowered her front half down to the ground, holding her wrists behind her back as if they were handcuffed, and pressed her face against the floor at the foot of the priestess's chair.

"We have been waiting for you, Loghann," the priestess said. At the moment I didn't want to argue about the name. I could see the sharp points of her aroused nipples pressing against the sheer purple fabric of her gown. "This is my gift to you."

The gold-mail skirt hiked up to display the elf's bare ass, cheeks spread to reveal the tight, dusky pink ring of her asshole. Below this, the naked swollen lips of her pussy glistened. Her excitement was obvious.

She was waiting for me.

Chapter 10

My hands moved to the button on my pants without my even thinking about it. My cock begged to be released. After getting so close with the nymphs and then being interrupted, I wanted absolutely nothing more than to pin the blond elf down and drive myself into the hot, wet slit of her pussy until she screamed.

I took a step forward and undid the button. The priestess leaned forward eagerly, licking her lips. Then I remembered what Ruhail had said the night we'd slept in the summoning circle.

Yes, she had laughed, the priestess will have plans for you.

I paused and the priestess watched me with her purple eyes dancing.

"What's the matter, Loghann?" she said. "Don't you like your gift?"

My eyes fell to the elf's upturned ass and the inviting pink opening above and below. Fuck, she was so wet.

"I like her very much," I said, my voice thick in my throat. "But I can't do this right now."

The elf whimpered piteously.

The priestess sat up straight in her oversized chair. "Why ever not?"

"I am worried about Ruhail," I said, closing my eyes to block out the temptation. "I promised her I would speak on her behalf when I had my audience with you. I thought I could help to clear her name. But now she's missing, and I can't let myself be distracted until I find out that she's safe."

"Oh, is that all?" The priestess laughed brightly.

I opened my eyes in surprise.

She let her head fall back until her small firm breasts popped up above the neckline of her robe, and my hands moved toward my crotch. It pulsed with desire for the priestess, despite the fact that I had just told her I was too worried to fuck her little elf slave.

The priestess began to speak in a strange, musical language. As she spoke the letters on the book glowed with purple light. She swayed back and forth like she was communing with invisible spirits. Suddenly she stopped, and she looked back up at me with her purple eyes wide.

"What's the matter," I said. "Is she okay?"

"She is safe," the priestess said. "She escaped through the tunnel with the nymphs. You didn't tell me you had been visited by nymphs."

Visions of the bubble-bodied little porn stars flooded my memory, and my balls ached all over again. I said, "In the cell. We were having a great time until your guard here interrupted us."

"And still you would not take advantage of this opportunity," the priestess said, awe coloring the edges of her voice. "Because you feared for the dryad's safety?"

"I saved her life once already," I said. "I feel responsible for her."

"And have you used her as you used the nymphs?" The priestess asked, her voice growing husky. "As you imagine using Iymbryl here?"

I closed my eyes and shook my head. I took a deep breath. "She offered herself to me, but she didn't want it. I couldn't."

"You didn't *want* to?" she asked. "It is your right as her bond mate. She belongs to you as surely as Iymbryl belongs to me."

"Of course I wanted to," I said, and my eyes fell to the elf trembling at my feet. "She is insanely sexy. But I didn't want to abuse my power over her. I wouldn't take her against her will."

"You are an unusual man, Loghann," the priestess said. The tanned skin of her chest was flushed in blotchy patches. She closed the book and set it on a table next to her, then she leaned back and pulled her legs up onto the chair. The sheer purple fabric of her robe fell up to her hips and her hand slipped between her thighs as she looked up at me.

"What about *her*?" I said, lowering myself to my knees behind the elf.

The priestess's lips quirked upward. "What *about* her?"

I slowly slid my left hand into the top of my boxers and pulled out my throbbing cock. It was huge, and the priestess gasped when she saw it. I couldn't ever remember having an erection like this, the skin was stretched so tight it felt thin and the nerves were painfully sensitive. With my other hand I gripped the elf's ass cheek and squeezed. She cried out, and her pussy clenched in anticipation.

"Does she want to be taken?" I said.

"Iymbryl wants what I tell her to want," the priestess said, breathing heavily now. "I could tell her to let a troll violate her backside and she would do it, then come crawling back to beg me for more."

I let my finger slide along her ass crack and into the hot, wet lips. Iymbryl moaned. I said, "Is that true?"

The elf panted on the floor. "I would happily humiliate myself for my Priestess."

If she wanted to be humiliated, I could get into that. I didn't remember ever having done anything like that before in my old life, but the appeal was undeniable. Especially since the elf had been so snotty with us ever since Ruhail and I arrived at the temple.

I pressed the tip of my cock against the inner folds of her pussy and felt her muscles tense against me. I said, "You're a dirty little slave. Is that why you let Voron fuck you?"

The elf leaned back into me pressing me deeper inside. I pushed her back off and slapped her ass. She yelped and the crack of our flesh connecting echoed off the bookshelves. A pink handprint shaped welt rose up on her pale skin.

"You know about that?" the priestess said, her fingers moving faster between her legs now, excited by my rough treatment of the elf. I licked my lips and watched her. She held my gazed as she stroked herself, completely unashamed. The priestess wasn't exactly as inexperienced as she pretended to be.

"Representing the virgin forest doesn't stop you from touching yourself," I said and slapped the Iymbryl's other cheek. She squealed, but kept her wrists dutifully clasped behind her back. I pulled her back against my cock and forced her to wait while I teased my tip along her swollen lips and clit. She didn't try to take any more than I was ready to give her this time.

"I cannot be touched by men." The priestess's face burned red, with excitement or embarrassment, it was impossible to tell. Maybe she longed to be humiliated too, and that's why she made her slave prostrate herself like a dog in heat. "Not until I am taken by the next Emperor, he must be the first. Iymbryl helps me to take care of the urges I otherwise must supress."

"Maybe you're not such a bad little elf after all," I said, rubbing the tender skin on her buttocks. She flinched under my touch and then moaned with pleasure. "Tell me, Iymbryl. If your Priestess didn't demand it, would you ever come to me voluntarily?"

She didn't answer. I smacked her again, so hard even the priestess winced at the noise. The elf groaned. Through gritted teeth she said, "Never. You disgust me."

"And yet you offer yourself to me just so the little virgin can pleasure herself at your humiliation?"

"Yes," she said, her voice trembling as if she expected another spanking. "Humiliating myself for *her* pleasure is the only thing that gives *me* pleasure. The worse the humiliation, the more surely I know I belong only to her."

"That is supremely fucked up," I said. I stroked the elf's fat lower lips with my fingers and I could feel how much she was enjoying this game. I slid my finger up, past the slit of her warm pussy, and around the dark pink hole of her ass. She froze, panting heavily. The priestess's purple eyes went wide, and an excited gasp escaped her lips. I leaned forward and whispered next to the elf's ear, "You know, right now, I want to fuck you just because I know you don't want me to. That's probably even worse."

"If that's what you want," the priestess said. "You have my permission."

"First I want to know how this works," I said. "How does she help you take care of your urges? Do you always watch?"

"No," the priestess said. She scooted herself back on the chair and opened her legs, so that I could see the sweet little mound and the glistening pink folds of flesh around her swollen clit. "Iymbryl shares my bed. She comes back to me after her exploits and touches me the way the men touch her, to prepare me for my marriage bed."

"Show me."

I shoved the elf forward roughly, and she gazed up at the priestess. The purple-eyed beauty trembled, as she looked from me to the blond elf, but she nodded her head. Iymbryl crawled forward and touched the priestess's thighs gently, moving her hands up and down the young woman's legs. The priestess leaned back and moaned as the elf slid two fingers inside her pussy and began to thrust them back and forth, slowly.

"With your fingers?" I said, gripping my cock in my hand and stroking myself as I watched the elf woman pleasure her mistress. "Never with your mouth?"

The elf stopped and looked at me over her shoulder.

"She kisses me, of course," the priestess said.

"Where?"

"My mouth," the priestess said. "My throat."

"Never lower?"

The priestess's eyes grew wide. "What do you mean?"

I groaned. This was too good to be true. I stood and stripped off my T-shirt, pulled my pants and boxers off. I wanted to feel her body against every inch of my skin.

Not taking my eyes off the priestess, I said, "Iymbryl, take off your mistress's robes."

"What?" The priestess said. "You can't—"

"Listen, Priestess, I will fuck your elf slave until she begs me to stop," I promised. "But I want you naked while I do it. And *I'm* not allowed to touch you."

The priestess bit her bottom lip and looked up at me, then down at my huge, throbbing erection. I had never been so hard in my life, and I wasn't going to waste it. She nodded. Iymbryl slid her hands up under the sheer purple fabric of the priestess's gown and pulled it slowly up over her head. When she pulled it all the way off, the priestess's golden hair fell around her shoulders and her small, firm breasts. Her pink nipples were hard and taut with excitement.

"Good," I said and I crouched behind the elf again. "Now take off Iymbryl's armor."

The priestess slid forward and undid the leather buckles holding the golden cage around the elf's breasts in place. Once it was unclasped, she lowered the lacy metal plate to the ground.

"Everything?" The priestess asked breathlessly.

I slid my hands up under the elf's gold-mail skirt and pulled her hips toward me. "No," I said. "The skirt and boots can stay. Get on your hands and knees, Iymbryl."

The blond elf obeyed me wordlessly. Once she was fully on the ground, I slid the skirt up over her hips and positioned myself behind her. I knocked her knees apart a little wider with the outside of my thighs and enjoyed the warmth of her skin against my legs. I felt her muscles shaking with the effort of holding herself low and spread for me.

I put one hand on her upraised tailbone and slid the other between her legs. She was so wet, her juices ran down my fingers when I touched her. Good. I rubbed her wetness over the shaft of my cock and pressed my tip inside her pussy. She knew better than to try to push herself onto me now. She waited, shaking.

I leaned forward over her back and gathered up the elf's long blond hair in my left hand, pressing deeper into her. She moaned. I said, "Are you going to be able to take it?"

She nodded.

"Good girl." I pulled her head back with my left hand and reached down to rub her clit with my right as I teased the tight little opening between her legs.

The priestess watched with her lips parted and her small chest heaving with excitement. To her I said, "Scoot forward and open your legs."

The priestess obeyed me too, forgetting in the heat of the moment that it was she who ruled this place. She leaned back on her elbows, pushing her ass up to the edge of the chair, her thighs open. Her naked mound, with a thin stripe of golden hair, opened too. Her small breasts, each barely a palm full, rose and fell with her eager breaths.

I tugged Iymbryl's head up higher and pushed her face toward the priestess's opened legs. I said, "Now kiss her."

The priestess's purple eyes widened, and she stared at me with her mouth open. "You want her to kiss me there?"

"Yes," I said. My mind ran with ways to make this more humiliating for the elf. "She's going to lick you. Like the dog she is."

The elf whimpered as she leaned forward and pressed her face into the priestess's hot little slit. She licked along the outer lips with long, lapping stroked of her tongue. The priestess panted, harder, and arched her hips against the elf's mouth. She moaned.

"I knew you'd like that," I said, holding the elf's head so she couldn't back up. Then I rubbed her clit to reward her for doing such a good job. There was no doubt Iymbryl was enjoying it, so I decided to push things a little farther. "You lick her everywhere, my little elf bitch, if you want to get fucked like a dog too."

I'd never considered myself a dominating kind of guy, but there was something almost primal in my urge to own and debase the guard. When she started lapping at the priestess's pussy desperately, her ass pressed against my cock, I felt a hard knot of desire forming in my abdomen. I couldn't believe this was real.

I shifted back to get a better view. The priestess's head had rolled back against the chair, and her eyes were unfocused. A passionate wail escaped her throat, and her cheeks flushed bright red. The elf flicked her tongue rapidly over the young Priestess's exposed clit. The louder the priestess moaned the faster she worked her tongue.

"Very good girl." My breaths came in sharp gasps and my cock seemed to swell even bigger than before. I slid myself along the wetness between Iymbryl's legs, teasing us both.

I rubbed the elf's tight little asshole with my index finger, and I felt her stiffen. But she didn't stop licking the priestess. I groaned. I could take her that way if I wanted to. It would be the ultimate humiliation. The thought of it made me insane with lust. But I restrained myself.

I had to save something for next time.

I wasn't even finished yet, and I had already decided there was definitely going to be a next time.

I pushed the head of my cock into her pussy and wrapped one arm around her waist to hold her still. The priestess was screaming now, her thighs shaking. The elf kept licking at her slit, just like the dog I had told her she was. I forced myself inside her.

She fell forward, face first, and moaned into the priestess's pussy, "Oh fuck, Kalia, he's so big."

Her pussy was so tight, the sensations took my breath away. I grabbed her hips and thrust again. She screamed. The priestess sat up on her elbow and wrapped her fingers in the elf's hair, holding her face between her shaking thighs. "Yes, Loghann," she panted. "Take her like that. Harder."

I didn't need any extra encouragement. I was so pent up, my body acted almost of its own volition. I drove myself into her tiny elf cunt over and over, as she kept licking the priestess. Soon both women were screaming and shaking, and I couldn't hold back any longer.

The orgasm grew and expanded until I erupted in a hot burst of cum that filled the elf and spilled out from between her legs. She wrapped her arms around the priestess's waist and sagged to the floor, exhausted. I slipped out of her and fell to my hands and knees with my cock still pulsing with my heartbeat.

"Holy shit," I gasped, laughing.

The priestess began to laugh, too. "What's so funny?"

"If you wanted to kill me," I panted, "there are easier ways to do it."

"Everything hurts," Iymbryl moaned.

"Did you cum?" I asked the priestess as I tried to catch my breath.

She blushed and nodded. "I have never experienced such intense pleasure."

I reached out and whacked the elf-guard's booted foot with the palm of my hand. "What about you, you dirty little mutt?"

She moaned and shook her head. "I think you bruised my insides."

I grabbed her by the ankles and dragged her toward me. She shrieked and tried to back away. I said, "Priestess, do you ever reward your slave for good behavior?"

The priestess laughed and nodded her head. She rolled onto her belly on the over-size chair, ready to enjoy the show. "Yes, Loghann. I have much to learn about this technique. I will watch."

"I'm not doing it," I said. I pushed up the gold-mail skirt once more and spread the elf's legs. "Get down here and do it yourself."

The priestess's eyes grew wide. "Me?"

"The best way to learn is to try," I grinned at her and slapped the elf's swollen mound with my fingers. She writhed and moaned under my touch. The priestess bit her bottom lip, and looked up at me through her golden lashes. Then she smiled back.

She crawled down off the chair on her hands and knees and got down on the floor between the elf's legs. I scooted out of her way, so the priestess didn't have to worry about touching me accidently. I leaned over Iymbryl's body, pinning her to the floor, and I squeezed her breasts in my hands. I pinched her nipples, gently at first and then harder, until her moans became screams, and she struggled to get away from me.

"What do I do?" the priestess asked nervously.

"Hold her legs apart," I said. "And then kiss her. Lick, tease, nibble, try it all over. Whatever she responds to, do more of that. You can humiliate with pleasure as well as pain. She's completely at our mercy."

The priestess giggled. "She's covered in your seed."

"Clean her up." I pinched the elf's nipples and felt her jolt. My cock was stirring again. "If you want to learn how to please your future emperor, you might as well develop a taste for it."

To my surprise the priestess dropped her face between Iymbryl's legs and dragged her tongue from bottom to top without any hesitation. She lapped up the river of cum flowing out of the elf's pussy like a cat lapping up milk from a bowl. Both women moaned and the blood rushed out of my head again. Iymbryl's hips bucked under the attention of her mistress, but I held her down. The priestess kissed, and licked, and sucked like she had been doing it her whole life.

I watched her with desire burning in my chest. When the priestess looked up at me from between the elf's trembling thighs, her cheeks flushed pink with excitement and her purple eyes dancing. I realized she was doing this as much for me as for her lover. I felt myself stiffen all over again.

"Why don't you make Iymbryl help you with that?" The priestess licked a strand of my cum from her lip, eyeing my erection. "Perhaps she should develop a taste as well?"

The elf rolled her head to the side and opened her mouth.

I took a brief moment to thank whatever gods or fates had brought me to this moment. As I sank my cock into the elf's throat and watched the priestess's darting tongue teasing her clit, I couldn't think of what I'd done to deserve this. If this was a dream, I didn't ever want to wake up. And if this was my new reality, I'd kill to protect it.

Then the time for coherent thought was gone. In an explosion like fireworks behind my eyes, I filled the blond elf's mouth with another gushing shot of cum and collapsed beside her.

Chapter 11

As we recovered from the impromptu romp, Priestess Kalia actually did get around to explaining a bit about her role at the temple and the dangers presented by the encroaching forces of the Chaos Lord, Drakkus. She pulled her sheer purple robe back over her head and wandered barefoot through the library, pulling down armfuls of books to stack next to her plush red reading chair.

Iymbryl and I dressed, too, and the elf shot me disparaging looks every time the priestess's back was turned. I grinned and mimed spanking her until she scowled and looked away. As fun as our little threesome had been, I had to admit I was intrigued by the idea of having each of the women to myself at some point in the future. The elf, in particular, if only because she seemed to want to hate me.

"Iymbryl," Priestess Kalia said as she carried over one more stack of books. "Please watch the corridor outside and ensure no one is listening."

The elf-guard gave me a final glare and stalked off to another door opposite the secret entrance we had come in by. She opened the door quietly and slipped outside, closing it tightly behind her.

"It was fortuitous of you to show up here when you did," the priestess said with a wry curl to her lips. "I was running out of ways to punish her. Voron's sexual appetites aren't what they once were. I was starting to worry that I actually would have to find a troll to violate her."

I shook my head. "I am not going to pretend to understand your arrangement. But anytime you need my help keeping her in line, I'm happy to offer my services."

"It's not so difficult to understand, really." The priestess curled up in her chair once more and pulled a thin, blue-covered book out of the stack and began flipping through the pages. "Iymbryl has always been high-strung. She's driven to succeed, to be the best at everything she does."

"I sympathize with her there," I said. "It leaves a person feeling a bit wrung out and hollow after a while. Like none of the successes really matter."

"Success is meaningless without failure," the priestess said. She shifted over on the chair and patted the cushion next to her. "Strength and power are nothing without submission. Underneath her tough exterior, she yearns to submit. She can't give herself fully in a romance because there are so few people she respects."

"She gets that with you, I suppose," I said, sitting next to her. The warmth of the priestess's thigh against my own sent a thrill of the forbidden through me. Was this allowed? I cleared my throat. "But what about Voron? I can't stand the way she simpers around that guy."

The priestess laughed. "That is my fault, I'm afraid. I ordered Iymbryl to break the vows she took as one of my guards and to offer herself as a slave to Voron's desires. It was the only way I could keep her from killing him. She absolutely loathes him. Of course, I like to know everything about what he does to her in case he—"

"Please don't talk about marrying that creep," I said. "I think I might vomit."

"Iymbryl submits to me alone," she said, looking up at me with her alarmingly purple eyes. "And someday, I will submit myself to the next emperor."

My heart beat against my chest like an animal trapped in a cage. Her gaze was like a shot of adrenaline in my veins. My mouth felt dry.

"What about the emperor?" I asked, my voice husky. "Who does he submit to?"

"I believe that is the kind of thing an emperor must discover before he is ready to accept the scepter," she replied. "Perhaps if you meet Emperor Illdrian you can ask him."

"I don't think that's the kind of thing I want to ask an emperor," I said, laughing. "What happens in the bedroom stays in the bedroom, Or the hidden library, I guess."

"Submission doesn't have to be sexual, Loghann," she said. Oh great, I thought, now she was calling me that too. The priestess continued, "The most powerful kinds of submission are not. To a higher power, for instance. Or to love and family."

Something in my chest tightened. "I wouldn't know."

"Don't you have a family?" she asked.

"I can't remember," I said, looking away from her. The words brought a mixture of emotions up to the surface of my mind, and I struggled to describe them. "I am sure I must. I feel like I am forgetting something very important about my mother. When I think of my father, there is just a kind of emptiness. A dissatisfaction that I know I carried with me to a lot of things in my life. A dissatisfaction I feel about myself, too. I get the feeling that he wasn't really a part of my life, or that if he was, he was an asshole."

"You don't behave like a man who is dissatisfied with himself," the priestess said. "You carry yourself with great confidence and strength of character. You seem to know who you are."

"Maybe." I sighed. "But I also have a feeling that I should be more than I am. I'm always chasing something, trying to be more. I can't explain it."

"Hmm." She opened the book so that it fell across both of our laps. "Perhaps it is Fate, then. Warning you of a great destiny."

The hairs on the back of my neck lifted, and I shivered. I said, "In my old world, I would have said you were crazy. Here, I'm not so sure."

"I wish you could remember more of your world," the priestess said. "I would like to ask you about it. Instead, I will tell you about our world. If you do have a great destiny ahead of you, you must be prepared."

She had opened the book to the centre, where a detailed map spread across both pages. It depicted a central mountain range with one towering flat-topped peak in the middle. Around the base of the mountains, a flat expanse of sand—colored in with a thin golden watercolor paint—stretched out until it butted up against an arc of crystal blue sea. On the other side of the sea, a lush, green forest filled the rest of the page.

"This is a map of the empire," the priestess said. "And each of these terrains represents one of the realms. The forested area here is the Ring Wood, the blue is the Azurian Sea, then the Silent Sands, the Lucidian Mountains, and the High Plains. Each realm is home to one of the ancient family clans, and is the source of one of the five major schools of order magic."

"Ruhail told me a little bit about this," I said. "The Ring Wood is home to practitioners of green magic, is that right? Magic that is connected to life forces?"

The priestess's purple eyes lit up. "That's right! I think I like your dryad. I look forward to meeting her when she decides to come out of hiding."

"You'll have to call off Voron," I said. "He seems convinced that she's evil."

The priestess waved my concerns away. "Voron has been my advisor for nearly two-hundred years. He has always been a bit paranoid. The last temple advisor was the same way. I suppose it's something about the position. They see darkness everywhere they look."

"Two-hundred years?" I said. "And here I was worried about taking advantage of you, the innocent virgin of the forest."

"I don't think I ever claimed to be innocent," the priestess giggled. "And I said I represented the virgin forest, not that I was sexually inexperienced."

"Just untouched by men," I said, and I felt myself stirring again. The place where our legs connected seemed to burn even through our clothing. "I'm touching you now, though."

She smiled up at me and blinked through long blond lashes. "Hmm. It's nice, isn't it?"

I tried to ignore the question. She was unavailable. Flirting wasn't going to get me anything except a raging case of blue balls, unless the priestess let me at the elf-guard again. I didn't want to push my luck. "Are you an elf, then? You don't have the ears."

"No," she said. "We priestesses are something different... I don't know how to explain it really. I suppose you could say I am the physical embodiment of the power of this realm. We are mortal, we live and die as other creatures do, and we are immortal, in that we are born again into a new body with all the memories of the past priestesses intact. Each priestess carries within her the limitless power of knowledge and magic in her realm."

"So what's Voron so worried about, then?" I asked. "What could possibly endanger you?"

"It takes time for a priestess to come fully into her power again once she is reborn." The seemingly-young woman tucked a strand of golden hair behind her ear and sighed. "It is only since the last blood moon that I have achieved the full strength of my potential. Until then, it has been Voron's duty to protect me. He takes his job very seriously. Too seriously, sometimes."

"The blood moon," I said. "You've mentioned it before. Voron, too. Is that when the dark forces began gathering?"

"The Lord of Chaos is always sending ripples and waves of discontent out into the world," she said. "But it was the last blood moon when his minions seemed to gather and entrench themselves, rather than simply passing through and moving on as they usually do. I am the youngest of the five priestesses awaiting the naming of the next emperor, and the last to come into my full strength."

"And Emperor Illdrian's strength is waning?" I asked.

The priestess nodded. "Perhaps Drakkus is getting desperate," she said. "He must strike before Illdrian passes on the scepter of power. For once we are united under our new emperor, we will be too strong for him to take on."

"But he refuses to do it," I said. "Because he is waiting for the return of his son."

"Yes." She looked up at me again with an unreadable expression in her eyes. "It is a dangerous time. Each realm is at its penultimate strength, second only to the moment of union with our next leader. But we each stand alone."

"United we stand, divided we fall," I said.

She blinked up at me. "Very true. So simple, and yet profound in its meaning."

"Wish I could take credit for it." I laughed. "It's a kind of proverb where I'm from."

"You are a very wise man to recognize the power of these words, Loghann."

"Sure," I said. "Can you not call me that, though?"

"But it is your name," she said.

"No. My name is Logan Greenwood. I know it's a funny coincidence, but I bear no relation to this

Loghann Grenwyld character you and Ruhail are always going on about."

"You carry the sword of Grenwyld," she said.

"I found it," I said. "It's a coincidence."

Priestess Kalia sighed dramatically and flipped through the book to another page. This one was covered in strange hieroglyphic writing that seemed to swim as I stared at it. The letters and symbols rearranged themselves on the page, twisting and shifting before my eyes. They reformed in a decorative script heading that, although it was difficult, I could just make out.

"Family Clans," I said.

The priestess's jaw dropped. She stared at me. "You can read this?"

"Yeah," I shrugged. "I mean, barely. That script is pretty hard to parse. But it's still English. Or whatever you call the language we're speaking right now."

"No," she said. "It is not. This is an ancient text, and the language here has been lost to all but the priestesses. We are the only ones who carry the cultural memory necessary to read the ancient books. This is why Voron may borrow the Book of Elders from me with no danger of him learning the secrets of a priestess's power."

"He's your protector, though," I said. "Why would you be afraid of that?"

"A priestess cannot be corrupted." The woman's purple eyes flashed. "We are the only ones safe from the call of darkness, other than an emperor bound to a priestess from each realm. A priestess's magic, turned to chaos, would be a weapon more powerful than anyone can imagine. We cannot allow our secrets to be known to anyone else, no matter how trustworthy they are."

"Oh," I said, glancing down at the book. It just looked like English to me. "I'm sorry. I didn't mean to read anything I wasn't supposed to."

"Go ahead," she said, pushing the book into my lap. "What else can you read? There is nothing dangerous in this."

"They look like names," I said, pointing to the page. "There is Grenwyld, and beside that it says 'spirit.' Blackthorne with 'earth,' Cascadia with 'water,' Hearthblaze with 'fire,' and Mystveil with 'air.' It's like each name is associated with an element."

The priestess's full lips parted in a wide smile. "Incredible. Yes, each clan has its roots in one realm, and each realm draws its strength from one of the five elements of power. I thought you didn't know anything about our world?"

"We have similar ideas where I am from," I said. "In some cultures, anyway. I'm afraid I've never been a very spiritual person. I can't explain it. But we use them in horoscopes and the same ideas work their way into a lot of stories."

"Perhaps our worlds are more connected than it seems," the priestess said thoughtfully. "Yes..."

"Okay, so Blackthorne," I said. "That's Voron's clan, I guess. Is that why he wouldn't like me carrying a sword of Grenwyld?"

"All of the elves who attend me in the temple belong to the Blackthorne clan," the priestess said. "Some more distantly than others, but they all have some Blackthorne blood. Even Iymbryl. Only the highest ranking family members are allowed to use the surname, though. Voron is one of a long line of Blackthorne advisors. Before him, his uncle served Priestess Maia, my predecessor. The advisor to Priestess Naomi of the Azurian Sea will be a member of the Cascadia clan."

"I see," I said. "And is there rivalry between the clans?"

"In a petty sort of way," the priestess said. "All of the clans and indeed the realms like to imagine themselves a step above the rest. In truth, we are all equal, and the balance between us is what creates the balance of the realms and therefore peace and order in the empire."

"The current emperor is a member of the Grenwyld clan," I said. "Does this make them more powerful? Are the other clans jealous of the Grenwyld clan's claim on the empire?"

"Yes and no," she said. "Throughout history, the Grenwyld clan has claimed more emperors than the other clans, but each clan has been represented. I believe the Grenwyld's tend to come to power more often because their magic comes from the spirit element, which is much less volatile than the others. The spirit element craves balance in a way the others do not. It is a naturally connective element."

"Tell me about the other elements," I said.

The priestess folded her hands over her belly and leaned back in the oversized chair. The points of her small breasts pressed against the tantalizingly sheer fabric of her robe. Even now that I had expelled the sexual tension that had been plaguing me since my arrival to this place, I longed to touch her. The infuriatingly chaste intimacy-by-proximity drove me insane. But, as the priestess, she remained untouchable.

I tried, and failed, to communicate that to the raging boner growing in my pants. I was forced to hold the book over my lap to hide it.

"Earth magic, or green magic, can be a bit wild and unmanageable," she said, closing her purple eyes and reciting as if by heart. "It deals with life and healing as well as sickness and death. Water magic is connected to emotions which can be fickle, it is both easy to manipulate and wildly unpredictable. Fire magic is connected to movement and energy, and is one of the most dangerous and the hardest to control as it changes course very quickly. Air magic is strange and hard to grasp, it is connected to the mind and intellect, but also fear and madness. Compared to these, spirit magic is very stable, but in contrast, it is challenging to connect to and requires a great well of inner peace in order to master."

"And the Lord of Chaos seeks to destabilize the realms," I said, "in order to shift the balance from order to chaos. It seems to me that these old clans would be a natural mark."

She opened her eyes. "How do you mean?"

"You know," I said. "Family feuds. A whisper here, a rumor there, the promise of a leg up in the next competition for imperial leadership. Old, powerful families in my world are always ripe with corruption."

She sat up, her posture stiffening. "It is strange that you should say so. This has been on my mind of late. You know, the Grenwyld clan is the only one never to lose a member to darkness. Until now, perhaps. There are concerns about Illdrian, fears that he may have fallen to madness and corruption years ago, and that his refusal to name an heir is a subtle attempt to undermine order and pave the way for chaos."

Another, different kind of chill crept over my skin. "Do you believe that?"

She shook her head. "My studies of the Book of Elders have indicated that he speaks the truth. He has heard a prophecy none of the rest can hear. His son, the real Loghann Grenwyld, will return. Unfortunately, the book also hints that war is coming, and that the new emperor may be too late to save us. Unless..."

"Unless what, Priestess?" The words stuck in my throat. The threat of this Drakkus guy was starting to feel all too real. Figures that I'd get tossed into a fantasy world on the brink of an apocalyptic-level war.

Priestess Kalia sighed. "I must ask you to leave me, Loghann."

I groaned in frustration. "Please stop calling me that."

"I'm sorry, Logan," she smiled. "Your name feels unfamiliar to my tongue, but you are right. It isn't fair to saddle you with the name of a savior who may never arrive."

She took the book from me and added it to the pile next to her chair. Then, pausing, she took it back and thrust it into my hands.

"Is this for me?" I asked.

"It is growing late," she said. "I'll have Iymbryl take you to one of my guest chambers. If you can read it, you might as well learn what you can of our history. I have some of my own research to do. You have given me much to think about."

"What about Ruhail?" I asked. "I know you've said that she is safe, but I would feel better if I could see that for myself."

The priestess stood and walked across the room to the door where Iymbryl stood guard.

"I will get a message to her," she said. "I promise you that."

She pulled the door open. The elf stood at attention with her spear pointing at the ceiling.

"Iymbryl," the priestess said, "please show Logan to a guest room. The one with the paintings of Priestess Maia, if you will."

The blond elf raised an eyebrow at her mistress. "That one? Are you sure?"

"No," the priestess said absently. "Not sure. Not yet. But it is best to be prepared."

She took me by the sleeve and led me into the hallway. I tucked the small book into my back pocket and shrugged at the elf. The priestess turned her back on us and began to close the door.

Just then, a spine-tingling howl rose from somewhere outside the temple. Iymbryl's face paled. The priestess opened the door and stared down the corridor, fear flashing in her purple eyes.

The library door slammed closed and both women broke into a run, heading for another door at the end of the hallway. Another howl joined the chorus, and I sprinted after them, wondering what in the hell was going on now.

Chapter 12

The wooden door at the end of the corridor opened up to a stone balcony overlooking the wild, dark sprawl of the Ring Wood. Voron Blackthorne and a tall male elf-guard with nut-brown skin and long white hair stood at the railing. The guard's jaw was clenched tight as he stared across the clearing at the trees. A sheen of sweat glistened on Voron's pale, waxy brow.

The sun was beginning to set, and the warm spears of golden light that had pierced the hidden grotto when Ruhail and I arrived were now tinged with rusty orange. The sky had darkened to a deep, bruised purple. Shadows stretched across the clearing as if they were reaching for the temple. Long fingers of blackness crept toward the river moat and the ornate bridges. More elf-guards, none of them in Iymbryl's scanty attire I noticed, stood with their spears crossed over the pathways leading to the temple.

At the edge of the trees, black shapes moved through the underbrush. Another howl trembled out of the forest, low and haunting. I felt the hairs on my scalp lift and prickle. More animals joined in, yipping and carousing at a distance. Voron leaned against the railing of the balcony, gripping the decorative stone banister with bloodless, white fingers.

"What is it?" the priestess asked. "Wolves? What are they doing?"

"Dire wolves," the tall, white-haired elf proclaimed. He held himself as straight as the spear in his right hand, and he looked twice as deadly. Yet he shivered as the next howl came. "I haven't heard them since the Battle at Silent Sands, under Emperor Sundamar, more than a thousand years ago. But I would know that sound anywhere. These are indeed dark times."

"It is as I predicted," Voron snarled without turning to look at the priestess. "I warned you that this was going to happen."

"To be fair," Priestess Kalia said, her shoulders stiffening, "you've been predicting the same thing for as long as I've been in power."

Voron wiped his forehead with the back of a long, bony hand and looked away from the scene below. He paused to shoot me a menacing glare then turned to face the priestess. "I need the Book of Elders, Kalia. I have not finished my protection spell yet. May I have it back, please? I must complete the ritual before the next blood moon."

The priestess sighed and turned to Iymbryl. "You know where it is?"

The blond elf nodded brusquely. She disappeared and reappeared moments later holding the ancient tome.

Relief sagged on Voron's face as he stepped forward to accept the book, but Iymbryl clenched her jaw and passed the book to Priestess Kalia. Voron's dull gray eyes blazed furiously. "These kind of games are why we are in this mess, Priestess."

"What games are you referring to, Voron?" The priestess's mouth turned downward in a frown. "You think I don't take my position at the temple seriously?"

Wiry tendons stood out on the sides of Voron's throat as he fought to control his temper. He ran a hand through his greasy black hair and forced a smile onto his sallow, thin-lipped face. "Sometimes I think you do not take me seriously, Kalia. I hope you will not live to regret that."

A violent cracking noise issued from the Ring Wood. Everyone on the balcony flinched. Iymbryl and the white-haired elf both moved quickly to protect the priestess. Voron stumbled backward, wincing as he put weight on his left leg. The red stone atop his staff pulsed once and dimmed. A creaking groan followed the crack and the treetops rustled against the darkening sky. The shriek of tearing wood rent the air and a massive, red-barked tree came rushing out of the forest and fell into the clearing with an earth-shaking thunder. In the depths of the trees, a massive shape lumbered.

My heart hammered in my chest. I had to restrain myself from pulling out my sword. It wasn't like I could do anything from up here anyway. I said, "What in the hell..."

A couple of trolls emerged from the darkness, blazing torches carried high. They lowered the flames to the fallen tree, and tongues of fire lapped at the red bark. As the blaze grew, a huge shadow in the tree was revealed. The beast was more or less bipedal, with heavily muscled arms and knuckles that dragged on the ground. Its grotesquely fat belly had a greenish tinge in the low light, and was covered in welts and warts and pustules. Its head seemed to melt into its massive, slumped shoulders so that the slavering jaw hung so low it appeared to grow out of the thing's chest. A wide flat nose with flaring nostrils reminded me of a boar, and above it, two squinty pig-like eyes were buried in thick rolls of greenish flesh.

"An ogre," the white-haired elf growled under his breath.

Huge wolves yipped and snapped at the thing's feet, more like the werewolf who had attacked Ruhail than like any wolf I'd ever seen.

"What are we going to do?" I said.

"We must get the priestess inside, immediately," the male guard said.

Iymbryl put a hand on Kalia's arm but the priestess stayed her.

The fallen tree now blazed like a bonfire, its flames reaching skyward like a row of dancers with their hands waving over their heads. If we didn't get the fire out soon, the entire forest might go up in flames. But the creatures stayed within the treeline, not seeming to dare to step into the grotto.

Lines of elf guards carried buckets of water to douse the flames while more guards stood watch with longbows and crossbows drawn, pointing into the trees. None of the monstrous creatures attempted to attack.

"What are they waiting for?" I asked.

"My magic holds them back," the priestess said. "Pure creatures of darkness and chaos cannot set foot on the holy grounds of the temple. We are safe yet, but..."

"But what?" I asked. "Priestess, we have to do something. We can't just sit here and wait for them to go away. What do they want?"

"Fool!" Voron shouted at me, gripping his staff like he wished he could clobber me over the head with it. "They want what all of the Chaos Lord's followers want. Control, power, the blood of their enemies flowing in hot rivulets over their bodies. They—*oof*."

Priestess Kalia thumped him in the chest with the Book of Elders.

"Go, Voron," she said. "Finish your spells. Strengthen our protections. This may be the last chance we get."

Voron opened his mouth to say something more, then seemed to think better of it. He pressed his lips together, snatched the book from the priestess's hands, and disappeared without another word.

I turned to the golden-haired priestess and put a hand on each of her shoulders. Realizing what I'd done, I snatched my hands away.

"I am not *that* untouchable, don't worry." She smiled and blushed. "Just... you know..."

Heat rose in my own face and I nodded brusquely, my thoughts still swirling with Voron's bitter expression. I didn't want to question the priestess in front of the senior elf-guard, but he seemed preoccupied with watching the crew on the ground.

I whispered to her, "Was that wise?"

She gave me a look that said now was not the time for this discussion. Aloud she said, “We do not have the numbers to form an offensive attack. We must focus on defense. Voron can enhance the protective spells surrounding the clearing. While I am alive, no creature of pure chaos can penetrate the grotto.”

I had a sick feeling in my stomach as I looked down at the trolls and wolves that gathered along the border of the temple grounds. Cackling came from deeper in the woods, and the flash of magic spells lit up the trees. More were coming. I didn’t like the way she had said that. *No creature of pure chaos...*

“What about someone or something that isn’t purely dark yet,” I asked, the words sticking in my throat. “What about neutral magic practitioners, or someone with order magic who has been turned? What about the traitor?”

“We are safe for now,” the priestess said, shaking her head sadly. “But if we have been betrayed, we may not be for long.”

“You must go now, Priestess,” the white-haired elf said. “It is too dangerous for you to be out here. If we lose you, we lose the realm.”

Priestess Kalia pressed her lips together and nodded. “There is nothing we can do right now but wait. Arlen, please monitor the situation and keep me advised on any concerning developments. Iymbryl and I will retire in my chambers. It is the safest place for me right now.”

“Thank you, Priestess,” Arlen said. “I will let you know if anything changes.”

He inclined his head to me, gave Iymbryl a sharp salute, and returned to his observation post.

"I'd like to stay," I said. "I'm pretty good with a sword. I have trained in my world. I could be of use."

"If it comes to that, I will be glad to have your protection, Logan," the priestess said. "That blade of yours, indeed all of the clan weapons, they have spells woven into the metal that make them superior for fighting against creatures of chaos."

"Even more reason that I should stay," I said. "I didn't notice that when I fought the trolls and the werewolf, though. What kind of spells?"

"Any wound you cause with that blade will fester and grow until the creature severs the infected limb or succumbs to the poison," she said. "This is true of any Grenwyld weapon."

"Grenwyld," Arlen turned his head to look at us again, his eyebrows piqued with curiosity. "Are you of the clan, then, young sir? I have not had the pleasure of fighting alongside a Grenwyld warrior for centuries."

I cleared my throat. "It is complicated, I'm afraid. But I do wield a Grenwyld blade."

"Good enough for me," he said. "If we must fight them, I will find you."

"You must rest," the priestess pleaded with me. "Whatever happens here it will not be over in a matter of minutes or hours. You will be useless to us if you are too exhausted to even lift your blade."

"She speaks the truth," Arlen said. "I predict the creatures await the fullness of the next blood moon to stage an attack."

I looked up at the strange triple moon now rising above the trees. None of the moons looked particularly red or bloody to me. "Which is... how long?"

"Tomorrow night," the priestess said, her voice tight.

I sighed and turned away from the excitement. I didn't like to admit it, but I was exhausted. The last night I'd slept had been on the ground in the summoning circle, which hadn't been the most relaxing set up. Then we'd hiked all morning, been imprisoned, I'd been taken advantage of by nymphs, questioned in the priestess's pavilion... and then there was what had just happened in the library. I was drained and there was no point in lying about it.

"Okay," I conceded. "You win. But only if you promise to wake me up if there's any fighting."

The priestess smiled and squeezed my arm, but there was no real joy in it. Her purple eyes were far away with worry. She said, "I promise you won't miss out on anything exciting."

I bid farewell to Arlen and followed Iymbryl and the priestess off the balcony. Our footsteps echoed along the empty corridor. We passed the library, which I realized looked more like a broom closet from the outside, and I wondered why she kept it so secret. Perhaps the priestess had as much to fear in her own temple as she did in the woods outside.

We rounded a corner into a warmly-lit passage hung with intricate woven tapestries. Six doors, three on each side, broke up the hanging artwork.

"This is the guest wing," the priestess said. She stopped in front of a solid wooden door with a frame carved to look like fall leaves and berries. "I think we'll put you here for the night, if you don't mind."

Iymbryl opened the door. The priestess stepped inside and I followed. The elf-guard remained outside, her lips flattened into a disapproving line. She looked away from me as I passed her, and I wondered what I'd done to earn her ire this time, or if she was just trying to provoke me. The priestess led me into the middle of the room and raised her hands slowly. As she lifted them, wall sconces flared to life with their magical, golden light.

"Will this do?" the priestess said. "I think you'll be comfortable here."

A window, covered in velvety red drapes, filled most of the far wall. A massive, four-poster bed stood on my left, flanked by two floor-to-ceiling oil paintings of an ethereally beautiful woman wearing a crown of red leaves. A fireplace, stacked with wood but unlit, made a centerpiece for the wall on my right. The stone walls were covered in more tapestries, depicting woodland scenes and luxurious banquets, and the floors were thick with rich carpets. Even without the fire burning, it felt warm and comforting in the room.

"I'm sure I will be," I said with a laugh. "This is more luxurious than anything I'm used to."

She put her hands on her hips and arched an eyebrow. "How do you know? You can't remember anything about your past life."

"I can't remember much," I admitted. "But I can remember enough to know that this feels like a dream come true. The temple, this room, you..."

Iymbryl cleared her throat from the hall. The priestess put a hand up to stop me from saying anything else.

"I must go," she said, and hurried out of the room. "Arlen will find you if they need help on the front lines. Sleep well."

"Okay," I said to her back. "Goodni—"

The elf-guard slammed the door closed. I stood there, staring at it, and wondered what the hell I'd done wrong.

"Women," I muttered to myself. "You get transported to another dimension and the hot ones are still crazy."

I shrugged my shoulders and decided to busy myself with making a fire. I didn't need it for warmth, but it gave me something to do, and would provide better light for reading before I settled in for the night.

I took the little blue book out of my pocket and tossed it onto an over-stuffed chair next to the fireplace. I pulled the sword sheath off my back and leaned it and the Grenwyld blade against the chair as well, then sat myself on the hearth. A little wooden box sat next to the fire irons. I flipped open the lid and found curled wood shavings and bits of crumpled paper that I assumed were meant for kindling. There were no matches—I guess this world hadn't invented them yet—but there was a little flint-and-steel kit that looked almost identical to one I remembered having in my camping supplies back home.

A memory! I reached for it with my mind, desperate for some concrete sense of who I was or where I was from. But as soon as I had latched onto it, the memory drifted away leaving me with nothing but a feeling of familiarity and the knowledge that I knew how to use the fire-starting device.

Maybe it was a good thing, I thought as I got the fire burning. Maybe the knowledge of two entirely different worlds is too much for the human mind to bear.

The wood chips and paper crackled as orange flames licked up around the logs in the fireplace. Once I was sure it wasn't going to burn itself down again, I stood and stretched, then sat in the over-stuffed chair. I flipped through the little blue book absentmindedly, with my thoughts turned instead to the idea of parallel worlds.

It wasn't an unfamiliar concept. I had a feeling there were unproven theories about the existence of other dimensions in my own world. It irritated me that I couldn't recall anything specific, but it comforted me to know that whatever had happened to me wasn't entirely impossible. I closed my eyes and pictured what it must be like, entire universes layered upon one another in space and time but completely oblivious to each other.

The crackling warmth of the fire combined with my bone-tired exhaustion hit me all at once, and I began to doze.

I don't know how long I slept in the chair, but at some point during the night, when the fire had burned down to a layer of smouldering coals, I came awake with a start. My neck ached, and I had been drooling on my shoulder.

I groaned and pushed myself up to my feet, shuffling over to the enormous bed. The paintings of the woman with the crown of red leaves seemed to follow me with giantess eyes. Something about her struck me. Like a plucked guitar string, it hummed and vibrated through my entire body. In the low light of the magical sconces and the glow of the fireplace, I felt certain that I knew her. Though the memory didn't stay, the sensation humming in my chest did.

I peeled off my clothes and crawled into the bed. I didn't have any pajamas, and preferred sleeping naked anyway. I pulled back the heavy quilt and gritted my teeth as I slid between the chilly sheets. As they warmed against my skin I wondered where the feeling of familiarity came from. Priestess Kalia had said she wanted me in the room with the paintings of Priestess Maia. Unless she had changed her mind, that must be who this woman was. There was no way that I could know the priestess of the forest temple who served hundreds of years earlier.

A coincidence, I told myself as I pulled back the bedcovers.

But as I fell back asleep, the feeling persisted. How many coincidences were going to have to happen before I admitted there was something else going on?

I drifted off with the woman's name—her real name, the one I knew her by—dancing on the tip of my tongue.

Chapter 13

I opened my eyes and stared up into blackness. The magical lights had gone out while I slept. Sitting up, I could see that the fire was out too. A cool breeze wafted through the room, and a sliver of moonlight filtered in between the heavy velvet drapes. Had the window been open before? I hadn't checked. Other than the rustling of the curtains against the floor and my own breathing, the room was silent.

I slipped my legs out from under the blanket and dropped my feet onto the plush rug next to the bed. The cold air against my bare skin sent goosebumps prickling over my body. I cursed and pushed myself up off the mattress and shuffled toward the window.

I shoved the curtains aside with my arm and looked outside. My view faced the opposite side of the temple grounds from the balcony. The elf-guards had created a perimeter of sentries on the ground. Craning my neck out the window, I could see archers mounted along the top of the temple facing the woods. Dark shadows shifted just outside the light of the guard's torches, but for now everything was quiet. I pulled my head back inside, reached up and tugged the wooden window frame down. It stuck for a second and fell with a rattle. I whipped my fingers out of the way just before they got pinched in the frame.

I chuckled as I thought about how embarrassing it would have been if I'd had to beg off of the war against chaos because I'd chopped my own fingers off trying to close my bedroom window.

I tugged the drapes closed and decided to build up the fire again.

When I turned around, though, I realized that wasn't going to be necessary.

The magic lights had flared back to life when my back was turned, and a small blaze crackled in the hearth. A golden-haired woman sat in the overstuffed chair next to the fire, with her feet curled up beside her on the cushion and a gauzy white nightgown stretched tight across her long, tanned legs. Priestess Kalia looked up at me with lids heavy over her purple eyes. Tears streamed down her cheeks.

"Priestess, what are you doing here?" I crossed the room in a hurry. "What's the matter? Has something happened?"

"No," she said. "Not yet. But I fear for what is going to happen."

As I got closer to the fire, the heat from the blaze warmed my skin and I remembered that I was completely naked.

"Oh, shit," I said. Blushing, I covered myself and looked for a blanket or something to wrap around my waist. "I'm so sorry."

I wasn't particularly shy, but despite our earlier romp, it felt disrespectful to be running around in the nude in front of the most powerful woman in the realm.

She stretched out her arm and caught my hand in her own.

"No," she said, and her voice hitched in her chest slightly. "Don't be sorry. Stay that way."

Her fingers were cold in mine, as if the warmth of the fire hadn't reached her.

"How did you get in here?" I pressed her fingers between mine. "Not the window, I hope. I would have opened the door for you."

Her eyes darted over my shoulder, toward the bed, and my heart began to beat faster. She said, "The paintings. It's why I wanted to you to be in this room."

"The paintings?" I spun to look at the enormous portraits of the former priestess. One of them, I now realized, had been knocked aside to reveal a darkened tunnel. "Another secret passageway, huh? I'm beginning to wonder about you priestesses..."

"We priestesses don't have teleportation magic like the elves." She tugged on my hand and I stepped closer to the chair. "The hidden passages are one of our most protected secrets. It is very rare for a priestess to reveal any of them to even the most trusted servant, let alone someone from outside the temple, and now you know of two."

"So does your little elf slave," I said. "I don't feel all that special."

"Don't you?" The priestess dropped her feet to the floor and stood, so close that the loose fabric of her nightgown brushed against my bare thighs.

She smelled sweet and herbal, like fresh-cut flowers. "Perhaps I can change your mind."

She traced her fingers along the inside of my palm and up the sensitive skin on my inner arm. Electricity hummed through my body and my breathing came faster. The top of her head barely came up to my chin, and I looked down on the braid of golden hair that wound around her head like a crown.

"Priestess," I said, swallowing a lump in my throat. "This is just asking for trouble."

"Do you fear for your self-control?" she asked, looking up at me with her wide purple eyes. She dragged her fingernails gently across my chest and down my ribs, stopping just above my hips.

My body responded immediately. The tip of my cock brushed against her nightgown as it rose. I gritted my teeth and took a deep breath. "No. I can control myself. If we can't be together, I can respect that. But it is cruel and unusual punishment for you to come to my room in the middle of the night just to give me a ball-ache."

"You don't like to be teased?" She bit her lip and dragged her nails lower. She was testing me. I knew it. I would have resented it a bit more if she hadn't just let me take my frustrations out on Iymbryl a few hours ago. She said, "Is that all?"

"What if someone finds you here?" I said, trying to ignore the fact that my dick was now pointing at her belly button like a divining rod. "Who do you think they'll blame?"

"Who are you afraid of?" she asked. "This is my temple."

"Even you have to follow the rules of your empire, Priestess," I said, clenching my jaw as her hands dropped to my thighs and began inching their way up. "And your advisor is just looking for an excuse to set his guards on me."

"Forget about Voron." She pushed me away from her as if she was angry, then reached up to the ribbon holding closed the neckline of her nightgown. Orange light from the fire lit the gauzy material from behind so that I could see the shadow of her curves illuminated like an angel in a stained-glass window. "Tonight he pores over the Book of Elders to strengthen our defenses against the gathering hordes. I am afraid, Loghann."

I decided now was not the time to argue about the name. I stepped forward and brushed a tear off her cheek with my thumb. "Is that why you're crying? You don't think it will be enough?"

"In a few days, we might all be dead," the priestess said, her voice cracking. "Chaos might take the Ring Wood. We will be the first of the realms to fall as we are plunged into an era of darkness and suffering."

"Maybe." My tongue stuck to the roof of my mouth. "And maybe not. We will not go down without a fight, Priestess."

"You will fight for us?" she asked. "Even though this is not your land and none of your concern?"

"I might not be from here," I said. "But this is where I am. I couldn't go home if I wanted to, and I don't. I haven't been here for long but I care about you and Ruhail, I care about protecting this beautiful forest, and your temple. I even care about your haughty little elf, but don't tell her that. Of course I will fight for you. What kind of man would I be if I didn't?"

Her fingers shook as she worried at the ribbon, passing it back and forth between her hands. She said, "It is not your fight."

"No offence, Priestess," I said, dropping my hand to cover hers and to stop the nervous movement. "But that is not your decision. It's mine."

The young priestess pulled on the end of the ribbon, and it unravelled slowly. The neckline of the nightgown widened and slipped off her soft, tanned shoulders. I pulled my hand away as the gauzy material fell down her waist, over her hips, and down to her feet. She stood naked before me and said, "Then I, too, am yours."

Blood throbbed in my temples and my groin as I stared at the priestess's body. I had seen her naked before, of course. There was no doubt that she was beautiful. But she was untouchable. I had watched her play with Iymbryl, and with herself, as a voyeur.

This was different. This was an offering fit for a god.

"I—I can't, Priestess," I said, even as my body begged to go to her. "That would jeopardize everything. If the realms aren't united under the new emperor, then Drakkus will win for sure."

"But there is no new emperor." Fresh tears streamed down her face. "Illdrian will not name a successor in time."

"Don't say that," I said. I reached for her shoulders and pulled her into my arms. The heat of her belly against my cock was like fire, but I tried to ignore it. "We can't give up yet."

"The Book of Elders foretells it," she said, shaking her head. "In the ancient language. It does not say specifically when, but it warns that one day an emperor will fail to name an heir. The priestesses have always known it would happen, and we have all hoped that it would not happen during our rule."

"It's not too late," I said. "Illdrian is still alive. There is time."

The priestess took a deep, shuddering breath. "The book says that in the event that the emperor does not choose his successor, the empire will fall. Unless..."

She closed her eyes, and I cupped her chin in my hand, forcing her to look at me. "Unless what. Tell me. Maybe I can help."

"Unless the priestesses make a choice for him," she said, her purple eyes scanning my face for my reaction. "All these years, I have been waiting, thinking that it would be Voron that we had to choose. He is the favorite among the old clans. And I knew that, because he is a Blackthorne, I would have to be the first."

My stomach turned at the thought, but I stroked her hair and let her speak.

"I almost went to him," she said. "The night before you arrived. I—I even had Iymbryl bathe and prepare me. I went to his chambers. I knocked on the door."

"Oh god, Kalia," I said, her name slipping off my tongue. "You didn't—"

"He didn't answer," she said, and let out a half-sob, half-laugh. "He didn't answer, and I ran back to my own room so quickly I don't even remember which way I went. It was as if Fate had intervened. I knew then, with all my heart, that he was not the one. I almost made a terrible mistake. Then the very next day, you arrived. And I knew."

As she said it, I felt I knew it too. It seemed crazy, though. And I wanted to hear her say it, in case I was wrong. I said, "You knew what?"

"It's you," she said, laughing with tears in her eyes. "You are the one we must choose."

"I'm not even from this world," I protested weakly.

"Last blood moon," she said, "I was reading in the Book of Elders, and I came across a passage about Loghann Grenwyld. The lost prince, it calls him. It must be him. It says that the lost prince will return, but that he will remain lost without the forest to guide him. I was brushing Iymbryl's hair afterward, and I joked with her that if the lost prince were to return I would guide him to the High Plains myself if it meant I didn't have to lay with Voron Blackthorne."

I held the priestess tight against my chest and felt the energy go out of me.

"Priestess," I said. "I am not your lost prince. If that is what you think, and that's why you are offering yourself to me... I can't. I cannot in good faith let you do that. It would be dishonest of me to take advantage of you that way."

"Logan Greenwood," she said. She drew back from me, and straightened to her full height. Still barely taller than my chin, but now with an air of authority around her that made me pay attention, she said, "Logan Greenwood, who comes from another world, and who is not Loghann Grenwyld but carries a sword of Grenwyld? I knew the moment that I saw you that you were the one I was waiting for. When you stood up to Voron in my pavilion, I was strengthened in my conviction. When I invited you to play with Iymbryl, I knew you were the kind of man I could give myself to—firm, commanding, and still respectful of boundaries. You are not intimidated by my power."

Her hair fell over her shoulders in a cascade of liquid gold, and her purple eyes flashed. Her small upturned breasts were taut with excitement, and the sight of her full hips and thighs and the small mound between her legs pushed all the chivalrous protests out of my head again.

"I'm glad," I said. It sounded stupid, even to my ears, but I couldn't think of anything better to say. Then I asked, "What if you're wrong?"

"If I'm wrong," she said, "the empire is damned. Because I will not submit myself to Voron Blackthorne. Not knowing that I could choose a man like you."

"I'm flattered, Priestess," I said. I was aroused, certainly, but such high praise was beginning to make me feel a bit nervous. "But I'm just a regular guy. I don't know if I'm emperor material."

She ran her hands over my torso again and bit her lip. Then her eyes widened. "Have you seen yourself? Here, I mean?"

"Like, in a mirror?" I said. "No. But it's only been a couple of days. I can't be looking that different from what I remember."

"I wonder..." She darted into the shadows of the room, next to the fireplace. I heard the whooshing sound of heavy fabric falling to the ground, then more lights blazed. Two torches, hung on either side of a tall, oblong mirror in an ornate black frame, cast a flickering light on the priestess's naked body. She said, "Come here, Loghann. See yourself."

I furrowed my brow at the sudden, strange direction this conversation had taken. But I humored her. That's what men are supposed to do when beautiful women take off their clothes and beg to be allowed to submit to you, right? I had to admit, I didn't really have a frame of reference for this kind of thing. I strode to her and stepped up to the mirror.

My mouth fell open. The man in the mirror looked a bit like me. More like what I'd imagine my taller, better looking, older brother might look like. Dark stubble covered my chin, not so surprising since I hadn't shaved in a few days. But the chin and jaw were a bit more chiseled than I remembered. My shoulders seemed broader. My muscles more defined. And yes, I wasn't imagining things. My cock was definitely bigger than it had been before. I said, "What the hell?"

"Is this how you remember yourself?" the priestess said.

I cocked my head to one side then the other, trying to figure out how the glass was warped. But the naked reflection of the beautiful woman didn't look distorted at all. I shook my head. "Maybe in my dreams. I look like me, but... better in every way."

"Our world is changing you." The priestess smiled up at me, as if what she was saying made any sense. "You are becoming your true self."

"My true—" I shook my head. "No, I know my true self. I've lived with him for twenty-eight years. This is not me. I've forgotten a lot about my past but I know who I am."

"You said yourself," she said. "You are always striving for something more, and feeling empty when you can't achieve it. Perhaps that's because you were limited in your old world. Perhaps you were cut off from the core of your magic."

"I don't have magic," I laughed. "I'm a human."

"Are you?" she said. Then she pointed at my ears.

I reached up and felt them with my fingers. Then I turned my head and tried to see them in my reflection. There was a point at the top, not nearly as pronounced as the elves ears, but more than I remembered. I said, "This is fucked up. I'm not an elf."

"No." She grinned broadly at me. "You are not an elf."

"What's this then?" I flicked at my ear and scowled at the handsome man in the mirror. "A fashion statement?"

She laughed. "You may be taking on some characteristics of the real Loghann Grenwyld. His father was an elf, and his mother was a priestess. I don't know how or why, but it seems to me you are meant to take his place."

I huffed and shook my head. "Well, it looks stupid."

"You don't look stupid to me," she said, padding away from the mirror on bare feet.

She stood in front of me, rose up on her tip-toes, and took my lower lip between her teeth. I lowered my mouth to hers. She gasped as I brought up a hand to the back of her head and wove my fingers into her hair, pressing her to my body. Her mouth was hot and sweet, as if she'd been eating honey, and my tongue slipped between her lips as if I could drink her.

The hard points of her nipples pressed into my chest, and her soft skin slid against mine like silk. I reached around her waist with my other hand, pinning her against me. My erection throbbed between us, suddenly eager to take the priestess up on her earlier offer.

She pulled back, panting. "Wait."

I let go and put my hands up, cursing myself for getting carried away. Of course she would have second thoughts once we got started. She was a virgin, after all. I said, "Sorry. If you've changed your mind, it's okay. I'll just—"

"No," she said, reaching for me. "I just want something else first."

She kissed my chest, burning my skin with the heat of her mouth. Then she lowered herself, kissing along the centre of my torso, dragging her tongue across my skin and leaving a cool, wet trail of saliva down my belly. She paused to kiss the top of the line of hair at my bellybutton, and I could feel her panting breath against my skin. Her hands caressed the outside of my thighs as she lowered herself farther.

I watched her in the mirror as her hips and thighs spread to kneel before me. Her hair fell across her naked back, and her round bare ass sat on her heels. When her breath touched my cock my entire body jolted. She ran her tongue from the base of my shaft all the way up the length and swirled it around the head. I moaned and put a hand in her hair again.

"Help me," she said, looking up at me through her golden lashes with those intense purple eyes. "I want to taste you again."

Oh god, yes. I had never wanted anything more in my entire life.

"Open your mouth," I said. My voice shook with the effort of holding back. I gripped her hair tight enough that she whimpered, but she didn't pull back.

She opened her mouth, and I moved myself so that the tip of my cock rested on her lower lip. I rubbed my head over her lips. Clear pre-cum glistened on her pink skin in the light of the torches. She licked her lips and groaned with pleasure. She said, "More."

This time when she opened her mouth, I guided her hand along my shaft and showed her how to stroke me as she sucked. She slid her fingers through the saliva, and worked it along my length while I watched her head bouncing in the mirror.

"Good." My breath came in short gasps as she took me deeper and deeper into her mouth. "Get it nice and wet."

When she had me pressed against the back of her throat, I held her head and pushed myself further in. She gagged, and I felt the muscles of her throat constrict against me. She made a whimpering noise and tried to back up, her hands pressed against my thighs.

"It's okay," I said, holding her still. "I've got you. Breathe through your nose."

She looked up at me with those purple eyes and nodded slightly. The sight of her full lips stretched around my massive erection was something I wished I could sear into my brain for eternity. I gripped her hair and pressed myself deeper.

Her eyebrows shot up, and she gagged again. Then her shoulders relaxed, and she took a deep breath in through her nose, dug her nails into my thighs, and leaned into my cock. I felt the head as it pushed past the tight muscles at the back of her mouth and down her throat.

"Oh fuck." I moaned again.

The little priestess seemed to have the hang of it now. She took me in and out, slowly at first. As she got more comfortable, she moved faster, and I felt a wall of pleasure pressing through my body like the wave of a tsunami. But before I exploded in her throat, I held her head and pulled out. "No. Go get on the bed."

Obediently, she stood. She said in a low voice, "Wasn't it okay?"

I spanked her naked ass, not too hard, but enough to show her I meant it. She yelped and leaned against my chest.

"Bed," I said. "Now."

She walked slowly away from me, and I watched her small, round bottom sway back and forth, one side pinker than the other. She sat on the edge of the bed and waited for me.

She bit her lip as I approached the bed, looking up at me with those big purple eyes. I said, "You're sure about this? There's no going back."

"Yes," she said. "I submit to you, completely."

I gripped her shoulders in both hands and pressed her into the mattress. She lay down, her small breasts pointing upward. Her chest rose and fell rapidly. Though her arms were relaxed at her sides, her hands were clenched into fists. She was scared. But her thighs fell apart slightly, as if she was eager as well as terrified.

I reached for one of the pillows and slid it under her ass. Then I propped her legs up and knelt on the edge of the bed between her knees. Her hair spread out around her like golden wings. I slipped my fingers gently inside her pussy. She arched her hips toward me. I pulled my fingers out and rubbed her clit in slow, even circles. It was her turn to moan.

"You're wet," I said. "Are you excited?"

"Yes," she said through clenched teeth, panting slightly. "Yes, I have been waiting so long."

I stroked myself with my left hand as I massaged her swollen lips, spreading her wetness everywhere. She jumped when I got back to her clit again, and let out a little yelp.

"It will hurt, you know." I rubbed a little harder now. Her thighs trembled, and a flush crept across her skin. She closed her eyes and rocked her hips, pressing herself against my fingers. I said, "Are you sure?"

"Yes, damn you," she said, grabbing me by the wrist. "I don't care if it hurts. You must take me."

I slapped her hand away and grabbed her by the hips, dragging her closer to me. I guided myself against the hot slit between her legs and pushed inside, just a little bit. She froze, waiting, her hands back on my wrists. Her chest pumped rapidly. She was like a rabbit caught in a trap.

But she'd said she wanted it.

I leaned forward, using my weight to force her thighs farther apart, and I put my elbows down on the bed next to her head.

"Look at me," I said, and I waited for her to open her purple eyes. "Tell me to stop if you need to."

She nodded. I let my hips drop slowly, sinking into her inch by inch. She cried out, and I paused. I could feel her chest heaving against mine, her breasts pressing against my ribs. She said, "More, please. Don't stop."

The way she pled for it drove me to the brink.

"Ask me again," I said. My jaw clenched. "Beg me to fuck you."

"Please, Loghann," she said, and I felt my cock pulse with pleasure. "Please fuck me."

I pushed my hands under her arms and wrapped my fingers over her shoulders to hold her in place.

"How hard do you want it?" I asked, rocking against her so that my belly pressed against her clit.

She arched her hips back, and whimpered. "I want it to hurt."

I held her shoulders tight and forced my entire length into her tight, virgin pussy. She screamed and bucked against me. I withdrew slightly. "Like that?"

"Yes," she said. "Yes, like that. Again. Please. Please."

I drove myself into her again, feeling her body wrap around me like my cock was being constricted. "Fuck, you're so tight."

She screamed again as I pumped my hips against her. She felt so small and vulnerable beneath me, and she whimpered like I was beating her, but she didn't tell me to stop. And god dammit, her cries made me insane with lust. My mind raced with forbidden fantasies as I hammered into the little priestess again and again.

If she wanted to submit, I would teach her to submit.

Suddenly, her screams took on a different tone, and I felt her body shaking beneath me. Her pussy pulsed and clenched along my shaft. She was coming despite the pain. I was close too; I don't know how I'd held off so long. I yanked her wrists up over her head, and pinned her to the bed, and fucked her like I wanted to break her in two. Her screams lurched with every thrust, but she never told me to stop.

I ravaged her.

When the first wave of my orgasm burst inside her, I grunted like some kind of animal. Before I was totally finished, I pulled out and crawled over her prone, panting body.

"Open your mouth," I said, my voice hoarse. I gripped my pulsing cock in my hand.

She did, immediately, her big purple eyes searching my face. I held her hair and squeezed the length of my shaft and aimed at her face. Another wave of cum shot out of me in a hot spurt, covering her lips and tongue. She lapped it all up, eagerly. Then she took me into her mouth and sucked her own juices off of me, moaning with pleasure.

When I couldn't take anymore, I pushed her back and sank onto the mattress beside her. She wrapped her arms and legs around me without saying a word, and we just lay there, trying to catch our breath.

"Priestess?" I said, finally.

"Call me Kalia," she said. "I think you've earned it."

"Kalia, then," I said, and I ran my fingers up and down her bare arms, watching the tiny hairs stand on end beneath my touch.

She sighed happily. "Yes, Loghann?"

I grinned, knowing I was probably going to make her mad. But I couldn't help myself.

"If this is how we save the world," I said. "I should have become an emperor a long time ago."

She didn't get mad. She turned to me and gave me an unreadable smile.

"You're not done yet," she said. "You have four more priestesses to tame before you get to be emperor."

Chapter 14

The next time I awoke, sunshine streamed in through the crack between the drapes. A spear of thin white light illuminated dust motes floating on invisible currents of air. Kalia's warm limbs were still wrapped around my body, and I had to move delicately to extract myself without waking her. I had just gotten out from under her arm and tucked her bare shoulder back under the blanket when I paused.

A rustling sound came from the foot of the bed.

I listened as whatever-it-was moved around on the floor, shuffling over the thick carpet as if it was in a hurry. Was it possible that an animal had gotten into the room somehow? The bedroom door was still closed, and the window didn't appear to have been opened again.

Maybe there was another kind of creature in here?

My eyebrows scrunched together as I tried to think of some fantasy races I'd read about or seen in movies, since so many of them seemed to be real in this world. Gnomes, dwarves, brownies, sprites... they were generally considered good, I thought.

Then there were goblins, kobolds, and gods knew what else. That would be less good.

I moved as quietly as I could over the top of the mattress. Kalia stirred in her sleep, but the mattress didn't squeak as I inched my way to the foot of the bed. Whatever it was still rustled around out of my sight. I gripped the edge of the mattress and peered down over the edge, hoping to catch the creature in the act.

I looked down into a pair of bright green eyes. There was a squeak and a scrambling as she tried to hide under the bed, but I caught the culprit by the back of her dress.

"Ruhail?" I grabbed the dryad around the waist and pulled her back out. "What are you doing here? Are you all right? I was so worried about you."

She pulled at my hands until I let go and backed up on her hands and feet like the world's sexiest crab. Her auburn hair was tangled around the top of her head and her leaf-dress was missing a couple of leaves, leaving patches of green-veined skin exposed along her torso. She stared up at me, her chest heaving, and said, "You were?"

"Of course I was," I said. "When I heard you had disappeared from the jail cell I was half-convinced Voron had done something to you."

"You can't have been too worried," she said, looking away from me. She traced a pattern on the carpet with her finger and avoided my gaze. "You didn't come to look for me."

"I wanted to," I said. The dryad's pale thighs caught my gaze and I tried not to follow them up in to the opening of her torn skirt.

She stuck out her bottom lip petulantly. "What stopped you, then?"

"Kalia assured me that you were safe," I said. "That it was best to wait for you to come to me. Was she wrong?"

Ruhail caught me staring and tucked her legs in beside her. She narrowed her eyes at me. Then she raised herself up to peek over the end of the bed at the sleeping priestess.

"No," she said with a sigh. "Priestess Kalia is never wrong about anything that happens in the Ring Wood."

"She said the nymphs helped you to escape," I said. "Where were you?"

"Inside the Heart of the Forest," she said. "I would have come sooner, but Voron placed alarm spells all across the temple ground. It would have been like trying to sneak through a spider's web without getting caught."

I reached out my hand to her. She stared at it for a moment, then she slipped her cool, slender fingers into mine. I pulled her up toward the bed, but she put a hand on my chest.

"What's the matter?" I said. "You don't have to keep sitting on the floor."

"You're naked," she said, her eyes darting nervously down and away. "And aroused."

"Oh, sorry." I tugged up the blanket to cover myself. "In my defence, you're half-naked and exceedingly cute."

"Haven't you already been satisfied?" She glanced at Kalia's sleeping form again. "After the way you..."

"The way I what?" I asked.

The dryad blushed deep crimson and tugged at the bottom of her dress.

I growled at the nervous woman and reached for her again. "How long have you been in here, Ruhail?"

She jumped back nimbly and continued to avoid my gaze. "I came in last night, through the window. There was a shift in the magical protections surrounding the temple shortly after dark. Voron's alarms were dispelled, and the barrier's around the perimeter strengthened. I waited a little while to be sure they would stay down, and then I snuck out of my hiding place in the Heart and climbed up to your window."

"You were here the whole time?" I said. The thought of the little dryad hiding in the shadows while I had ravaged the priestess sent another rush of blood coursing to my groin.

"I didn't mean to spy," she said. "It was terrible timing. But once I saw her go to you I knew I couldn't interrupt. I know what this means, Loghann, that she has chosen you. When we met, I thought there was a chance..."

"You knew this would happen?"

"None of us wanted Voron Blackthorne to be the next emperor," she whispered faintly, as if admitting it might be enough to get her in trouble again. "When you appeared, with your name, and a sword of Grenwyld. I hoped you would be an alternative choice for the old clans. I didn't know that Kalia would take matters into her own hands quite so... thoroughly."

"I hope you enjoyed the show."

The dryad bit her lip and pressed her thighs together in a way that made me want to pry them apart and see for myself just how much she had enjoyed it.

But she said, "I must give the priestess my message. About the traitor."

All the sexy daydreams flooded out of my mind and a new sense of urgency replaced them.

"Of course," I said. "I forgot completely."

I reached across the bed and shook Kalia gently awake. She moaned and rolled over so that her small pink nipples stuck up from the top of the blanket. With her eyes still closed, she said, "Is it morning already?"

"Kalia," I said. "We have company."

The priestess sat bolt upright, her golden hair mussed sexily around her pink cheeks and bare shoulders. Her purple eyes darted at the door, and then back at me. I pointed at Ruhail.

"The dryad," she exclaimed. "Oh, how wonderful. And you are every bit as beautiful as Loghann said you were."

The dryad looked down, and her blush intensified. "He said that about me?"

At the moment, she looked like she had been dragged through the bushes by a mob of angry imps, but I still had to agree. Her pale skin, and full hips and breasts begged to be fondled. But we had something important to take care of first, and Ruhail had made it clear that she wasn't interested in humoring the lusty dreams of a man from another world.

"The message from the emperor," I prompted. "You were almost killed trying to deliver the damned thing, remember?"

"Yes," the priestess said, pulling aside the blanket. "Voron's spells should hold them off for a while longer, but if we've been betrayed, it is imperative to know so that we can stop the traitor from damaging the protective spells."

"I'm sure Voron knows his stuff," I said. "But we can't be too careful."

Priestess Kalia stood up from the bed and strode across the room to pick up her nightgown off the floor. She slipped it over her head and tied the ribbon at her throat, and held out her hand to the dryad. In the early morning light the gauzy material of the nightgown could barely be described as fabric. It was more like a thin, white web that completely revealed her body underneath. Neither of the women seemed to have any qualms about the fact that the priestess was essentially naked.

Ruhail approached and took the priestess's hands in her own. They stood, facing one another, with their eyes closed and their hands clasping each other's wrists. A milky white mist began to form in the space between their bodies, and letters and symbols floated in the mist.

The dryad kept her eyes closed, but the priestess opened hers, her purple gaze flashing over the message like she was trying to solve a puzzle. The color drained out of her face and she pressed her lips together. She shook her head slowly and muttered, "It can't be."

"What is it Kalia?" I asked, stooping to pick up my pants from the foot of the bed. "What was in the mist?"

"Mist?" Ruhail asked. Her eyes popped open and she began to say something but the look on the priestess's face stopped her.

"Priestess." I snapped my fingers in front of her face and she broke contact with the dryad stumbling backwards. "What was the message?"

She wrapped her arms around herself and began to shake. She whined faintly, like she was in pain, and her lips paled to a ghostly gray color. "How could this be? I didn't know... I had no idea..."

Ruhail's eyes jumped between us and she began to look frightened. "What happened? Did I—"

She seemed to cut herself off, not having any idea what could have gone wrong.

I gripped the priestess by both shoulders and guided her toward the over-stuffed chair next to the fireplace. I said, "Ruhail, please build us a fire. She's cold."

The dryad nodded and rushed over to the window where her staff was hidden behind one of the heavy velvet curtains. She hurriedly piled some logs into the fireplace and swirled her staff over them. The shimmer of her magic fell down on the logs like snow and green flames sprouted up like leaves bursting from the dead wood. Soon the warmth of the blaze spread into the room. I rubbed Kalia's shoulders and wrapped a blanket around her. She stared dazedly ahead and didn't speak.

Ruhail sat on the hearth next to the fire and watched the priestess with concern drawn into every line of her face. After a time she said, "What did you mean by mist, Loghann?"

"When you were giving her the message," I said. "There was a white mist between you, with letters and symbols floating in it. Didn't you know?"

She shook her head. "I have seen many such messages delivered, and I have never seen any mist."

"It's like the green mist around your staff when you use magic," I said. "Or the weird red glow that Voron's staff makes when he's angry."

"You can see my magic?" she said, her green eyes widening.

"Of course," I said. "Is that so strange?"

"I can't see my magic." She wrapped her fingers around her knees and hugged her legs against her chest. "Or anyone else's. I've never heard of anyone who could."

"What?" That shocked me. "I just assumed—"

"You said my magic is green?" Her eyes shot up to mine and her pink lips trembled. "And Voron's is red?"

"Yeah," I said. "I thought it had to do with the kind of stone you have in your staffs."

The dryad shook her head. "But we have the same stones. All magical artifacts use spirit crystals to channel the elemental forces. They have no color."

I stared at her staff. "But yours is green."

"It's not," she said. "It's clear. You must have some innate ability to see elemental magic. It's strange, but not impossible, I suppose. Except..."

I was only half listening. I stroked the priestess's cheek and tried to get her to look at me, but it was as if she was trapped in her own mind. My heart beat harder in my chest. Something was wrong. Fear seized me suddenly that she had made a mistake, and that by giving herself to me she had broken something inside herself. My eyes burned. "Kalia, please. Come back to us."

I couldn't handle the guilt if I had given in to her crazy whim, and was now the reason that she was—

"It's him, Loghann," the priestess said, her eyes still in a dreamy, faraway place. "Voron Blackthorne. He is the traitor."

"Voron?" I snarled. Fear was replaced by a surge of rage that sent heat coursing through my limbs. "I knew he was a pompous prick, but a traitor? I'll kill the bastard myself."

"That's why his magic is red," Ruhail said. "He's a Blackthorne, his magic should be green like mine. You saw his corruption."

I cursed myself for not saying something earlier. We could have had him arrested as soon as he cast that spell against Ruhail that weakened her so badly.

"He has the Book of Elders." The priestess began shaking so hard I thought she might be having a fit. "We must get the book back. With it he could unweave every protective spell in the Ring Wood. Even without knowing the ancient languages."

"Where is he?" I grabbed my T-shirt and pulled it over my head, slung the sheath and sword over my back, and began hunting for my shoes. "Ruhail, stay with the priestess. I'll find him. I'll get the book back."

Suddenly the door flew open and Iymbryl strode into the room.

"What is going on here?" she roared at me, pointing her spear at my chest. "What have you done to the priestess?"

Gone was the surly sex slave in the gold chain-mail mini skirt and decorative chest plate. The blond elf was dressed in full battle armor, like her brethren along temple battlements. She no longer looked haughty and up-tight. She looked like she could tear the head off her enemy and drink his blood without batting an eye. I reminded myself never to truly cross any of Kalia's guards.

"Nothing," I said. "I swear."

"Iymbryl," the priestess wailed. "I'm so sorry. I have subjected you to the worst kind of humiliation."

The color rose in the blond elf's cheeks. She said, "What are you talking about?"

"Voron Blackthorne," the priestess said, "is a traitor. I have exposed you unwittingly to his corruption with my desire to—"

"Never mind that," Iymbryl said. "What do you mean he is a traitor?"

"The message I brought from the emperor," Ruhail filled in quietly from her place next to the fireplace. "It named him as a slave of Drakkus."

"That greasy little piece of worm shit," Iymbryl slammed the butt of her spear against the floor. "I'll kill him!"

"We must get the Book of Elders from him," the priestess said, pushing herself to her feet. "He must be in his study."

"Stay here," I said. "Iymbryl and I can handle this."

Iymbryl gave me a scathing look. "I will handle this. You will stay here."

"Stop it, both of you." Priestess Kalia stood up straight. A fire burned behind her purple eyes and the high color had returned to her cheeks. "You are all coming with me. If he has already attempted an unweaving the only way any of us will be safe is if I can repair the damage he has done."

She didn't wait to hear what we had to say. She stormed out of the room with her golden hair and her gauzy nightgown flowing behind her. Ruhail pushed past Iymbryl and I to follow the priestess with her staff held high. Iymbryl glared at me.

"We're on the same side," I said.

"We'll see about that," she said, rounding on me with her spear. "Everything started to go wrong when you appeared, didn't it? If anything happens to Kalia I am holding you responsible."

She shoved me out of the way with an armor plated shoulder and strode after the priestess.

I rolled my eyes and ran after her. Sheesh. Put a little body armor on and suddenly she's She-Ra, Princess of Power.

We rushed through dimly lit corridors I would never be able to retrace until, eventually, we made it back to the hallway Ruhail and I had first entered on our way to see Voron Blackthorne. This time there was no giggling, or sounds of sex-behind-closed doors. A silent rage surrounded the priestess, so thick that no outside sounds seemed to penetrate it. Even the clinking of Iymbryl's armor was subdued, somehow.

I stood on the priestess's right side and Iymbryl stood on her left. Ruhail hovered behind us, casting a spell that shrouded us—to my eyes—in a fine green mist, presumably some kind of protection spell. Priestess Kalia held her hands out before her and shoved them forward like she was pushing the air away.

The door to Voron's study exploded backward in a shower of splintered wood. I rushed into the room first with my sword drawn. Iymbryl was close behind. A shelf full of books lined one wall. His paper strewn desk was tucked into the corner. Outside, the window behind his desk, in the thin morning light the creatures of darkness were stirring. A shout rose up from the guards stationed outside.

Iymbryl and I whirled around, trying to find where the sleazy elf was hiding. I checked under the desk, and she pulled open cupboards and closets. He wasn't there. We rushed into the corridor to check neighboring rooms, but there was no sign of the advisor.

"It is too late," the priestess's voice called out to us as we ran, panting through the halls. "He is gone, and he has the book. The unweaving has already begun."

"What does that mean?" I said. "Can't we stop it?"

She came out of his study, her shoulders sagging with defeat. She said, "Without the protective barriers around the grounds, the temple will fall in a matter of days. I cannot repair it fast or thoroughly enough to thwart the armies of Chaos."

Ruhail cried out and covered her face with her hands. Iymbryl gritted her teeth and stomped over to the window where she stared out at the fighting which was already beginning. Her shoulders were stiff as she said, "I am needed outside."

My mind churned with the sudden change in our fortunes. Last night I'd believed I was the luckiest man in the world. Now the reality of Kalia's choice hit me in the chest like a battering ram. The realms were at war, and they had no one to lead them. Chaos would take the Ring Wood and then, one by one, each of the realms would fall.

Unless the people and creatures of order could be rallied together under a new leader. Unless I took up the call.

"Kalia." I took a deep breath and looked the priestess in the eye. "You chose me, and I am not going to fail you."

"I was too late," she said, tears streaming down her cheeks once more. "We are too late."

"It is not over yet," I said and I squeezed her against my chest. "I promised to fight for you, my priestess. And I will. I have a plan."

Chapter 15

Ruhail stood with Kalia at the window, with her arm wrapped around her. A green mist wrapped around them both and I had a sense that the dryad was using her healing magic in an attempt to sooth the tortured priestess. I felt an ache at the back of my throat, all the words I didn't know how to say that might help Kalia feel better. But this wasn't my world, and as an outsider I knew they would just come across as hollow placation.

But actions speak louder than words, and I was ready to act. I was ready to beat Voron to death with his own staff if it came to that. The way he'd used and misled the Priestess, and by extension the people of the empire, repulsed me.

"Where would Voron have gone with the book?" I said. "Could he disappear and reappear outside the temple grounds?"

"No," the priestess said. "That power only works within the temple itself. He would have to leave on foot."

"We need to discover where he's gone if we are going to retrieve the Book of Elders," I said. "Iymbryl, help me look. There might be a clue in this room."

"This is your plan?" She sneered at me, but she did start looking.

"No," I said. "But it gives us something to do while we think. First, I need to understand something. If Emperor Illdrian knew of Voron's betrayal, why didn't he say anything?"

"The old families are already muttering about his fitness as a ruler," Ruhail said, looking over her shoulder at me with her bright green eyes brimming with tears. "If he had spoken against their favored candidate it might have pushed them to drastic measures."

I noticed something on the stone tiles next to the desk and bent for a closer look.

"That makes sense," I said, pulling back the rug. "If the lost prince hasn't returned and his only option was Voron Blackthorne, procrastinating the decision was probably the safest thing for the empire. But it seems like he should have done something."

Two sets of gouges in the stone, partially hidden by the rug, had caught my eye. I dragged my fingers along the stone as I listened to the women speak.

"He did do something," Priestess Kalia said. "Months ago, each of the realms received a call for us to send a trusted messenger to the High Plains. I sent one of my own guard, a man recommended to me by Voron himself. The same messenger arrived only days before you and Ruhail. Voron intercepted the message and claimed to have dealt with the culprit already, a minor staff member from the kitchens. It seems to me Illdrian must have foreseen Voron's interference and sent another summons. How did you come to receive the call, Ruhail?"

"The Heart of the Forest gave me the order, Priestess," the dryad replied. "I was terribly afraid. I have never travelled outside of the Ring Wood before. But I was aided along the way with other elementals who knew of my quest. The emperor was very grateful to me for making the journey. I was honored to have been chosen."

"We are very fortunate that you survived to deliver your message," Kalia said. "We must assume that the emperor has at least attempted to warn each of the priestesses about Voron's betrayal. Unfortunately, we must also assume that Voron is not the only one of the old family clans who have turned. It is as you forewarned, Loghann. The old families are vulnerable to corruption. Our entire empire may be rotting from within."

The marks on the floor were deeper than they appeared at first, made by something very heavy or very strong.

"Our worlds are not so different," I said absently, inspecting the gouges carefully. "Iymbryl, what is this, do you think?"

The elf guard huffed in irritation, but she stomped over and crouched next to me. I ignored her theatrics. We were on the same side, whether she liked it or not, and I knew her attitude came from her love of Kalia so I couldn't really hold it against her. She rubbed the grooves with her fingers and frowned. "They look like claw marks."

"Does Voron keep a pet?" I said. My mind wandered uncomfortably to the dire wolves pacing the perimeter of the temple grounds. "A big dog maybe?"

"Elves do not keep pets." She scowled at me. "We do not believe we are above any creatures of the forest."

I refrained from commenting on the fact that she allowed herself to be kept as a pet by the priestess. I didn't think that would win me any brownie points. Instead, I nodded. "Voron doesn't seem like the loving owner type, probably for the best."

"One cannot own a creature of the Ring Wood," she said. "Whether lovingly or not."

"Okay," I said, raising my hands in defence. "Forget it. What could make a mark like this, though?"

"Too big to be a fox," she said. "Too small for a bear. Wolf, perhaps."

A chill crept over my skin. It was as I had suspected.

"Ruhail was attacked by a werewolf," I said. "And two trolls, on her way to deliver her message from the emperor. Could the werewolf have been here? Could it have warned Voron of our arrival?"

Iymbryl stood suddenly. She roared and threw her spear at the advisor's bookcase. It stuck and thrummed where it protruded from the wall. A creaking noise came from the wood, but the spear held.

"If Voron has been corrupted," Iymbryl said, clenching her hands at her sides. "It is possible that any manner of dark creature could have visited him in this room. He would have the magical ability to hide their presence for short periods."

"It's true," the priestess said, her voice strung so thin it sounded like it might break. "I was too trusting. I never checked in on him. He could have hidden many things from me."

Iymbryl stomped a foot in frustration. "We don't have time for this. I must go help my brothers and sisters prepare for battle. With strategy we may be able to hold them off long enough for the priestess to secure the protection spells again."

Kalia shook her head. "He is unweaving them too quickly. I will always be a step behind. But I will try. We must get that book away from him, Loghann."

"I plan to do just that," I said, pushing the rug back over the claw marks with my foot. I stared at Iymbryl's spear. There was something strange about the way it hung in the shelf like that. I strode across the room toward it. "But I need to find out where he is, first. Which means we need to buy ourselves some time. That's where my plan comes in."

"What is it?" Ruhail asked. She kept her arm around the priestess's waist, but she turned to face me with hope in her green eyes.

"When we first met," I said to her, "you mentioned that there were creatures of order and creatures of chaos. And there are neutral practitioners, too."

I wrapped my hands around the spear shaft and tugged. It wouldn't budge. I pulled down on it. Nothing.

"Get out of the way," Iymbryl said, and she began to heave on the spear, too. I was gratified when she couldn't pull it out either.

"Yes," Ruhail said. "In most realms, the creatures of order are the most numerous but the creatures of chaos tend to be more powerful. This is one way that a balance is maintained."

"That's what we are seeing here, is that right?" I said. "There are more of us, and we could gather more from the forests. We could outnumber them."

The dryad began to comb her fingers through the priestess's long golden hair. Her shimmering green magic still made a bubble around them. I hoped that it would help Kalia to heal from the trauma of this betrayal. I gritted my teeth and prayed that I would be the one to find Voron and bring him to justice.

"Perhaps," she nodded. "But not all creatures of order will fight, it is not in our natures."

"But we need them," I said, driving my fist into my palm. "If they don't fight the Ring Wood will fall. We have to try, even if they only offer defensive magic. Ruhail, we must send someone to spread the word. Someone who can travel quickly and silently through the forest, who won't be in danger if they come across creatures of chaos."

She blinked her big green eyes at me and stepped back from the priestess. She swept her tangled, auburn hair away from her pale face with a nervous hand. "M-me?"

"No, I want you with me," I said. "I have another, more dangerous task for us. I need your help."

"Who then?" Iymbryl said, giving the spear another pull. A weird noise came from somewhere behind the bookshelf. She jumped back as if she was worried it would fall on her. She stared at the shelf with her eyebrows drawn together. "We need every guard here, at the temple," she said, a bit distractedly. "We cannot spare anyone."

"I was thinking of the nymphs."

"Nymphs?" Ruhail's eyes grew wide and she shook her head. Then she blushed. "That's... Actually, that might work. They are terribly hard to keep focussed on important tasks, but I think if you asked them they would do it. They are infatuated with you, Loghann."

I didn't miss the flash of embarrassment in her eyes as she said it, or the thrill I got from hearing that the sex-crazed little nymphs were still thinking about me.

Iymbryl cursed at her spear, took a flying leap and kicked it sideways. The wooden shaft bent easily, as if it were swinging on a hinge, and she went sprawling across the room. A groaning sound shook through the room, and the bookcase opened like a doorway that had been levered open by a crowbar.

"What the..."

I helped Iymbryl to her feet, and the two of us peered into the dark channel inside the bookcase. I said, "It looks like you aren't the only one with secret passageways, Priestess."

"It is not a secret from me," she said, paling slightly. "I have always known of this path. But we have never told the advisors of what lies behind the bookcase. You don't think he—"

"Look," I interrupted, pointing at the floor. More gouges marked the stone where an animal had scrabbled at the other side of the door. "Something came this way. And it looks like whatever it was made its way into the study. Voron must have known about it too. Where does it lead?"

"The same place as you would have ended up had you gone down the stairs rather than up on the way to the library," The priestess's voice trembled. "The belly of the temple. It is... it is not a pleasant place."

I drew her toward me and placed a finger on her lips. Kissing the top of her head, I spoke into her golden hair. "We will investigate this, but first I want to tell you the rest of my plan."

Kalia nodded and leaned against my chest. I wrapped my arms around her and spoke to Ruhail.

"How many nymphs are there?" I said. "Can we ask them to leave immediately?"

"I will go back to the Heart of the Forest and send out a message to them," she said. "There are hundreds of nymphs in the Ring Wood."

She grabbed her staff as if she meant to leave right away.

"Wait," I said. "I want to come with you."

"You cannot," Ruhail said, her eyes widened with almost comical horror. "Only servants of the Spirit of the Forest may enter the Heart."

"Okay, okay," I laughed grimly. "I'm not going to force my way in. Go then, and return here immediately. You and I are going to the Dark Woods."

"The Dark Woods?" The priestess looked up at me with a haunted look in her purple eyes. She shivered in my arms. "When the creatures of chaos are emboldened like this? It is too dangerous."

"I trust Ruhail to protect me," I said, winking at the dryad. "She's got personal stakes in the matter. Besides, it's the only place I know of with the kind of creatures I'm looking for."

"This is madness," Iymbryl shouted, and for a moment, I thought I saw a flash of concern in her ice-blue eyes. She glowered at me. "You might not be much use, but you are certainly of no use at all if you are dead."

A howl lifted on the air outside and a chorus of dire wolves, werewolves, and other dark creatures rose in a frenzied crescendo. I rushed to the window to see what they were doing, but they stayed in the shadow of the trees.

"Do they fear sunlight?" I asked, peering out the window.

"Many do." Iymbryl joined me and pointed to a commotion near one of the ornate wooden bridges leading to the temple gates. "But not all. Look, the guards are skirmishing with some imps over there."

"We must move quickly then," I said. "It will get worse at nightfall."

The elf-guard nodded and for once didn't seem to have some smart-ass remark to follow. "It will get worse. The daylight hours are when we will rest and prepare for the next attack. When the blood moon rises tomorrow night, Drakkus's army will be at its strongest."

Ruhail shuddered involuntarily.

"Why do you want to go to the Dark Woods?" she asked, touching my shoulder to draw me away from the window.

I couldn't blame her after what had happened to her the last time we were there. I didn't really want to go back myself. But I had a feeling we were going to have to, if we were going to get the help we needed.

"I think we need to try to sway the neutral players in the Ring Wood," I said. "And I thought we could start with the Arachana."

Everyone stared at me. The looks on their faces told me this might not be the cleverest plan.

"You want to ask the spider folk for help?" Ruhail said with a gasp. "You can't be serious."

"They are powerful," I said. "And even creatures of chaos fear them. Isn't that right?"

The dryad nodded, but the look of fear on her face didn't disappear.

"Well, with the priestess's blessing, I'd like to try," I said. "If Drakkus has sway over members of our side, we need all the help we can get."

"It is a foolhardy plan," the priestess said, shaking her head. She collapsed onto a hard wooden chair next to the doorway into the hidden passageway. "Their Queen is a monster. You will most likely die. But if we do nothing, we will surely die as well. I don't like it Loghann, but you are right. It may be our only hope."

"Why do I have to be bound to a man who is so determined to get himself killed?" Ruhail wailed at the ceiling. Then she wiped her eyes and pointed at me with a long pale finger. "I really wish you *had* tried to force yourself on me like all the other bond mates I've had."

"How would that have been any better?"

The priestess covered her mouth with one hand and made an undignified sound somewhere between a snort and a sob. Iymbryl laughed dryly.

"Because if you had abused our bond," she said. "I could have severed the bond myself, by killing you. The Spirit of the Forest does not abide abusers of her generosity."

My eyes opened wide as I remembered the dryad's early flirtations.

"You *were* trying to tempt me, then." My jaw dropped as I considered the implications. "You wanted me to take advantage of you so you could kill me?"

"Oh, don't look like that," Ruhail said, crossing her arms over her substantial chest and sticking out her lower lip. "The moment you refused me I knew it would be immoral of me to keep trying. Even forest spirits have a code to work within."

"But you did try," I said. My mouth went dry. "You really would have killed me?"

"Only if you had deserved it." She turned away from me. "But you were a perfect gentleman. So I remain indebted to you and I will only be able to sever my bond to you the old-fashioned way. Apparently by prying you out of the jaws of an oversized arachnid."

"Loghann has been infuriatingly noble, hasn't he?" The priestess's eyes slid toward Iymbryl, who turned and alarming shade of pink and looked outside the window again. "It's one of the reasons I knew he would be the perfect candidate for our next emperor."

I shook off a chill.

"That's it," I said, waving the women away. "I'm not sleeping with anyone else in this crazy world unless they beg me for it, good and thoroughly. You are all crazy."

Ruhail huffed indignantly and the priestess laughed.

I stood by the mouth of the darkened channel and peered inside. A cold, dank air wafted out of the blackness. It had the same tingling sense of danger and adventure I had felt on the stairs toward the library. Something in the pitched tugged at me, like that was the way I was meant to go.

"Kalia," I said. "Where does this lead. Could we get out of the temple grounds this way?"

The priestess's eyes widened. "Yes. You could. How did you know that?"

"Just a hunch," I said. Then I turned to Ruhail. "Go back to the Heart of the Forest. Get the message out to the nymphs. We need every creature who is willing to fight for us or defend us to come to the temple. Aligned with order or neutral, doesn't matter. Then meet me back here. You and I are going to go on an adventure."

The dryad cast a wary glance at the dark tunnel behind me, then she nodded and ran out of the room with her tangled auburn hair flying behind her.

Chapter 16

While Ruhail was talking to the nymphs, Priestess Kalia and Iymbryl helped me to gather some more appropriate clothing for the challenge ahead. Soon, I was suited up in hardened-leather armor that had been stained a deep green. The armor appeared almost black in the low light of Voron's study. Iymbryl had brought me a proper scabbard and showed me, without laughing too much, how to wear it around my waist without tripping on it.

She quirked an eyebrow at me. "You say you have trained with a sword before?"

"I have," I said, refusing to let her get under my skin. I knew that was what she wanted. "In my world, we don't have to carry them with us, though. Fencing and sword fighting are practiced as sport, not in battle."

She rolled her eyes. "And what do you use in battle then? Rocks?"

"Let's just say if Drakkus had weapons like we do," I said, "this battle would be finished already. And this entire empire would be little more than a crater in the ground leaching poisons into anything that survived the first attack."

Priestess Kalia gasped. "That's horrifying."

"I don't believe you," Iymbryl said, and she produced another sword out of a pile of armor and weapons she had brought to the study from around the temple. "Prove it."

"You want me to fight you?" I backed away from the elf like I was scared.

Priestess Kalia, perched on the edge of Voron's desk, watched with her purple eyes wide with excitement. "Yes, Loghann. Show her that you are a true hero."

"I never claimed to be a warrior." I twirled the blade around my wrist, fumbling it slightly. Iymbryl's lips twitched, and I laughed silently to myself. I said, "And you've got hundreds of years of experience on me."

"He is frightened of me," Iymbryl said. She pulled her chosen weapon from its sheath with a controlled movement, lacking amateurish dramatic flourishes. "Don't be. I will not hurt you."

"I should hope not," I said. "I'll make a poor offering to the Arachana if I'm missing any of my limbs."

The blond elf laughed heartily, the first real laugh I think I'd heard from her since we met. She said, "At least you are brave as well as frightened. The latter might save your life."

"I handled two trolls and a werewolf with this blade," I warned mockingly as she advanced on me.

"Trolls are stupid." She took up an *en guard* position. "And the werewolf got away."

"Yeah." I grinned. "But it was limping."

"All right, boy soldier," she said. "Get in position. I'll go easy on you."

I lifted my sword and did a little warm-up shuffle.

"How about a bet?" I leered at her lasciviously. "You don't go easy on me. But if I can get at least one touch in, I get two hours with you where you aren't allowed to say no to me."

She scoffed. "I would never agree to that. Priestess, how do you suffer this fool with a straight face? I would be doing you a favor if I finished him right now."

"Do not even joke of such things, Iymbryl," the Priestess said, but a small smile played at her lips. I wondered if she knew what I was up to.

I waggled my eyebrows at the elf and did some complex and ineffectual stretching maneuvers. "I think your mighty protector is the one who is scared, Priestess. Perhaps you need to order her to take my bet."

Priestess Kalia laughed and crossed her legs, leaning backward on the desk like she was settling in to watch the show. "This is between the two of you. I will not order Iymbryl to do anything."

"I am not scared," the elf snarled. She made a fake lunge at me and I jumped back. She laughed. "And when I get the first touch? What is my reward to be?"

"I'll let you spank *my* bottom," I said.

She narrowed her eyes and flicked her long blond hair over her shoulder. "Maybe I will. I want the same deal. Two hours where you cannot say no to me."

Then she grinned with such malevolence I had a moment of second thought. I glanced at the Priestess for help.

"Don't look at me," she said. "You started this. I think it's a fine wager."

I took a deep breath and squared off against the elf, my heart thudding in my chest. As Iymbryl rolled her shoulders and bounced on the balls of her feet I began to worry that I had made a mistake.

I was a fine fencer by modern Earth standards. I knew I'd won more than my fair share of competitions. I couldn't remember any of them, mind you, but the knowledge was there as surely as I knew what my face should have looked like.

Iymbryl, on the other hand, had been training for hundreds of years *and* she was an elf. She probably had magically enhanced reflexes and armor that granted her special abilities.

At least, that's how it would work in a video game.

Just in case, I said, "No magic, flats of the blade only."

"Agreed," the elf woman said. "Priestess Kalia will adjudicate."

She turned to bow to the priestess, and I did the same.

Kalia clapped her hands together and shouted, "Begin!"

Iymbryl did not wait. She darted in on my left side and slashed down toward my legs. I spun on my heel and blocked her blade with mine a fraction of an inch before she landed the strike. I pushed her blade with mine and the singing of metal against metal filled the room.

She took a step backwards, as if retreating for her next attack. Her weight shifted as she feinted, and I leaped out of the way as she lunged forward on the same leg. She laughed, "You are fast, boy soldier. I will give you that."

"You are taking chances you wouldn't take if you thought I was a real swordsman," I said, backing up to give myself a bit more space. "I should be insulted."

"No." She flipped her sword up over her head and caught it in her left hand. She raised her eyebrows at me. "You should be worried."

Damn. That was a neat trick.

Sweat trickled down the back of my neck in the new, too-warm armor.

I watched Iymbryl's feet for some sign of what she was going to do next. But she didn't move. She took up a defensive position and waited for me to attack.

I wasn't as comfortable fighting against a left-handed opponent as I was a right-handed one, and she had probably assumed that. But I wasn't completely useless at it either. I decided to play to her probable assumptions.

I advanced and lunged, thrusting toward her chest from the same angle I would have used if she was holding her sword in her right hand. I adjusted slightly at the last minute as if I was correcting a strike made from muscle memory. She parried exactly as I would have in her situation, crossing her blade against mine and forcing it away. Exactly what I had hoped she would do.

I pulled my sword back at the last second, and her aggressive parry put her off-balance without the resistance of my blade to stop it. Her back foot stumbled forward to catch her weight. I pivoted on my left foot and thrust at her side.

The elf deflected my blade and spun deftly out of the way.

"Nicely done," she said. "Perhaps you have some experience with a blade after all."

Without waiting for me to respond she jumped into an attack, rapidly striking at me *left-right-left* with each step. I stumbled backward, parrying each of her strokes, but barely. She paused slightly after the fifth such blow. I was backed up against the wall and had nowhere to go.

It was time for a desperate maneuver I'd only ever seen in movies and probably couldn't pull off in real life.

Without stopping to think long enough to talk myself out of it, I dropped and rolled past her on her left hand side.

She must have made a backhanded swing because I felt the blade of her sword slap my ass as a millisecond before I shot to my feet and pressed the tip of my sword against the back of her neck. We both held our points of contact, breathing heavily.

"I win," she said. "First touch goes to me."

"It was pretty close," I said, even though I didn't really believe it. "Let's ask the adjudicator."

"Iymbryl got first touch," Priestess Kalia said, and she clapped her hands together excitedly. "She wins the bet."

I wiped the sweat from my brow. That's what I got for getting cocky. I had let this whole hero thing get to my head. Hopefully the elf wouldn't tell everyone she met how useless the wanna-be-emperor was with a sword.

I cringed, my cheeks burning.

Then I reached out my hand to shake hers. She'd beaten me fair and square.

"Don't feel too badly," the blond elf said smugly. "You fought well. I will take good care of you when you fulfill your obligations to me."

I dropped my sword and groaned.

"Loghann got in a touch, though." The priestess's purple eyes twinkled. My heart beat a little faster. She said, "So he also wins his bet."

"What?" Iymbryl shrieked. "That is impossible."

My eyes widened and a grin spread across my face.

"It's true." I whirled back to the elf. "The conditions of my bet were that if I got in at least one hit, you would give me two hours where you couldn't say no. Your conditions were that if you got the first hit, you won two hours from me. We both won."

Iymbryl threw her sword to the ground with a clatter. "This is foolishness. I never should have agreed to this bet."

"Don't worry." I smiled benignly at her. "I'll take good care of you as you fulfill your obligations to me."

The elf moved toward me like she was going to punch me, but I stood my ground. She narrowed her eyes and said, "You have to survive the Arachana first, boy soldier. They might be able to knock that smile off your face."

"Just in case they don't," I said, "you might want to start being a little nicer to me. I think addressing me as Sir would be a good place to start."

"Never," she growled.

"Well then, that's where we'll start once you belong to me," I said.

All the blood that had been coursing through my body with the exercise suddenly rushed to my crotch. Oh, I was looking forward to teaching Iymbryl a thing or two about authority.

The fact that she was likely thinking the same thing really did nothing to tame my desires.

Priestess Kalia laughed and slid off the desk. She approached us and gave each of us a kiss. "Don't fight, you are both my heroes."

"Where is that gods-be-damned dryad?" Iymbryl picked up her sword and tossed it in the pile of weapons and armor next to the door. "If she had hurried, we wouldn't be in this mess."

"Oh it will be messy," I said. "I promise you that."

Iymbryl whipped something at my head and I ducked. It flew over me, through the doorway, and out into the corridor. There was a thwack and a squeak.

"Oh no," the priestess said, attempting to hide a giggle. "Here she is."

Ruhail stomped into the room with what looked like a medieval jock-strap hanging off her forehead. Her staff blazed with electric green fire not unlike the look in her eyes. She said, "What is the meaning of this?"

"I think it's, uh..." I made a circular motion around my crotch. "You know, for protecting the—"

"I know what it is," she snapped. "Why is it on my head?"

"I was trying to hit Loghann," Iymbryl said by way of apology. "He ducked."

Ruhail picked the leather cod piece off her forehead and flung it to the side. I noticed she had fixed her hair and repaired her leaf dress when she was gone. If I wasn't mistaken, the leaves covered a little less than they had before. She glared at me when she caught me staring, and I looked away quickly, feigning disinterest.

"How did it go?" Priestess Kalia asked, grabbing the dryad's hand and ushering her into the study. She pursed her lips and gave Iymbryl and me a warning look. "Did the nymphs cooperate? They can be very impulsive creatures."

"They have already left." The dryad leaned on her staff and sighed. Her eyes darted toward me and away again. "Once they heard what was on offer, they were eager to agree."

"That's wonderful," the priestess said. She pulled Ruhail into an embrace and kissed her lightly on each pale cheek.

The dryad blushed. "I just hope Loghann won't mind too much."

My ears perked up at that. I narrowed my eyes at the auburn haired beauty. "What exactly did you offer them?"

"Quality time with the new emperor." Her blush deepened. "You will be a very busy man once Illdrian passes the scepter of power to you."

Ruhail bowed to the priestess and stood with her staff next to the yawning doorway of the secret passage hidden in the bookshelf. She bounced on her toes and waited for me to finish my preparations.

"If he passes it to me," I reminded her, sheathing my sword and picking up a small leather buckler shield. "So far I have the support of one priestess, one realm. We'll need to save the Ring Wood if I'm to have any hope of convincing the other priestesses that I'm a good candidate for the emperorship."

Iymbryl leaned against the bookshelf next to the yawning doorway into the secret passage. She crossed her arms over her armored chest and curled her lip in a derisive sneer. She said, "If you can't, we'll have bigger things to worry about than some oversexed nymphs."

"We won't know until we try," I said.

I took Priestess Kalia in my arms and wrapped her small body in a tight embrace. She felt fragile against the stiff leather armor I now wore. I lifted her chin with my fingers and bent my mouth to hers. She moaned and melted into my arms.

The heat of her body on my hands and the soft, shifting fabric of the gossamer-thin dressing gown made me wish we had more time to explore the power of our new bond. I longed to push her back on Voron's desk and take her again while the dryad and the elf watched. The yearning burned like a ball of fire in my belly, and the heat of my desire coursed through my veins like its own kind of magic.

But I knew I had to prove myself worthy of the priestess's faith in me. If I survived, the gift of her body would taste even sweeter than it had last night. She had taken a chance on me, and it was up to me to prove to the realms that Kalia had not made a mistake.

The way she moved against me, I could tell that she was thinking the same thing. When I released her, I felt fortified. A pale, green shimmer glowed around my hands as if my connection to the priestess was giving me a new strength. It was strange, but since the priestess had given herself to me, I felt more at one with this world. The hazy memories of my past life seemed to fade away, leaving only bits and pieces of knowledge behind—things I knew to be true but couldn't actually recall.

I wondered if she had already shared some of her power with me, and if her strength would be enough to help me convince the Arachana to fight beside us.

The others didn't mention my glowing hands, so I guessed it was something only I was able to sense, like Ruhail's glittering magic or the angry red blaze of Voron's dark spells. But the sight of it renewed my confidence in our mission.

Reluctantly, I turned away from the priestess and said to Ruhail, "Are you ready?"

The dryad gripped her staff tightly and nodded. "Yes, we should go."

"Take care of her, Iymbryl." I clapped the elf-guard on the shoulder. "And yourself. It would be a shame if you died before we could make good on our wager."

She slapped my hand away and glared with bright, icy-blue eyes. "I was taking care of her long before you showed up. Worry about keeping yourself alive, and I'll take care of the rest."

"I trust you will," I said. I ignored her anger and gave her shoulder a squeeze. She didn't slap me away that time.

Priestess Kalia floated across the room and nestled herself in next to the blond elf. I knew she was in good hands, and I was grateful for the fierce warrior's loyal protection of the temple and my lover.

"I will go to my pavilion and begin strengthening the protective spells on the temple grounds. I'll attempt to repair any damage that Voron has done," the priestess said. "But please hurry, Loghann. I don't know how long I will be able to keep up our defenses."

I fixed the buckler shield on my back and slung a bag of provisions over my shoulders.

"We'll do our best," I said, stepping up to the mouth of the dark passageway. Cold, damp air seeped out of the darkness, and I felt a chill. But underneath the ominous sensation, there was a tremor of something more. An urge to explore, the promise of adventure. "Good luck, Priestess."

"And to you, Loghann," she replied softly. "Beware in the tunnels below the temple. There are passages beneath us that are far deeper and far darker than even my memories go back. Challenges await you. Let your heart guide you, for whatever you are looking for amongst the roots of the ancient trees will find you. If you hold even a sliver of darkness within you, you may be dead or corrupted before you make it back to the surface."

"I will ensure that doesn't happen, my lady," Ruhail said firmly. "While many creatures can stray from the path of order, we dryads are stronger than most. I owe Loghann my life, and I will gladly give it up before I see him twisted by the hand of chaos."

I gripped the handle of my sword, and the blade hummed in response. My heart swelled with strength and purpose.

"That won't be necessary," I said. "My path is clear. I will destroy Drakkus and his followers or die trying, but I will not be corrupted."

My voice echoed off the walls and disappeared into the passage before me, like a warning to whatever awaited us beyond the light of the study.

I should have felt scared.

My memories were faded, but I knew I had never done anything like this before. Still, there was something growing inside me that seemed bigger than whoever I used to be. It was as if my body had become a vessel for something much more than the simple man I had been before.

Now I was a man strong enough to rule with the power of the five realms, a man who would conquer the elements and use them as a shield to protect this empire from the gathering darkness.

I was a man with a destiny.

And my destiny awaited me beneath the forest temple.

Chapter 17

Ruhail conjured up a swarm of fireflies to light our way as I led us through the sloping tunnel. At first, the passage was made of stone with fluffy green moss growing like mortar between each square brick, not much different from the rest of the walls in the temple, except that it hadn't been cared for and kept up in the same way. As we wound our way down, though, the gray stone darkened with moisture, and after a time, it became slick and black. My new boots slipped against the sloped ground. The faint, trickling sound of running water came from somewhere ahead. The soft thump of Ruhail's staff against the stone floor created a lulling rhythm that set our pace.

The light of the fireflies cast an eerie glow on the wet stones, and the air that wafted toward us from the depths was getting colder. It had a strange smell, like rotting vegetation and the acrid tang of rusted metal.

We walked in silence. Every step I took felt like cranking a wheel, ratcheting up the tension in my chest. Something was going to happen down here.

I just hoped it would be something that would help us, not make things worse.

"I hate this place," Ruhail said suddenly, with a shiver in her voice. "How can you step so confidently? I can feel us moving farther and farther from the heart of the forest."

"Do you think we are underground yet?" I dragged my finger along the slick stones and rubbed the moisture between my fingers. The wet black look of the stones made it seem like something ominous but it appeared only to be water. "There is an energy here. Can you feel it? Like we are being pulled deeper beneath the temple."

The soft thump of Ruhail's staff was my only answer. I glanced over my shoulder at her. The dryad walked with her eyes closed, surrounded in a pale glittering mist. In the cold, her nipples had hardened into sharp points that strained against the confines of her leafy dress. A couple of fireflies darted around her face, making shadows dance in dizzying circles over her pretty features. When she opened her eyes, her pupils stretched wide like a cat's in the dark. She said, "I sense something. But it is not green magic. It is not good or orderly. We must be very careful, Loghann."

"We will be," I said. "But we are meant to go this way. I just know it."

A soft sigh escaped her lips.

"I hope you are right," she said. And then, "Oh!"

I opened my mouth to ask her what had startled her, but my next step fell through empty air. My arms pin-wheeled as I tried to keep my balance on the edge of the crumbling stone ledge. Below me, a deep black pit yawned hungrily. Ruhail caught me by the arm and dragged me backward before I could fall. I overbalanced and crashed down onto my tailbone. Pain exploded up my spine. I made a rather un-heroic grunt and closed my eyes against the burst of fireworks going off in my head.

"Whoa," I said, panting. "That was close."

The dryad crouched next to me, glowing even brighter than before. She stared at me with her full lips pulled into a frown. "Are you all right, Loghann? I am sorry."

"Sorry for what?" I laughed, rolling over to rub the sore spot on my backside. "Saving my life? I thought that was your job."

My eyes widened as I realized what I'd said. Ruhail didn't say anything. She pressed her hands against my chest and green light burst from between her fingers. A warm, fuzzy feeling filled my body and the pain in my tailbone dissolved in a fizz of sparkly green magic. She said, "Is that better?"

"Yeah," I said. My heartbeat throbbed through my body like a blinking neon sign screaming Still Alive! "But Ruhail. You saved my life. You're free of our bond now."

She nodded once, curtly. "Yes, well. I couldn't just let you walk off a cliff, could I? Let's carry on. The ledge wraps around the wall there. I think we have to—"

I grabbed her hands and looked into her eyes. "You'll stay with me?"

"Of course I'm staying." She pulled her hands out of mine and pushed herself up to her feet. "Who knows what kind of trouble you'd get into on your own?"

I rolled onto my knees and stood, brushing the damp and dirt off my pants with a still-shaky hand. Ruhail's magic seemed to glow brighter than before, as if part of her power had been leeched away and had now returned. I said, "It worked though, didn't it? You're free?"

"Yes," she whispered. "And thank you."

I shook my head. "For what?"

"For saving my life when you did," she said, casting her eyes downward at the ground. "And for not abusing your power over me."

I put my arms on the dryad's shoulders and kissed the top of her auburn-haired head. "I would never do that. And besides, if I had, you would have had me assassinated, so..."

"Yes." She turned her spring-green gaze up to my face, a faint smile dancing on her lips. "But I would have hated to do it."

I grinned. "That makes me feel much better."

"Loghann?" Fireflies bobbed around the dryad's face, making her eyes sparkle. She bit her plump bottom lip and waited.

I leaned closer to her and inhaled the fresh-grass scent of her skin. "Yes, Ruhail?"

"Would you like to kiss me now?" Her breath tickled the side of my neck and sent a chill running down my spine.

I whispered in her ear, letting my lips brush gently against her skin. "Very much so."

I wanted to do much more than to kiss her, and she damn well knew it.

She turned her face toward me with her eyes closed.

I pulled away and stepped deftly backward. Two could play hard to get, and we had an operation to complete.

When her lips touched nothing but empty air, her eyes flew open. I blew her a kiss from the other side of the corridor. Her jaw dropped. "What are you—?"

"You had your chance." I shrugged. "Now we have a dangerous mission to focus on, some terrifying creatures to negotiate with, an evil advisor to hunt down and destroy, and a temple to save. Kissing will have to wait."

She gripped her staff and stomped toward me, her green eyes blazing. With each step her heavy, round breasts jumped and jostled and strained the integrity of the skimpy leaves of her dress. "I have never in my life met anyone as infuriating as you, Loghann Grenwyld. If the Arachana don't eat you on sight I might have to have a talk with their leader myself."

Ruhail pushed past me and crept out onto the crumbling ledge next to the wall, fireflies buzzing angrily around her face. None of them stayed to light my way. I cursed and followed the dryad before I was left to navigate the precipice in the pitch black.

But I grinned to myself as I shuffled along the ledge. I'd hoped the sexy dryad might be more attracted to me than she let on. Now that she had confirmed as much, it was all I could do to keep my overactive imagination in check. It wouldn't do to fall to my death before I had a chance to peek beneath those leaves.

I didn't know what it was about this world, but something about the danger and intrigue had my libido working overtime. I had heard near death experiences could increase your sex drive, but this was ridiculous.

I gritted my teeth and forced myself to concentrate. Ruhail and her fireflies rounded a sharp corner and left me in the dark. I leaned back against the wall but the shield on my back kept me off-balance. My heart hammered in my chest as I slid my foot sideways along the crumbling ledge to make sure I had enough room to take another step. I prayed my sword wouldn't catch on the rough stone wall and send me over the edge.

"Ruhail?" I called. She wasn't mad enough to abandon me in the tunnel, was she? "I can't see anything."

She didn't reply. The sudden blackness was disorienting, and my eyes filled the void with floating blobs of color and weird phantom shapes. Closing my eyes didn't help, the shapes were still there. I inched my way forward, testing with my right foot and then shuffling my left along behind it. The crevice seemed to have a kind of gravity. It tugged relentlessly at me as if waiting for me to slip and plunge into its depths. When I came to the corner, and my foot fell into empty space again, my stomach lodged in my throat.

I swallowed hard, feeling around the edge with my right arm, and focussed on getting around the bend. Halfway there, bent at an awkward angle with my right foot and arm grasping for purchase on the other side and my left trembling to maintain my balance, a noise rose up from within the void that sent icy chills down my spine.

At first it was like a single voice, whispering. The sound bounced around the walls of the tunnel in a strange, hollow echo. But what started as a single whisper grew into a susurrus of overlapping voices as other whisperers joined the chorus, all of them speaking at once.

Where are you going, young prince?

Come to us. Don't be afraid...

You are lost, young prince.

But we have found you...

I scrabbled around the corner and was relieved to find the ledge a little wider. The faint glow of the dryad's fireflies gave me just enough light to see by. I hurried as fast as I dared to where the crumbling edge connected to solid ground. Once safe, I collapsed onto my hands and knees and sucked in a lungful of air. If I never had to scramble across a death-defying precipice again, it would be too soon.

The eerie whispering drifted after me. The voices swirled around my head, rushing toward me and then fading as if the speakers were invisible attackers coming at me from all sides.

"Ruhail," I said again. "Please tell me you can hear this too."

The dryad stood in the tunnel with her back to me, her shoulders tense. The light of her staff was thin and dull, as if I was seeing it through a veil.

She can't hear you, the whisperers said. *She can't see you.*

Ruhail's auburn-haired head tossed left and right, like she was searching for something. She raised a hand to her mouth, like she was calling out, but no sound reached my ears.

"What the hell is going on here?" I demanded and I pushed myself to my feet. "Who are you? What did you do to her?"

We are. We are. We are...

"You are what?" I stumbled forward and placed hand on Ruhail's milk-white shoulder. Or I tried to. My hand went straight through her, as if she was a ghost. Or I was. In the pitch black tunnel beyond, the shadows moved and shifted.

We are coming, the voices hissed.

The dryad stared into the darkness, frozen in fear. Pale gray shapes, hunkered on all fours, crept out of the shadows toward Ruhail. They looked like huge hairless rats, their bodies starved and emaciated. Their skin hung off them in wrinkled sheets, binding and bunching between their limbs. Pink tongues lolled out of long, toothy muzzles. Their black, dead-eyed stares were locked on the petrified woman. My stomach curdled as they got closer. Their human hands and feet had clawed fingers and forearms streaked with blood. The stench of rot and rust thickened in the air.

Ruhail tensed like she could sense the things. Her eyes darted back and forth. She lifted her staff in an attempt to illuminate the darkness. But her magic was blocked here, getting weaker by the second, and the dryad didn't seem to be able to see the creatures coming toward her.

"Move, Ruhail!" I shouted and waved my hands in front of her face, panic seizing in my chest. "Run!"

She stared straight through me.

Join us, young prince, the whisperers said. *We have been waiting ever... so... long...*

I put myself in front of Ruhail, even though she couldn't see me. If I had somehow become incorporeal, I had no idea if I could do anything to protect her against the monsters.

Still, I pulled the buckler shield off my back and gripped the hilt of my sword.

"What are you?" I shouted at the saggy-skinned creatures. "Get away from her!"

The nearest beast bared its teeth, and a wet growl rumbled from its emaciated chest. The gray skin of its muzzle peeled back to reveal black gums and yellow canine teeth. Its dull, black eyes pinned me with a soulless glare.

Come with us, the voices hissed.

The creature lunged.

I pulled my sword from it sheath and jumped forward to meet the rat-thing with my shield raised. I slammed it in the jaw with the edge of the buckler, spun to the side, and whipped the sword down toward its shoulder. The blade of the Grenwyld clan glowed hot white and sliced through the thing's sickly gray flesh, exposing pulsing red muscles and pale tendons.

An unearthly animal howl shrieked through the tunnel as the monstrous creature reared back on its hind legs and swatted at me with its bony, clawed hands.

The blade! The whispers rose to a piercing wail that stabbed into my brain like a hot iron poker. *Why does he have the blade?*

I dodged backward and struck again, ignoring the voices. If I could hurt these ugly fuckers, there was no way I was going down without a fight.

Flesh sagged from the thing's massive frame. I whipped my sword across its body and carved a chunk of dangling skin off the bottom of its belly. It shrieked again, and the other rat-things backed up like they were having second thoughts.

Stop him. The voices howled. *Stop him!*

My bleeding opponent dropped back to all fours, its disturbingly human fingers digging into the stone floor until its long, clawed nails shattered. It roared at me like a grizzly bear warning off a competitor during mating season.

Holy shit. It wasn't an oversized rat, it was a bear.

A bulge of purple entrails poked out of the hole I'd made in its wobbling belly and dragged on the ground. It stumbled backward, its wrinkly pink head low and threatening, but it seemed unwilling to attack again.

Another naked bear crept up on my flank. I could feel its hot, fetid breath as it rose up on its hind legs, looming over my shoulder. It swatted at me. I lifted the buckler and braced myself for the blow. A crushing weight slammed into my arm and shoulder, and the shield clipped the left side of my head. It was like getting hit by a lead Frisbee. My vision blurred and my ears rushed with a sound like a river of blood. I shook my head, trying to regain some sense of where I was and what I was doing.

If I fell now, everything would be lost. And the first one to suffer for my failure would be Ruhail.

The thought of these disgusting creatures sinking their teeth into the pristine flesh of the beautiful dryad filled me with revulsion. It burned through my pain and cleared the black clouds creeping into the edges of my vision.

This was a challenge. It wasn't a play fight with a haughty elf. This was how I would prove myself worthy of Kalia's belief in me; how I would prove myself worthy to be the next emperor.

I was ready.

The hairless pink feet of the creature took a shuffling step closer. I kept my shield up, hiding from its beady black-eyed gaze. I wanted it to think I was hurt. I wanted it to come closer.

The ragged, wet sounds of the thing's snuffling breath set my teeth on edge. I placed my body like a barrier between the creature and Ruhail. Could she tell I was there? That I would protect her? I hoped she wasn't too afraid. I gripped the handle of my sword tightly and waited for the thing to get close enough for me to strike.

The bear dropped to all fours and dipped its head to peer beneath my shield. Its pink lips quivered. Its dark gums dripped with thick, frothy saliva. A snarl rippled its muzzle, and the yellowed teeth snapped at me, faster than the thing should have been able to move. My instincts screamed to jump backward, out of the way of its powerful jaws. But that would expose Ruhail, and I would die before I let it hurt her.

I drove my sword forward into its lunging face. The tip glanced off the yellowed teeth, splitting its black gums into a gaping red wound. It roared and whipped its muzzle to the side. I stabbed it again. The blade pierced its left eye, and a broken white and pink glob fell out of the bear's face as I withdrew my sword for another strike. A blinding red light exploded from the hole left in the bear's skull and a shrieking wind howled up around us like we were suddenly in the middle of a cyclone.

The whispered voices wailed and moaned and began chanting in a language I didn't understand. I shielded my eyes from the intense blaze of crimson magic and stood my ground between the injured creature and Ruhail. What the hell was going on? Shadowy shapes moved behind the bear that bled light. More roars joined the cacophony, some enraged, some pained and terrified. The whispering voices seemed to be egging them on, urging the beasts to attack.

I swung my sword in an arc, warding them away. The blade left a trail of white light like the tail of a shooting star that cut through the oozing red magic. The red darkened like drying blood and faded to black. The whispers faded to silence. The naked bear-rats disappeared. Ruhail and I stood alone in the tunnel.

She looked at me, and her spring-green eyes widened like I had appeared out of thin air.

"Loghann?" she said, reaching a pale hand toward my face.

Blood trickled from a gash on the side of my head where the shield had thumped me. My shoulder ached, and my skull felt like it was full of rocks. But all things considered I felt okay. She stepped toward me, and her cool fingers caressed my cheek.

She grabbed the front of my shirt and pulled me toward her, her full red lips parted. Her chest heaved with panicked breaths. I thought she was going to kiss me, and this time I wasn't going to argue. But the moment our bodies connected, her knees went weak and she pitched against my chest. I scrambled, with my shield in one hand and my sword in the other, and caught her in the crook of my arm.

I lowered her gently to the stones of the tunnel floor, cradling her head against my arm.

"Ruhail?" I patted the side of her cheek gently. "Are you okay?"

She moaned and her eyelids twitched. Her eyes stayed closed. A crease formed between her eyebrows and her lips pulled into a frown.

"Loghann," she said, moaning like she was having a bad dream. "Be careful..."

"It's okay," I said and shook her shoulder. "They're gone now. You're safe."

A warm wind blew through the tunnel, and the sweet scent of maple leaves and berries wafted on the air. I looked up in surprise. A woman stood over us, wearing a crown of red leaves in her dark brown hair and a gown the color of mulled wine. She was older than she appeared in the paintings in my bedroom, but it had to be the same woman.

"Priestess Maia?" I said, my jaw dropping. "What are you—?"

"You are not safe," she said. Her dark eyes flashed with fear. "Not for long. Come with me. Carry her if you must."

I sheathed my sword, fastened the buckler onto my back, and bent to pick Ruhail and her staff up off the ground. The dryad weighed about as much as the leaves that made up her skimpy dress, which was a good thing because the mysterious woman didn't wait for me. She disappeared into the darkness of the tunnel so quickly I had to run to keep up.

In the back of my mind, I wondered if it was a good idea. Priestess Maia must have been dead; she had to be if Kalia had taken her place. Unless she was the priestess of the forest realm currently married to Emperor Illdrian, in which case, why would she be there in the tunnels with us? It could be a trick, some dark forces trying to lure me away from my quest. Or she could be a spirit sent to guide me. Without Ruhail to help, I had no way of knowing for sure.

I wanted to trust the woman. Kalia had said to follow my heart, and there was something about the red-crowned woman that drew me to her. It wasn't just that she was beautiful—all of the women in this world seemed to be—but there was something so familiar about her. In fact, she was the first woman I'd met here that I didn't feel desire for. I just wanted to be close to her. I had to believe this was the right choice. I needed to know what those creatures were, who the voices belonged to, and how they had managed to separate the dryad and me from one another like that.

From behind, the cold air of the crevice tugged at me like it wanted to draw me back into its maw. Swallowing my unease, I carried Ruhail deeper into the tunnel, following the scent of berries and autumn leaves.

Chapter 18

We wound in and out of a maze of tunnels that seemed to get darker and danker the deeper we went. The woman's burgundy dress appeared as a flickering of color barely visible amongst the thickening shadows. I held the dryad tightly to my chest. My sword slapped against the side of my leg as I ran, and Ruhail's staff dug into my shoulder blades where I had wedged it underneath one of the straps that held my shield on my back. My lungs burned, but I never quite seemed able to keep up with the mysterious stranger.

Eventually, we emerged from the tunnels into a cool, black cavern. I sensed more than saw the space open up before me. Cold drafts moved through the chamber as if it was connected to a much larger network of tunnels and caves.

The cavern was dark, but not quite as dark as the tunnels we'd just run through. My eyes slowly adjusted to the low-light, finding edges and shapes hiding in the shadows. A dim blue glow illuminated the edges of toothy stalactites and stalagmites. In the center of the cave, a smooth black surface like polished glass glistened in the strange light. A pool of water, I guessed. The glow appeared to come from tiny phosphorescent mushrooms, growing in clumps like little bunches of flowers between the cracks in cave walls.

The red-crowned woman had disappeared.

"Hello?" I called out. My voice echoed around me, amplified by the enclosed space. "Where did you go?"

My arms were beginning to ache despite the fact that Ruhail barely weighed anything at all. The adrenaline that had surged through my veins during the fight was seeping out of me now. In its absence, I felt like a wrung-out sponge.

So much for being a big hero, I thought. How am I going to protect the forest temple and get the priestesses of the realms to rally behind me if I can't even fight a few mutant bears-rats without getting winded? Too bad this wasn't a video game. I could use a stamina upgrade. Maybe cash in some skill points for a new talent perk.

I laughed bitterly to myself.

"Do not despair," a woman's voice said. I looked around the cave but couldn't see the former priestess. Her soft words rippled across the water toward me, washing me in a feeling of calm and comfort. She said, "Come to the pool. I have much to show you."

"But Ruhail," I said, clutching the pale, limp dryad to my chest protectively. "She needs help."

"She will be restored. I will take care of both of you."

The woman's voice was so strange and otherworldly, like notes plucked on a foreign instrument.

And yet it was familiar, too. Something itched at the back of my mind, some connection I was missing. Something from my past life? That didn't make any sense. But what else could it be?

I placed Ruhail gently on the cave floor and lay her staff beside her. Her soft auburn hair spread out around her beautiful face, the milky white skin of her cheeks and neck standing out like porcelain on a finely made doll. The green leaf-like veins that traced along her arms and legs looked like whimsical paintings added for effect rather than something organic. Her chest rose and fell with even breaths. I ran my fingers over her soft shoulders and resisted the urge to kiss her frowning lips.

Then I knelt next to the pool and looked around expectantly. "Well? Show yourself."

Soft, tinkling laughter filled the cave. "Look down, child. Look into the pool."

Startled, I glanced at the still black water spread out before me. The woman's face stared up into my eyes from the depths, shifting and rippling like a half-remembered dream. The sense of familiarity grew until it was an ache in my chest. I said, "Who are you? Why do I feel like I know you?"

"Don't you remember?" she said, and I thought I detected a hint of sadness in her voice. "No, I suppose you wouldn't. I didn't look much like this the last time we met. You haven't seen me in my true form since you were too young to remember."

"So I do know you," I said. "From where? I don't remember much of anything before a couple of days ago."

"You once had a photograph of me," she said, a melancholy smile playing at her kind mouth. "Sitting next to your bed."

I shook my head, trying to remember. As if rising up from the deepest recesses of my mind, a faint image materialized in my memory. A room full of medals and trophies and the intense longing that came with them, the need for more, the need to prove myself. I remembered the shelves of books, and my escapes into fantasy worlds any way I could get them—stories, movies, video games. My bed. And the family photo next to it. Me, a smiling toddler...

And my parents.

"Mom?" My voice caught in my throat. It was impossible, and yet as the word left my mouth a whole flood of memories came rushing back. My mother the way she had been before my father had left, the way she had faded over the years, the husk of a woman she had become recently, the desperate way I had wanted to help her and to get as far away from her as I could.

Shame resonated in my chest as I remembered trying to get ready for my date with Jessika while my mother was passed out on the couch in the living room of our shitty, run-down trailer in Pine Ridge mobile home park. I remembered the text message I had gotten from her on my way home from my shift at Finger Lickin' Chicken: *I'm so sorry.*

The realness of this sudden rush of memories made my current situation feel completely *un*real. I gazed around the cave. The light from the mushrooms reflected off the crystalline pool and rippled in faint blue waving shadows over the rough ceiling. I inhaled the damp, earthy air and felt the coolness of it in my lungs. I licked my lips and tasted the salt of my sweat drying on my skin. There was no doubt in my mind that this place was real. But how could both realities exist?

I looked into the water again, and this time the full weight of a lifetime of memories hit me as I gazed into the face of my mother. I said, "Is it really you?"

"Yes, Loghann," she said, and tears glistened in her eyes. "I'm so sorry. I never meant for you to find out like this."

"Find out what?" I asked. My voice ached with restrained emotion. The last time I'd seen my mother I had thought she was dead, and that memory was suddenly fresh in my mind. Despite seeing her reflection in the pool, I couldn't shake the sadness inside. "And why are you calling me Loghann? My name is Logan."

She shook her head. "No, my son. We had to pretend when we lived in that other world, but we do not have to pretend any longer. You are Loghann Grenwyld, the lost prince of the empire."

"What?" Cold washed over my skin like someone had thrown a bucket of ice water in my face. "I grew up in a fucking trailer park in fucking Evergreen Hills, Colorado. I run a consulting business in Denver. How could I be the lost prince of anywhere, let alone this place? There are three moons here. This isn't even the same damned planet!"

"I know it is hard to believe." She took the crown of red leaves off her head and ran her fingers through her long brown hair. Her expression was drawn and tired, and she closed her eyes. "We were only trying to protect you."

"We?" I said. "What do you mean we?"

"When you were born," she said, "your father and I were given a gift from one of the fae folk in the northern isles, a prophecy."

My mouth went dry, and my heart beat faster. "My father? That jackass left us before I could walk."

"He didn't want to." Tears streamed down her cheeks, and she shook her head again. "Oh, Loghann, I wish I could have told you this sooner and eased the pain you've carried for so long. Your father never wanted to leave, but he had to. He had an empire to protect. The magic of the realms binds him to this world, even more strongly than it binds you and me. I was able to stay with you all these years, but the effort wore me down until I couldn't continue any longer. Earth is a terrible, soul-sucking place for magic wielders. I know you felt it too..."

I remembered the feeling that something was missing, that I never quite fit in like other people did. Even when I found success in the city, it never felt right. I never felt whole. Tears burned my eyes as I said, "I always thought there was something wrong with me."

"You adapted better than I could have hoped," she said, her voice as tight and thin as an elastic band stretched to breaking point. "But it is not where we belong. I tried to numb those feelings any way I could, and I fear I failed you when you needed me most. When my magic broke and I was forced to return, there was nothing left to hold you in that other place. Now you're here, and it may be too late—"

"What do you mean, too late?" I said. The image of my mother shimmered and disappeared. "No, don't go!"

I reached out my hand to stop her, and my fingers plunged into the ice cold pool. Beneath the surface of the water, a new image was forming. My mother and father bent over an ornate ivory cradle with tears in their eyes. A wizened old hag dressed in shredded gray robes lay prostrate at their feet.

My mother's voice filled the cavern. She said, "When you were born, we were given the gift of a prophecy from an elder of the northern fae, a very rare and invaluable gift, for the seers of such prophecies die in the telling."

I realized now, the old woman in gray must be the seer. Her milky-white eyes stared up at nothing, her wrinkled hands curled into tight fists over her chest.

"The seer told us that our new baby would someday grow up to be the most powerful emperor the realms have ever seen," my mother's voice said. "But only if you received the scepter of power before your two hundredth birthday."

"I'm only twenty-eight," I said. "That gives us lots of time."

"Time moves much slower on Earth than it does in this world, my son," she said. "Here, you were born on midsummer's eve, two-hundred years ago."

My heart lurched in my chest. "What?!"

"That means you have less than three months to stake your claim as emperor," she went on. "If you do not take power by midsummer's eve, Drakkus will overthrow the empire and we will enter a new era of chaos. Already he grows stronger. His boldness suggests that he, too, knows there is something special about this year's solstice. It is possible that he has his own seers, and that he has been warned of your potential to overthrow him. This was the prophecy the fae seer died to deliver to us, and the prophecy that drove your father and I to hide you in another world."

"Then I just need to get to the High Plains in the next three months," I said. My breath hitched in my chest as I thought of seeing my father again. My father the emperor? I shook my head. It was too bizarre to contemplate. "We can send him a message, can't we? Tell him I'm coming. He can tell the other clans and—"

"We can tell no one, Loghann," my mother said, sadly. "Prophecies cannot be shared with anyone who is not present for the seer's vision. You were an infant when we were given this gift, but it is enough for me to tell you now. We have never been able to explain to anyone else why you and I went missing, or why your father has held out hope for so long. They think him mad, Loghann. Even if he did tell them now, no one would believe him."

I clenched my hands into fists and pounded them against my thighs. "We can tell him at least, can't we? Give him some hope after all these years?"

"I will try," my mother said. "But I can feel myself weakening already. When my magic pulled me back to this world, my soul sought the fount of my strength. Once, I was Maia, priestess of the forest temple, power of the forest. This pool was my secret place."

"Your soul?" I didn't like the way she said that.

"You saw me die on Earth, my son, and I am dying here as well. I must use the time I have wisely." A soft breeze touched my cheek, as if I had been kissed by a ghost. She whispered, "Your father has never given up hope that you would return. He still holds his faith in you. I must ensure you have all the tools you need to make your claim before Drakkus gains more power."

"What are we going to do?" My voice broke with the frustration. "I don't even know how I'm going to save the Ring Wood, let alone the empire."

"Do not despair," she said again. "If you defeat Drakkus's general in this realm, his army will be weakened. This will buy you time to gain the support of the next four priestesses. Time for pity and hesitation is a luxury you do not have. You must not doubt yourself any longer. If you do, you will surely fail."

"That's reassuring," I muttered.

Even the childish petulance felt achingly familiar to me now, and I regretted the words as soon as they left my mouth. I had been so sure my mother had abandoned me to her depression. Now that I knew what she had lost, it amazed me that she lasted as long as she had in the trailer park.

"Your power grows the longer you are home, Loghann," she said kindly. I felt an invisible hand on my shoulder. "You are on the right path. And I will ensure the Arachana will help you to defend the forest temple."

"How can you do that?" I said. "Ruhail had me half-convinced they were going to eat me the moment I set foot in the Dark Wood."

"They would have every right to," she said. "But you shall carry the mark of their Queen, and they will not dare. Place your shield and sword in the pool, my son."

Slowly, I withdrew my sword from its sheath and slipped it beneath the crystal clear surface of the water. I pulled my buckler off my back and slid it into the pool as well.

It didn't occur to me to question my mother's request. Everything about this encounter was strange, like something from a dream. Yet it resonated with some primal instinct inside me that told me everything she had said was true. I really was the lost prince of the empire. I was the rightful heir to power. Priestess Kalia had known it, and had given herself to me. She believed I would save the Ring Wood, and deep in my heart I believed it too.

As these thoughts swam through my mind, the image of my sword and shield beneath the water seemed to shimmer and change. The colors distorted and the shape shifted.

"Take them now," my mother's voice urged. "The Arachana will know that you are my chosen warrior, and they will not dare to harm you. Their Queen owes me a favor, many centuries past, but she will not forget her duty to me."

I lifted my shield first. As the water ran off its surface, a silver sheen glimmered in the strange blue cavern light. A geometric design, like a tribal symbol depicting a long-legged spider, had been etched in the silver surface. A collection of deep-green gemstones in the shape of a sword decorated the spider's abdomen.

"It's beautiful," I said. I placed the shield on my back and pulled the sword from the pool. It, too, now gleamed like highly-polished silver, but the blade itself had transformed into something more similar to the long, thin fencing blades I had trained with. Its handle fit better in my hand. When I tested the blade against my finger I found it deadly sharp and unusually strong. "What kind of metal is this?"

"It is an ancient ore," my mother said, "the sources of which have been long depleted in this world and known only to the oldest clans. Its name and craft are lost to us now. This is the First Sword of Grenwyld, the oldest artifact of your father's clan, and your father meant for you to have it. He hid its true form with magic, and now I reveal it to you. This sword will not break in battle or bend to another blade. It will slice through any lesser material. In the presence of some creatures of chaos, additional magical protections may aid you. We do not know everything there is to know about this blade, but we do know that you are the one meant to wield it."

"Thank you, mother," I said. It felt strange, but right to accept these gifts. Something inside my chest was stirring, like a power awakening. "I will do my best to deserve them."

"You will prevail," she said, her voice strengthening in its conviction. "But it will not be easy. You must be ready to attack Drakkus with everything you have. Everything you do from this point on will be a strike against him. As future emperor, it is your responsibility to protect the lands of the five realms and their people. You must convert as many to your side as you can, for the corrupted walk among us. Every man you forge a friendship with, every creature you provide aid to, every woman you take to your bed, and every child you sire, brings strength and power to your name and will add to the magic inside you."

The water began to shimmer again, and I stared into the vision, blood pumping through my veins. Flames burned beneath the surface and a dark, shadowy form emerged from the billowing smoke and tongues of red and orange fire. A huge, demonic beast took shape in the center of the flames. Thick black horns jutted from its massive skull. Fanged teeth gnashed in its open mouth. A long, forked tongue darted out between the teeth as the monster grinned at the chaos. A glow of red magic shimmered around his form like a layer of protection. I knew exactly what this thing was.

"Drakkus," I said. "Where is he?"

"Drakkus's realm is in the underworld, a monstrous hellscape that mirrors our own realms. Usually, he and his minions can only cross over into the empire during a blood moon. But he has been working some kind of evil magic that weakens the protections of the realms, creating thin spots in the veil between our worlds. The creatures you sensed in the tunnels back there, they were in the Chaos Realm. Somehow you were able to pass into their world and inflict damage upon them."

"There were voices," I said. "Whispering to me, calling me to them. Ruhail didn't seem to hear them, but she could sense the creatures that attacked us."

"I have never heard of such a thing happening before." My mother's voice was tight with concern. "They should not be able to physically affect anything in our realm without crossing over. You should not have been able to interact with them at all. And yet you fought them. I saw it all from the Spirit Plane. You must be very careful, Loghann. The rules as we know them are changing, and Drakkus may have ways of attacking our realms that we do not yet know."

"It must have something to do with Voron Blackthorne," I said, gritting my teeth at the thought of the greasy, sallow-skinned elf working his magic against Priestess Kalia's temple. "He has stolen the Book of the Elders from the temple. Kalia said he would use it to weaken her defences."

"You have to stop him." The air became cold and my mother's voice trembled. "Get the book back before he hands it to Drakkus. If the Lord of Chaos unlocks the ancient spells inside that book, we are all doomed."

"I plan to," I said. "And I will kill him myself for his treachery. I must go now, mother. Thank you for everything." A tightness clenched my throat, and I swallowed hard. "And I'm sorry. I misunderstood you in our old life, and I resented you. I wish I had been a better son to you."

"You are a better son than I ever dreamed of having, Loghann," she said. Even without a physical form, I sensed she had tears in her eyes. "You are stronger and more powerful than you will ever know, and you will be the forebear of a new era of good and order in this world. Your blood will be the strength of the people of this world for millennia. But you must destroy Drakkus. Only you can stop him."

"I promise," I said. My voice cracked.

"In each realm, the elemental powers are specially connected to magical cores within your being. As the priestesses of each realm submit their power to you, you will unlock the ability to access those power sources." Her voice was growing weaker now, and I strained to hear her as she continued. "The magic of the Ring Wood grounds your power and gives you roots to your ancestry as a member of the Grenwyld clan. In the Azurian Sea, you will connect to your emotional core. The Silent Sands will show you the way to full control of your magical energy. The Lucidian Mountains will reveal the potential of your mind and intellect. And on the High Plains, you will achieve transcendence of spirit. Once you have done this, you will be ready to defeat Drakkus. Do not engage him before your power is complete, or you will fail and the empire will fall."

"I understand," I said. "Thank you."

"I must go now, Loghann," she said, her voice barely a whisper. "I will use the last of my power to heal the dryad. She, too, will give you much strength if you accept her as one of your wives. If she offers herself to you, it is your duty to take her as your own. I know it will seem strange to you after I was forced to raise you in that backward, uptight place. But the women of the realms belong to you as the emperor, they long to submit to you. It is the natural way of things here. Each union you make will strengthen you, your partner, and the empire."

Blood surged to my cock instantly, and I looked at Ruhail laying on the stones beside the pool. Her legs were slightly parted, and the ragged edge of her leaf dress barely covered the apex of her thighs. Her full breasts rose and fell as she breathed. I was ready to take the dryad now. Part of me wanted to take her while she slept, to use her like doll she looked like. And if all the women of this world belonged to me, I could do it if I wanted to...

But not with my mother in the room—Spirit Plane or not. This world might have different rules, but there were some lines I wasn't going to cross.

I said, "I understand."

"Goodbye, my son," my mother's ghost said. "Remember, no matter what happens, I am proud of you."

I gentle caress touched my cheek. Then a faint glow surrounded Ruhail, and the dryad began to stir. Her hands ran up and down her body, and her fingers tugged at the leaves of her dress. One breast tore free of the flimsy material, and I ached with longing as I watched her. She moaned in her sleep again, but this time it didn't sound like she was having a nightmare.

A warm wind that smelled of maple leaves and berries swirled around the cave, whipping up a smattering of dust and debris that scattered against the cave walls. Then it disappeared, and Ruhail sat up with a gasp, her spring-green eyes locked on mine. One hard, exposed nipple tantalized me, like a little pink berry against her pale white flesh.

"Loghann," she breathed, spreading her legs open wide so that I could see the invitingly wet slit beneath the hem of her dress. "Come to me..."

Chapter 19

"We don't have time for this," I said, even as I crawled toward her over the hard stone floor of the cave. "We have to find the Arachana."

"We have time," she said, reaching for me. "I thought you were dead, Loghann. I thought I had lost you."

"I thought I'd lost you." I knelt between her thighs and pushed her back on to the stones. My cock strained against the hardened leather armor painfully. I bent over the dryad and sank my face against her neck, kissing the perfect white skin there. She moaned gently and arched, crushing her chest against mine.

I leaned back and dragged my fingers over her body and tore the flimsy leaves away from her skin. Her other breast sprang free and I grabbed them in my hands and pressed them together, pinching her hard little nipples between my fingers until she cried out. I pinched harder, and she grabbed my wrists, writhing against the stones. She gritted her teeth and said, "It hurts."

"Do you want me to stop?" I asked, not letting go. The fat, white mounds of flesh spilled out over my hands, making me want to squeeze even harder. Her body trembled beneath me and her legs fell open.

"I want you to make me yours," she said, biting her lip. "However it pleases you."

I groaned and gave her nipples another pinch until her cries echoed off the roof of the cave. Then I pulled the rest of the leaves off her body, exposing her thighs and the plump mound of bare flesh between her legs. The lips of her pussy were pink and swollen. I put my hands on her thighs and pushed them up toward her chest. "Hold your legs there," I said.

She obeyed instantly, pulling her legs back and lifting her ass off the floor so that her sex was spread wide open to me. I fumbled with my armor and managed to extract my throbbing erection from the leather plates. I pulled it all away until my engorged shaft swung between her thighs.

Ruhail's eyes widened. She said, a little nervously, "You're bigger than I thought."

I swiped a finger over her clit, and she yelped. I said, "Are you changing your mind?"

She bit her lip and shook her head.

"Good," I said. I fingered the tight opening of her pussy, rubbing her wetness around. Then I placed my left hand on her belly to hold her still and thrust three fingers inside her.

"Oh!" she screamed, and rocked her hips up to meet the palm of my hand. Her eyes closed and she spread her legs wider. I stroked the inside of her pussy with my fingers and pressed her clit with my palm. Her juices spilled out over my fingers like she had been ready for me for hours. I spread them all over her lips and between the firm round cheeks of her ass. My cock rubbed against her thigh as I leaned forward.

Her eyes opened wide again as I rubbed my finger around her asshole. I said, "If you dryads don't need to use these, why do you have such nice, tight little holes back here?"

She bit her lip and shook her head like she was afraid to answer.

"You don't know?" I said, pressing the tip of my finger just inside. Her muscles clamped down around me. "I have an idea."

"I've never—" she started, and then shook her head again. "That's not how we—"

"How do you know you won't like it if you've never tried?" I pushed my finger in a little farther. Ruhail's hips bucked and her muscles tightened. Her breasts bounced up and down as she panted. But she kept her legs held back for me, and her pussy juices dripped down between her ass cheeks. I said, "If you're going to belong to me, you're going to have to learn how to like what I like, isn't that right?"

Her cheeks burned as red as her hair, and she nodded slowly. Her bright green eyes never left my face.

I kept my left hand on her belly and slid my finger into her ass all the way up to the bottom knuckle. Her mouth dropped open and she groaned. "There you go," I said, and I pulled my finger in and out of the tight little hole. "It's not so bad is it? You must like it, or you wouldn't be so wet."

She blushed even deeper and looked away. "It's embarrassing."

"Are you going to tell me to stop?" I kept stroking her asshole, teasing it with the tip of my finger. "Or are you going to let me fuck you the way I want to?"

Her pussy twitched and pulsed, and I looked down at her, enjoying her discomfort and the submission written on her face. Her green-eyed gaze slid back to mine, and her lips parted slightly as if she might object. Then her mouth opened as if she might object. But she said, "I belong to you. You don't have to ask."

I pressed the head of my cock into the hot, wet slit between her legs. She gasped. I kept my finger inside her ass.

"Is it embarrassing because you like it?" I asked, pushing myself deeper into her pussy. The pressure from inside her backside made her feel impossibly tiny as her body stretched to accommodate my throbbing shaft. I forced myself to take it slow. I backed my finger up and inserted another next to it, teasing the opening with two fat fingertips. She whimpered. I said, "Or because you think it's disgusting?"

"Both," she said, her voice strained. "It feels so unnatural."

"But..." I prompted and thrust my fingers deeper into her ass.

"I do like it," she said, closing her eyes and turning away from me in shame.

"You're a dirty little slut," I said, and she whimpered again. "That's why you like it. Why don't you admit it?"

"No," she said weakly.

"I saw you playing with yourself when those nymphs sucked me off." I pumped my fingers in and out, stroking my own cock through the thin layer of flesh stretched between her holes. Her body writhed beneath me, her heavy breasts pressed powerlessly against my leather-armoured chest. Her shoulders trembled, but she kept her hands on the backs of her thighs, keeping her legs spread wide for me. "Is this what you were picturing me doing to you?"

She bit her lip and shook her head. "No!"

I forced another finger into her ass and groaned. The pressure against my cock was almost too much. I pushed my fingers as deep inside the dryad as I could reach, stretching her hole so tight it didn't seem possible. I thrust deeper with my shaft, harder, my balls aching to release. A cry escaped her throat. I fucked her harder just to hear it again.

"Oh gods." She bucked her hips, forcing my fingers farther inside her ass. She said, "I've never been so full. It hurts."

Taking the hint, I pressed myself balls-deep into her pussy and drove my hand in and out of her backside like I was jerking myself off inside her. She squealed, struggling against me and rocking her hips like she couldn't decide if she wanted to escape or wanted me to fuck her even harder.

She was mine. She had said she wanted it any way I wanted it, and I didn't want to restrain myself.

I pinned her to the hard stone floor and drove my hips into her like I was some kind of Viking raider of old, taking his reward from the whores of the ransacked towns. Ruhail's gasps came hot and heavy in my ear as I pounded her. The more forceful I was, the more she tightened against me.

"Oh fuck," she screamed, suddenly, and her muscles twitched and pulsed frantically around my fingers and shaft. "I'm coming, Loghann. I'm coming, don't stop."

"I'm not going to stop until I'm finished," I growled.

But even as I said it, the pressure of my fingers inside her ass and her tight pussy wrapped around my cock built up until I couldn't take it anymore. An explosive gush of hot cum burst out of me, filling the dryad and squirting out around my cock like a geyser.

"Oh!" she screamed and bucked against me one final time. "There's so much!"

Panting, I pushed myself off of her. My slick, wet shaft hung between her legs as she continued to hold them open for me.

Sticky, white semen covered her plump mound and drained down around her asshole, which twitched and gaped as the muscles tried to adjust to the absence of my fingers.

Ruhail's big round breasts were flushed as pink as her hard little nipples. The pale green veins on her delicate white skin stood out more clearly with her arousal. Her green eyes watched me cautiously above her blushing cheeks. She pressed her lips together.

I laughed. "You wanted to be mine?"

She nodded her head emphatically. "Yes, Loghann."

"I think I've marked my territory," I said, enjoying the sight of the well-used dryad. She smiled shyly. Just seeing her covered in my cum made me want to fuck her again. My cock twitched, and I laughed again. "This world is insane."

"Is it insane for me to want you to abuse me like that?" she asked, blushing again.

"If it is, I want more crazy in my life." I said. The fact that she was still holding herself exposed to me was like icing on the cake. "If I get power from sex, Drakkus doesn't stand a chance. And neither do you."

Her eyes widened. "Drakkus! I almost forgot—"

"Don't worry," I said. A buzzing warmth filled my chest and a halo of green magic surrounded Ruhail and I in our messy, post-coital state. I could feel the both of us strengthening. The way the dryad looked at me said she felt it too. I said, "I didn't forget. When you gave yourself to me, you gave me access to your power and you have received access to some of mine. We are both more powerful for your submission."

Slowly she let go of her legs and sat up, cross-legged on the stone floor. She closed her eyes. "You are right. I feel a connection to you, like the life bond but different. I haven't felt this strong in centuries."

"You are mine and only mine, now, Ruhail," I said, pulling the naked dryad to her feet. "No one else will ever touch you again. This bond is stronger than any life bond."

She nodded and leaned against my chest. "The old magic is faded. I don't think I could be bonded to another, this link to you is too strong."

"Good," I said, and pushed her toward the pool. "Now let's get cleaned up. We have some spiders to talk to and a battle to win."

I wrapped my arm around her shoulders and scooped her up off the floor. She giggled happily. "Yes, master Loghann."

"Oh, I like that," I growled, nuzzling my face against her neck and biting gently at the delicate skin. She moaned and leaned her head back expectantly.

Then she shrieked as I tossed her into the water.

Ripples of light from her splashing danced across the surface of the cave's ceiling as I stripped out of my armor to join her.

Chapter 20

As my mother had warned, I wasn't able to tell Ruhail why the magic had worked the way it had. The words wouldn't come out of my mouth no matter how hard I tried, even if I attempted to be tricky about it. Whatever force bound the secret seemed to be able to sense my intentions.

But it didn't matter. The little red-headed dryad clung happily to my side like we were honeymooners striding along a tropical beach rather than warriors creeping through a dank, black tunnel glowing with phosphorescent fungi and crawling with insects. She had used her magic to conjure a new dress for herself. It didn't escape my attention that this one was even less substantial than the last, or that she appeared to have found new, semi-transparent leaves to make it with.

"Why don't you have to stitch this one together like before?" I asked as we walked. The tunnel was now taking an upward slope, and the walls were becoming more earthen rather than the black, wet stones of the underground cave system.

"I didn't have to do it that way before," she said. "But I was newly bound and didn't want to show you too much of my power in case you were the kind of man who would try to abuse it."

"You just wanted me to abuse you sexually?" I teased, smacking her plump bottom.

"No," she said, swatting my arm with the back of her hand. "I didn't want that, either. It's different you know, when you *can't* say no to something like that. I have been bonded many times in my life—"

"This is the last time," I said.

"Yes," she smiled. "Thank you. But it's never occurred to any of my past bond mates that I might not want what they wanted. They didn't care."

"I'm sorry for what you went through," I said, and I meant it.

She strode alongside me, her wooden staff glowing with a green light only I could see. Ruhail turned to me. "It's not your fault, and the last time I was bonded was years ago. Centuries, really. It doesn't matter anymore. But you see, knowing you can say no and choosing not to is different. It was exhilarating to be taken so roughly, Loghann. I felt so alive, so..."

"Slutty?" I said, laughing.

"Yes," she breathed. "It felt good."

"You know, when we first met," I said, "I thought you were a prude."

She laughed too. "I always have been, a bit. The only time I ever had sex was when I was forced to by some bumbling bond mate, never because I wanted to. But with you I feel different. Free to be completely vulnerable."

I knew why she felt that way, after what I'd learned about who I really was in this world. Instinctively, she and all the other women in the five realms would be drawn to the strength of my power and the magic inside me. I could feel it there, too, like a white-hot orb burning in my chest, waiting to explode.

But I didn't know how to use it yet, and that bothered me.

How would I learn to harness this growing power in time to unleash it upon Voron Blackthorne and the general of Drakkus's assault on the forest temple?

I pushed those doubts away and shoved through a bundle of roots hanging from the roof of the tunnel. I didn't have time for doubt or self-pity. I had to believe that I would be able to figure it out when the time came.

The burning in my chest intensified as if the power inside me was trying to send me a message. This was the right choice. I was on the right track.

"Well, I'm happy to have made you into my little slut," I said, winking over my shoulder at her. "And I look forward to teaching you all kinds of new ways to submit to your depraved new master."

She wrapped her arms around me and pinned me against the tunnel wall with a kiss. Her hot tongue probed my mouth hungrily and, despite the fact that I knew we were in a hurry and we'd already wasted enough time with our fooling around, my hands gripped her narrow ribs and slid up to squeeze her lusciously heavy breasts.

But fate had other plans for us.

There was a thump from above. and dirt crumbled down around our heads. We looked up in alarm. The earth above us shook like something huge was walking on the surface overhead.

"What is that?" she said.

I extracted myself from her embrace and said, "Let's find out."

I stumbled into the tunnel ahead. Blackness surrounded me.

"Send me some fireflies, will you?" I called over my shoulder. "I can't see anything."

A swarm of glowing bugs swirled through the air around me, lighting the way just enough, so I could see I wasn't going to stumble into another black hole. The earth above my head trembled, and another shower of dirt fell around my shoulders. I rubbed my eyes and coughed, pushing my way forward.

The tunnel angled up sharply and was covered in loose stones and boulders, as if there had been a rockslide here. Or like someone had filled in a passage they didn't want anyone using anymore. I had to climb like I was scrambling up a cliffside in the mountains outside Evergreen Hills.

Now that the fog in my mind had cleared, I remembered vividly the solo hiking and camping trips I'd done over the years. I felt more confident in my skills and abilities now that I could actually remember them. I wasn't just running on instinct anymore. All the things I'd learned over the years were right there for me to draw on—my archery and fencing lessons, outdoor survival skills, my love of running. The memories of who I was flooded through me as if I had unlocked a secret well of strength I hadn't known I had.

I surged ahead, scrambling toward a spear of light piercing into the tunnel from far above.

"Wait for me." Ruhail's voice sounded far away. "Don't go up on the surface yet. We don't know what's up there."

I paused, leaning forward mid-climb, with my weight on my hands and my feet wedged onto a narrow ledge of stone. I called back to the dryad, "Do you know where we are?"

She didn't answer immediately, but I could hear her scrambling through the tunnel and cursing each time the earth thundered above us.

"How did you get up there so quickly?" she said, and I turned to see her standing at the base of the rockslide.

"I don't know." My limbs buzzed with pent up energy. "I feel powerful, like I could fight one of those ogres single-handedly or run for miles without tiring."

"Please don't do either of those things," she said, clambering up beside me. "I don't know where we are yet, and if this is the Dark Wood you might need that energy for facing the Arachana. Their queen will not bow before a weakened man."

"Who are you calling weak?" I teased. "I feel stronger than I've ever felt in my life."

She pursed her lips at me. "You might feel differently if one of those ogres pounds you on the head with its club, don't you think?"

"Fair enough," I said, climbing again. "But for the record, I don't plan on getting pounded by any of Lord Drakkus's minions."

The beam of light was stronger now, illuminating all the stones and a thick carpet of mossy growth between them. At the top of the tunnel, an ancient wooden door with a circular metal handle was embedded in the earth. The beam of light came from between the slats in the wood. The trap door wouldn't have been out of place in the Shire. But whatever was stomping around up there was no hobbit.

Ruhail took a deep breath. Her nose wrinkled. "Smells like ogre. You might get your chance, whether I like it or not."

I grasped the metal ring in my fingers and pressed my shoulder against the trap door. I looked back at the dryad. "Say when."

She closed her eyes, and the green mist of her magic thickened and then spread out in long tendrils, like wisps of smoke. The mist seeped through the cracks in the wooden door and burrowed into the mossy earth above our heads. The thundering on the surface seemed to be getting fainter.

"Now," she said, her eyes opening in a flash. "Quickly. Stay low."

I heaved my weight up into the door and felt the wood groan against my shoulder. Ancient hinges creaked, and for a moment, nothing happened. My thighs shook as I pushed upward. Sweat beaded against my brow and trickled into my eyes. Then the door lurched open. I stumbled over the threshold and smashed my shin against a boulders. Pain exploded in my leg and my brain, and I bit my tongue against the stream of curses that threatened to spill forth and give away our location.

Gritting my teeth, I slid out of the narrow opening. I stayed on my belly and held the door for Ruhail, while I studied our surroundings. In the distance, a huge lumbering shape that must have been an ogre or some other giant creature, crashed through the trees. It moved away from us, thankfully, and didn't seem to have noticed the sound of the trap door's hinges over its own thundering footsteps.

Ruhail slipped nimbly out of the hole in the ground. She stayed low and moved as lithely as a vixen on the hunt. I eased the door closed behind her and pushed myself up into a crouch, keeping my eyes on the place where the ogre had disappeared. The dryad grabbed my arm and pulled me toward a towering, red-barked tree that was so gnarled and knotted it looked like someone had smashed three trees together and twisted them up into a length of rope that dangled from the canopy above us.

The dark, murky woods seemed to enclose upon us as we crouched next to the tree, waiting to see if there were any other creatures of chaos lurking in the shadows. I said, "There's no light. Where was the sunlight coming from?"

"What sunlight?" Ruhail gazed up at me with her bright green eyes intent upon my face. Her fireflies hovered around us, casting pale glowing circles across her fair complexion. "It's been dark as pitch since we left the cavern."

"In the tunnel," I said, sighing in exasperation. "That spear of golden light coming through the cracks in the door."

"I saw no light, Loghann," she whispered. Her gaze darted over my shoulder and scanned the black trees behind me. "I believe you are being guided by something beyond my senses. I just hope it is something we can trust."

Mother. I swallowed a lump in my throat. I wouldn't see her again. I would never get to say all the things I wish I had said when she was still alive. But could she be using the last of her magic to lead me on the path to success? I had to believe it was true. I said, "Do you know where we are now? This feels like the place where I found you."

She nodded. "It is the Dark Woods, early evening."

"The day is lost." My chest tightened. "We must have wandered those tunnels for far longer than it felt like. We have only hours until the blood moon rises and Drakkus's army attacks."

Ruhail paled and bit her lip. Tears formed in her eyes. "We are not far from the clearing where the werewolf and its trolls had planned to..."

Her voice trailed off, but I knew what she was thinking. Had I not stumbled upon their encampment, gods only knew what kinds of horrible things the werewolf general might have done to her. She shuddered.

I pulled her close and kissed the top of her head. "Don't think about it now. It's over. Right now, I need you to lead me to the Arachana. We don't have much time."

She leaned against my chest and sighed.

Then she tensed and pushed me away from her, backing up and looking into the tree canopy overhead. Her eyes were wide with terror. The leaves rustled and a faint clicking noise echoed around us, like someone tapping their fingernails against a hard surface. I reached for Ruhail again and took her hand. She shook her head and pulled her fingers from my grasp, gripping her staff tightly. She motioned toward the treetops with her eyes and gave me a hard look. I pulled my shield off my back and slid my arm into the brace on the backside. As quietly as I could, I slid my sword from its sheath.

The trees shivered. I backed toward Ruhail, ready to protect her from whatever was coming. Her magic surged forth and surrounded us in a pale green haze, hiding us or guarding us, I couldn't be sure.

Long, pearly white strands fell from the treetops, landing around us like the anemic stalks of strange cave flora. My guts clenched as I realized what this meant.

"No need to come looking for us." A soft, seductive voice resonated from leaves above us. "We are already here. We are *always* here, watching, waiting..."

The voice sounded eerily like the haunting voices I'd heard back in the tunnel. But it was different now, the voice of one instead of many. And unlike those mysterious voices from beyond the veil, I knew who was speaking to me this time.

"Then you know why I come," I said, my voice tight. "You know who I am?"

A huge black shape dropped in front of my face, like a person wrapped in a stiff, plastic body bag. I jumped back, barely managing not to scream. The thing's shiny chitinous abdomen was stretched so tight it seemed I could burst it with a prick of my sword. Yet the long, daggered legs that gripped the strand of web silk moved so deftly I knew that if I tried I would be dead before I could withdraw my blade. Dozens more of the things descended to the forest floor, and I choked back a scream. In my mind the "spider-folk," as Ruhail had so quaintly referred to them, had been somewhat humanoid. Eight-legged centaurs, maybe. These were just massive spiders like nightmare creatures from a horror movie.

The one before me hovered inches from my face, its fanged mouthparts twitching and the delicate pedipalps quivering as if in anticipation of its next meal. Above the mouth, barely visible in the fine black hairs covering the creature's face, was a cluster of glossy black eyes. The eyes fixated, unblinking, on my own.

"We know the weapon you wield," the creature said, and the voice penetrated my mind without physically coming from the its quivering mouth. "Why don't you tell us who you are?"

My fingers ached from clutching my sword. The words I wanted to say got halfway up my throat and stuck there. More black shapes skittered out of the trees, some smaller than the one speaking to me and some much, much larger.

"Tell them, Loghann," Ruhail's voice trembled and though I couldn't see her, the fear I sensed in her steeled me to what I had to do.

I cleared my throat. "I am Loghann Grenwyld, and I request an audience with the Arachana Queen. Priestess Kalia needs her help."

A hiss rose from the darkened clearing, and the enormous spiders lurched and twitched hideously on their threads as many voices tried to speak at once.

The spider in front of me let out a piercing shriek, barely audible to my human ears, which seemed to stab directly into the most primal neurons in my brain. Cold fear drove through my bones like an ice pick, and my limbs froze. There was nothing I could do against an army of these creatures. I had been a fool to come here. But even as these thoughts arose unbidden from my unconscious mind, I gripped my sword and tensed for battle.

"Silence," the creature screamed.

All the other spiders fell to their impatient clicking. Their leader cocked its hideous head at me, and I saw my pale face reflected in the shiny surface of its cluster of eyes. It said, "You fear me?"

Its voice was soft, grotesquely sensual coming from that face. I gripped my sword and swallowed hard. I nodded, "I am not a fool."

It made a strange noise in the back of its throat—if spiders even have throats—that might have been laughter. "And still you come to beg our help? Perhaps you are a fool."

Ruhail whimpered behind me, and I wondered if she was also face to face with one of these monsters.

"Without your help, the forest temple will fall to chaos," I said, fighting against my urge to scream and flee. "You may not love order as the priestess does, but I believe you respect balance."

"Do you?" The creature's voice hummed inside my skull like it was putting it there by some psychic means.

I flinched but stood my ground. "I have to, or else we are lost."

The spider reached toward my face with one of its long, black legs. It stroked the side of my cheek with the dagger-like appendage, and my skin burned beneath its touch. A chill crept across my shoulder blades and down my spine as its barbed foot tugged at my clothing.

It hooked the back of my armor and wrenched me toward its open, quivering mouth. Its fangs pulsed and venom hung from the needle-like pinchers. I roared and tried to free my sword arm, but the creature's other legs wrapped around me and held me in an iron grip.

Behind me, Ruhail screamed.

I struggled against the monster, but nothing I did seemed to have any effect. Its sharp legs poked and prodded me, spinning me to and fro like a fly. Strands of sticky white web clung to my limbs and bound my arms to my torso. The next time I tried to shout webs shot across my face, suffocating the sound in my throat.

I writhed like an insect in a web, which was exactly what I was, until suddenly my captor climbed its lifeline back into the trees.

With a lurch and a tug, my feet lifted off the ground. I flipped upside down as the spider drew me up into the canopy. And the last thing I saw before I disappeared into the blackness of the Dark Woods was Ruhail, bound and gagged and tied to the great red-barked tree with pearly white ropes of spider silk.

Chapter 21

We rushed through the forest canopy with green leaves rushing past my face and branches snapping against my exposed flesh. I was strapped to the creature's back like an egg sac and it—she?—did not seem remotely encumbered by my weight. I kept my eyes closed as much as I could to avoid being blinded, but the rocking and swaying made me sick to my stomach. With my eyes closed, the chittering of the spiders drilled into the primordial core of my lizard brain and filled me with horror.

I attempted to distract myself by feeling for the hot, magical centre in my chest, the source of my power. I didn't know how to access it at will yet, but knowing it was there pulsing like a star, comforted me. My racing heart slowed to a regular rhythm and my breathing became calm and even. My muscles relaxed. My arms were pinned to my sides, but the pommel of my sword was within my reach. Power surged like a current from my arm into the blade. Could I do it? If I tried now I would fall to my death. So I wrapped my fingers around the sword's grip, and I waited.

After a time, the spider slowed and dropped out of the trees on a safety line made of silk. My stomach lurched until she controlled the descent with her razor-like legs. As her body swayed along the rope, I caught glimpses of the approaching forest floor. When we were close enough that I thought I might survive the fall, I imagined all that hot, white energy inside my chest moving along my arm and into the blade. I imagined the blade glowing like a white-hot iron poker. Miraculously, I felt the magic move to do my bidding. My arm buzzed like it was full of electricity, and the sword hummed in its scabbard. I heaved on the handle. The spider-silk that bound my arms to my body disintegrated in a shower of silken strands.

The creature carrying me let out a shriek like rending metal. As my sword burst out of the bindings, the rest tore from my body like shreds of old fabric. I plunged headfirst toward the forest floor.

Without any conscious action on my part, my body flipped mid-air as I fell. I landed with a thud that shot through my knee-joints. I clamped my teeth together with a painful crack. But I managed to stay upright with my sword and shield in my hands.

I stood in the middle of a clearing, surrounded by blackened trees. Thick sheets of white web wove between the branches. Winding funnels led like twisted corridors deeper into the dark woods beyond. Bones littered the torn-up earth around us; some were small—like birds, rabbits, and foxes; others were larger—like deer, wolves, and bears. The black eye sockets of a human, or elf more likely, stared morosely at me from the scraggly underbrush. A fat, red millipede crawled out of its nostril and between a gap in its teeth. I shuddered.

Another shriek from above sent chills racing down my spine. The massive spider dropped to the ground next to me, her front legs raised like hooks above her head. I crouched low, with my shield and sword at the ready. Hers was a threatening posture I had seen in nature documentaries, designed to make her look bigger and scarier than she actually was.

And she was already pretty fucking scary.

I leaped backward with inhuman strength and momentum, flying to the other side of the clearing and scattering a pile of bones in every direction. The magic I had been promised was clearly working its way through my body, but I had no control of it. I landed in an awkward heap beneath the burned out husk of an ancient tree, rolled sideways, and somehow managed to scramble back to my feet before the spider attacked.

She lunged for me, her pinchers gnashing in her ugly face. The dagger-like legs moved with impossible speed. I caught her first blow against my shield and swung at the middle joint of one of her legs. It was as if my body was being controlled by a force outside myself, like I was a puppet on strings wielded by a master. I tried to relax and let the magic do its work. The less I fought it, the faster my limbs moved.

But the spider met my speed with ease. Her legs flashed toward me, darting in scooping motions, as she tried to hook me with the barbs on her legs and drag me toward her dripping fangs. More spiders dropped out of the trees, closing the circle around us to prevent my escape. I was badly outnumbered, but with the sword thrumming in my grip, I felt strangely invincible.

I gritted my teeth and growled at the monster. "Come on then, fight me."

"I knew I should have bitten you." The spider hissed inside my mind. "That sword is giving you ideas above your station, peasant."

"Peasant?" I sneered and circled to her left. "What does that make you, then? Vermin?"

An unholy uproar came from the ring of monsters as they all clacked their mouth-parts and moved in closer. I swiped at the underside of my opponent's abdomen. She deflected my blade with a powerful side thrust from her front leg. The metal sang as it crashed into the chitinous armor plating on her limb. I cursed under my breath. She was too fast, and there were too many of them. My blade glowed with a faint white light in the darkened woods, illuminating the shiny edges of the spider's bodies and their glossy black eyes.

I probably wasn't going to feel very invincible when they were sucking my liquefied guts out like I was a human-flavored juice pouch.

But right now, it was all or nothing. I braced my shield arm in front of me and charged at the spider, roaring like some battle-crazed Celtic warrior of old. With my sword arm raised above my head, and the blade glowing ever brighter, I smashed into the spider's face. She screamed hideously and lurched backward. I had caught her off guard. The other spiders shuffled back in surprise, their many-eyed gazes darting back and forth between one another. Without hesitation I swung my sword arm downward, slashing at the narrow section of exposed flesh between my opponent's head and abdomen.

But before I could strike the beast something warm and wet spattered against the back of my hand, covering my arm and the blade. Resistance met my movement as if I was pulling against an elastic band. My muscles screamed in protest as I fought against the sticky webs.

"Enough," a crisp feminine voice said. The sound cut through the shrieking of the spiders, and the still silence that followed rang in my ears like echoes. "I will have no blood shed this night, unless it is I who spills it."

The surrounding spiders crouched low to the ground, stretching their long, blade-like forelegs in front of them as if they were bowing. My opponent staggered backward and fell to the ground as well. I sensed their beady black eyes had locked on something behind me. The hairs on my scalp stood on end and my arms broke out in goosebumps.

This must be the Queen of the Arachana.

I turned slowly, prepared to face the biggest, most monstrous spider of all. But nothing could have prepared me for the sight before me. My heart dropped into the pit of my stomach and my mouth went dry.

A woman stood in the middle of the clearing, amid the bones and blackened trees. Her skin was the color of moonlight, and her flowing hair was as black as night. It tossed about her face as if she were in the midst of a torrential storm that could not touch the rest of us.

She wore a lace gown that seemed to be woven from spider silk, and her bone-white body was clearly visible beneath the gossamer strands. The purplish shadows of her nipples and a dark swatch of hair between her legs were all that broke up the deathly white pallor of her flesh.

That and her lips, as red as fresh blood, and the fine black fangs that protruded from them.

She had the long, pointed ears of the elves and the shiny black eyes of her arachnid companions.

My brain screamed at the sight of her, torn between the near perfect beauty of her form and the sheer terror of her presence. A half-remembered line of poetry from my high school English class floated through my thoughts. She was William Blake's 'fearful symmetry' made flesh.

The woman beckoned to me with long bony finger tipped with a black fingernail like the razor-sharp chitin on the spider's bodies.

"Your majesty," I said, and I gripped the handle of my sword and took a step forward, cautiously. "I have come to beg your assistance on behalf of Priestess Kalia of the forest temple. Please hear me."

"Begging has never suited me." Her lips curled cruelly up on one side, exposing the length of her black fangs. "Do you usually beg with a weapon in your hand? I may change my mind."

"Your creat—" I stopped when the smile dropped from her face. Glancing over my shoulder I revised my statement. "Your soldiers attacked me. I was only defending myself."

"They were transporting you to me," the queen said, and her black eyes pierced me with a look that said it would be deadly to defy her. "On my orders."

I cleared my throat. The future emperor of the five realms should probably have practiced his diplomacy skills before visiting the kingdom of a hostile neighbour. I said, "Perhaps they could have communicated that to me."

"And who are you," she asked, "that you feel worthy of such courtesy?"

"I am Loghann Grenwyld," I said, the name flowing more easily from my tongue now that I'd said it a few times. "Priestess Maia was my mother, and she promised me you would accept my audience. That you owed her a favor, long past due."

"Your shield bears my mark." The queen's black eyes narrowed and her sharp, white cheekbones glistened in the light of my glowing sword. She held out her thin, spider-like hands. "Let me see the blade."

I hesitated, but the burning energy inside my chest flared to light in such a way that I knew I was meant to abide by the request. Trust was important to this woman. I had to trust her before she would trust me. I stepped closer to her and laid the blade across her palms.

Her black eyes watched me as I stepped back to a respectful distance. On impulse, I knelt before her, on one knee, as if I were a knight paying homage to his queen. She licked her red lips thoughtfully and, holding the sword in one hand, she drew her fingers across the edge of the blade. Thick black blood, like ichor sprang from her finger. Her eyes widened in surprise. She left a dark smear across the shining metal, and the sword glowed brighter still.

"Arise, Loghann Grenwyld," she said, her voice low and pensive. "Tell me of this request."

I stood, and she held the blade toward me, with its tip pointed at her belly and the handle at me. I took it gently and sheathed it, nodding my thanks.

"You must know that Drakkus' minions have been encroaching on the Ring Wood," I said, and the Arachana Queen crossed her arms over her narrow chest as if this irritated her. She dipped her chin sightly. I continued, "Now, they have the temple surrounded and the Heart and Spirit of the Forest are in danger."

"The Priestesses have always been able to defend the temple on their own," the queen said. "Their magic is much more powerful than mine."

"Perhaps," I said, looking around at the queen's hideous soldiers. "But perhaps not by as much as you let on."

The faint flicker of a smile passed over the queen's face, and she stepped closer. "You are cleverer than I gave you credit for, Loghann Grenwyld. But I wonder, do you know what they call me?"

I shook my head.

"The call me The Widower," she said, stepping closer to me again, close enough that I could feel the cool, misty source of the magic surrounding her like a fog. "Slayer of Men. I am Queen Venemia, the only neutral witch powerful enough to create her own race of people in the history of the Ring Wood. Next to the priestess, I am the most powerful magical force in this realm."

"What about Drakkus?" I asked.

Queen Venemia made a sound in the back of her throat like nails tearing into a chalkboard. She hissed. "A false god."

"Priestess Kalia was betrayed by her most trusted advisor," I said. "He was corrupted by Drakkus's growing power. The priestess fears that, with Voron Blackthorne's skill and knowledge, the Chaos Lord's general will breach the temple's defenses in a matter of days."

"So the priestess sends her savior to beg my help," she said, her voice hardening, "with a sword in his hand?"

I bowed my head to the queen. "She knows that you are the only one strong enough to help her."

Queen Venemia stroked the side of my cheek with one of her dagger-like fingernails. The point of one dug into the bottom of my chin like a knife as she tilted my face up to hers. Mere inches away, I could see the drops of clear green poison dripping from her fangs. She said, "You have a power about you, child of Grenwyld. You are fortunate that I do not take lovers anymore. I do like to feast after I fuck and you reek of sex. Like a corpse ripe for the sucking."

"Uh, thanks?" I said, my throat clenching against the words. "No offence, but in that case, celibacy sounds like a fine choice."

She laughed, and her spider soldiers clicked their mouth-parts and chittered along with her, making my skin crawl like there were thousands of baby spiders crawling over my skin. Inside her mouth, rows upon rows of tiny white teeth flashed in the darkness.

"I like you, Loghann Grenwyld," she said. "I will help your priestess, and not just for the kindness your mother showed me once, all those years ago."

"Thank you, Queen Venemia," I said. "We will be forever grateful."

"But I will warn you once, and only once, child of order, child of light." She bent and whispered in my ear. A tremor tingled through my body and straight to my groin. She said, "Never mistake my kindness for goodness. I still have a taste for mortal flesh. Tread carefully among the monsters."

"I will remember that," I said, swallowing hard. My body's betrayal appalled me, but the woman was a force of nature beyond anything I had ever experienced. Fear of imminent death in her presence somehow made me hungry for her. "If I ever uncover the secret of immortality, though, it might be you who will have to watch her step."

She stepped back, grinning ferociously, her black hair writhing like a storm cloud around her face. She raised her hands in the air, and I could see the gray and white swirls of her magic like vortices of power rising up from the earth. Her face became wan and sunken, and her lips peeled back in an animal snarl around her long, black fangs. The spider army clicked and shrieked and more spiders dropped down from the trees around us. I gazed around in horrified wonder as hundreds, maybe thousands, of the creatures amassed upon the forest floor in a glistening, wriggling mass of shiny black abdomens and sharp, blade-like legs.

"Rise up, my children," Queen Venemia intoned in a voice that seemed to come from everywhere at once, "We have been called upon to right the imbalance between order and chaos, to demonstrate our true power. Tonight we fight for the forest we call our home, and for the priestess who respects the boundaries of our territories. Tonight, we feast upon Lord Drakkus's brood and drink the blood of chaos!"

The piercing scream of thousands of Arachana rose and shook the branches of the Dark Wood. As the spiders scurried into the trees and through the underbrush like a swarm of pestilence of biblical proportions, I felt a flash of pity for Drakkus's minions.

But when I remembered what Voron had tried to do, my pity burned away in a rage. Drakkus's soldiers would spare no pity for Kalia, Iymbryl, Ruhail, or any of the rest of them.

I would not rest until every last one of them had fled or lay dead on the floor of the forest.

Chapter 22

Queen Venemia swept me up in a vortex of pale gray mist and deposited me in front of the tree where Ruhail had been imprisoned. But when we arrived, the webs that had bound her were torn to shreds and Ruhail was nowhere to be seen. I felt a surge of pride at the dryad's feistiness, but it was quickly replaced by worry when she didn't reappear.

I put my hand to my mouth and called out into the trees, "Ruhail! Where are you? Come out!"

The great red-barked trees whispered amongst themselves in the breeze. Shadows shifted in the reddish light of the moons. I glanced up at the burnt-orange orb burning between two white crescent moons on either side. This must be the blood moon. Tonight, the Drakkus and his minions would stage their attack.

"Perhaps she is afraid of me," Queen Venemia said without pride. She cocked her head and picked up a strand of broken web, rolling it between her fingers. "Most creatures of order are."

I turned my gaze to the forest floor, hoping to see some sign of her. But the dryad was so light, she probably wouldn't leave footprints, and the earth was so churned up here it was impossible to see any evidence of which way she'd gone. The only thing I noticed was a strange shape poking out of the undergrowth next to the tree she had been tied to.

I crouched down and swept the broken webs and the dry shrubs away. My heart hammered in my chest when I realized what I'd found. "No," I said. "Not again."

"What is it?" the Arachana Queen asked, hovering over me like a ghostly shadow.

I pulled out the same gnarled branch that I'd found in the forest on my first night in this world. It looked like a walking stick. But now that I understood about the dryad's magic, I knew what it was. "Her staff," I said, my voice thick. "She's been taken."

I gripped the staff in my hands and whirled around the clearing. Deep gouges in the earthen forest floor had destroyed the mounds of moss and clusters of wildflowers that grew elsewhere in the forest. Had we and the spiders churned up the clearing like this? Or had something else been here?

"I did not give order to harm the dryad," the queen said. Rather than sounding defensive, she seemed irritated that anyone would go against her orders.

"No," I said. "I don't think it was one of your soldiers. There was an ogre here not long before we were intercepted by your army. Could it have circled back and found her?"

Queen Venemia sniffed the air, her thin white nostrils flaring. Her glossy black eyes scanned the trees.

"The stench of chaos has been thickening for weeks," she said. "I do not pay it any mind anymore. But yes, I sense them. An ogre. Trolls, too. Probably dire wolves, though it is hard to separate their scent from the natural wolves who live in the Dark Wood. I cannot tell which way they have gone, though."

My blood pulsed through my veins like waves pounding against a rocky shore. I had promised to keep Ruhail safe, and now she had been captured by the same creatures who had almost killed her the last time. I tried to focus my rage inward, to fuel the burning power inside my chest. A faint green mist formed around the staff in my hands.

Show me, I thought. Show me which way they've taken her.

As I gazed into the darkening woods, a fine green trail began to materialize in between the pools of reddish moonlight. Adrenaline surged through my chest, and I gripped the staff tighter. "I know where they've gone."

"What are you going to do?" Queen Venemia asked, turning her eerie black eyes on me. In the shadows, her face became sunken and more menacing than she had appeared back in her webby grove. She said, "I must accompany my soldiers. I can take you with me if you like."

Four parallel claw marks raked the red bark of the tree next to me, and a chill passed over my skin. I shook my head. "No. I must help Ruhail. Go to the temple. If you cannot find Priestess Kalia, seek out the elf guards Iymbryl and Arlen. Tell them where I've gone and that I will join the fight as soon as possible."

"And what of the priestess?" The spider woman's fangs flashed ominously as she licked her lips. "What will she think of your shifting priorities?"

I fixed the Arachana Queen with a hard-eyed stare and felt the magic flare inside my chest. Her eyes widened, and she took a step back.

"She knows me." I said. "She will understand. Saving the Ring Wood is my priority and Ruhail's safety is a part of that."

"You are more powerful than I realized." She reached out and stroked my cheek with one of her long, needle-sharp fingernails and smiled. "Perhaps more powerful than you realize, too."

I shook off the compliment. It didn't do anything to help the current situation, and I didn't really want to explain the fact that I was only starting to understand how to manipulate the powers she sensed. It was better for her to think I had control. I said, "Queen Venemia, I need your leadership on the front lines of the battle. I promise to join the fight as soon as I can."

"Very well, Prince of Grenwyld," she said. "I will fulfill my agreement with you. Then the debt I had with your mother will be settled. Next time we meet, we will meet as equals."

I took her cold, white hand in mine and brought it to my lips. I kept my eyes on her glassy black orbs as I pressed my mouth to her skin. "I consider myself warned, great Queen."

Her wet red tongue flashed out between her lips, and she bared her teeth at me in an expression that was not quite a smile. She stepped closer, and I felt her body shiver beneath the thin, lace gown. Despite the fact that I knew she was threatening me, I felt my body respond to her presence. Her gaze glanced down, and she made the horrific clicking sound in the back of her throat that her soldiers had made earlier.

"I do like you," she said. "Don't die before I get a chance to play with you. That would make me very angry."

"I will try not to," I promised, and a thrill of fear rushed through me at the idea of attempting to dominate the spider queen. Would my magic ever be strong enough that I could take her as one of my consorts? If I survived this war with Drakkus, maybe.

"I suppose I should get into my armor, then," she said.

I thought of tearing the gossamer dress from her body and tying her up in her own silken bonds. I gritted my teeth and said, "Is that not what you're wearing into battle?"

She laughed, exposing the rows and rows of sharp teeth once more. One thing was certain. There was no way I'd let this woman give me a blow job.

A thick, gray fog swirled up from the forest floor, whirling around Venemia like a cyclone. In it, her silken dress dissolved, revealing her bone-white body. Large, high breasts seemed to defy gravity beneath her razor sharp collarbones. Her torso was long and lithe with the well-defined muscles of an apex predator. Her wide hips pushed her sex out invitingly, but the tiny triangle of black hair between her legs seemed like a warning sign. *Abandon hope, all ye who enter here.*

After giving me a little peek, the fog swirled over her limbs again. As it dissipated, it left behind a hard, black chitinous armor covered in barbs and spikes. Her breasts were now plated in shiny, black spikes.

Her shoulders prickled like a punk hairstyle from the '70s. A helmet covered her wavy black hair, its crown coming to a point between her eyebrows like a widow's peak worthy of Count Dracula in the old black and white films. Venemia looked like a vampire dressed for the battlefield, ready to display her enemies' heads on pikes. She even carried the pike, a deadly-looking black spear tipped with a curved blade that bore a striking resemblance to an enormous spider fang.

"Fight well, Loghann Grenwyld," she said, and parted her red lips in a smile. "Fate rewards those who take charge of their own destinies. And so do I."

With that, the gray fog swirled around her in a ferocious funnel which grew until its top met the branches at the bottom of the canopy. It disappeared, from the bottom up, and when it was gone so was Venemia.

I shook my head to clear any remaining intrusive thoughts about the spider queen. With her gone, it suddenly seemed much easier to think about the problem at hand. Ruhail had been taken and I needed to find her before something terrible happened.

The reddish-orange beams of the blood moon spilled through gaps in the forest canopy, leaving pools of bloody light in patches along the forest floor. The rest of the forest was black as pitch. But as I stared into the trees, and my eyes adjusted to the low light, the faint green trail seemed to glow brighter.

I clutched the staff and attempted to force my magic into it, the same way I had been able to with my sword. But something in the staff resisted my magic. It was like pushing against a rubber sheet, giving for a bit and then becoming tauter and tauter until suddenly it sprang back and my magic was forced back inside my chest. I slid the staff behind my shield and found the green trail persisted even when I wasn't holding onto it. Good. That made things easier.

I drew my sword and crept into the dark shadows as quietly as I could. Following the green light meant I could focus my thoughts on what else was going on in the surrounding forest. I didn't want to stumble into one horde of Drakkus's minions while following the trail of another. My sword glowed a gentle white, illuminating the ragged path the ogre had taken through the woods. I hoped the sword wasn't actually glowing, and was rather lit with magic only I could see.

Otherwise it was going to be hard to sneak up on Ruhail's captors.

How far had they taken her? She'd said we were close to where they'd brought her last time. Would they bring her back there, or to a new location? Why had they taken her if the secret of Drakkus's spy inside the temple had already been revealed?

My muscles shook as I raced through the forest, and questions raced through my mind. Whoever or whatever had taken Ruhail, they had a good head start on me. I was going to have to pick up the pace if I had any hope of finding her before it was too late. Especially if I was right, and the black-robed werewolf was in their party.

The dryad had given herself to me, and it was my job to protect her. The thought of any of those beasts so much as touching her made my skin flush with rage. If they hurt her, I swore to the power of this strange red moon that I would hunt down every last one of Drakkus's followers and string them up by their guts.

And I would start with Voron Blackthorne, the betrayer, the one who had made this awful war possible.

Thoughts of revenge sustained me as I loped over fallen logs and boulders torn from the earth. It looked as if an army had passed through this way. It wasn't some lone actor, or small band of riff-raff, that had captured the dryad. She was being dragged along by a mob of Drakkus's soldiers.

My lungs began to burn in that old familiar way that I had grown to enjoy in my marathon training. I was pushing myself hard, but not so hard that I couldn't handle it. The extra weight of my weapons and armor made me slower than I would have been in a normal race, but I knew I had the stamina to run at this pace for as long as it took to find Ruhail.

The longer I ran, though, the more I began to wonder where in the seven hells this mob was taking her. I followed the glimmer of green magic through the Dark Wood and out into the still-dark-but-less-ominous Ring Wood. I glimpsed patches of breadshrooms growing beneath a massive red-barked tree and remembered Ruhail crawling on her hands and knees to reach one for me when I was hungry. As I continued on, I had a sinking suspicion I knew where this group was headed.

Tonight was the blood moon, the night Drakkus would send his soldiers in to attack the forest temple. I was headed straight into the thick of his forces, and I was on the wrong side of the battlefield. Ruhail had called the werewolf 'Drakkus's general.' If it was here, and it was the general of this attack, I was going to have to make some kind of plan before rushing into their flank waving my sword around like an overly enthusiastic Lord of the Rings cosplayer at a sci-fi convention.

The farther I continued the more familiar the woods felt. There was an eerie stillness here tonight, though. No birds sang, no small animals rustled in the bushes. It was too quiet. Either Drakkus's army was smaller than I expected or something else was going on here.

The shimmering green trail became stronger the closer I got to the forest temple. That must be a good sign, I thought, it means she's still alive. And even without her staff, her magic should be more powerful the closer she gets to the heart. But for some reason that thought didn't give me comfort. What did they want with her? If they hadn't killed her yet, was it because they had something even worse planned for her?

I tried to shake the sensation of dread that settled around my shoulders like a lead blanket, weighing me down and sucking the energy out of me. As doubt overtook my mind, the trail of green magic began to fade and panic stabbed through my chest.

No. I clenched my left hand into a fist so hard my nails bit into my palm, and the pain brought me sharply back to reality. *She's not dead yet,* I told myself, *and I'm going to rescue her.*

Just then, a cluster of greenish-yellow orbs appeared in the distance, bobbing their way through the trees toward me. The lights weaved and darted erratically, but they were definitely heading my way. Hope swelled in my chest. The fireflies! If they were here, Ruhail must be close. But why had I lost her trail?

The glowing insects surrounded me in a friendly haze of dancing light, but their movements were quick and urgent, more spirited than the follow-the-leader game we had played upon my initial arrival.

Ruhail had been in trouble then, too. Whatever was happening to her now, I could only assume it was worse than her situation with the trolls and the werewolf. I swallowed hard and nodded.

I pulled my shield over my shoulder, making sure the dryad's staff was still secure on my back, and gripped my sword in front of me.

"Lead me to her," I whispered. "I'm ready."

The fireflies danced and wavered around my face, swirling in a dizzying flurry of activity. Then, one by one, they shot forward along the path Ruhail's glittering magic had been leading me. With a subtle *pop! pop! pop!* they each disappeared at a place on the path about three yards ahead of me. What the hell?

I strode forward slowly, keeping my eyes on the place, where the glowing bugs had vanished as if through an invisible door. My arm sweated beneath the straps of my buckler. My knuckles ached from clenching the grip of my sword. The blade blazed a brighter white with each step I took, as if reacting to something I was approaching but couldn't see.

Then, suddenly, I *could* see something. An iridescent sheen hovered in the air in front of me, like the oily rainbow surface of a soap bubble. I looked left and right. The strange wavering surface continued as far as I could see. Looking up it was the same. I reached out with my sword hand, holding the blade sideways, and pressed against the surface.

The white-hot energy inside my chest flared like a nuclear blast. I stumbled backward like I'd been hit by a battering ram, gasping to catch my breath. The backs of my eyes felt like they'd been melted into my skull.

When the burning sensation ebbed, it was like that molten core of magic inside me had crystallized into diamond. I couldn't see it, not exactly, but I sensed it there in my mind's eye, as if my heart had been transformed into a spirit crystal like the one camouflaged within Ruhail's staff.

My power felt harder, too, more focused somehow. Like all I had to do was think about what I wanted to do and the magic would obey.

Show me what lies beyond the barrier, I thought, feeling a bit foolish. But I was desperate, and anything was worth a shot.

My jaw dropped as the iridescent barrier crackled and broke apart. Pieces of the material shattered and fell, raining down on the forest floor like pieces of a broken rainbow. And on the other side was a hellscape like nothing I had ever imagined.

Behind the wall, hordes of dark creatures milled about. Their grunts and squeals, and the cackling of insane laughter floated out into the forest, filtering into the unnatural stillness I had sensed earlier. It must have been some kind of cloaking spell, and I had broken it.

The creatures didn't notice me at first, and I stared at the army in horrified silence. A troll with a boil the size of a grapefruit on the top of his head heaved a wheelbarrow full of oil behind a group of skinny goblin-like creatures, leaping and jumping about and juggling torches. A mountainous thing covered in ragged gray cloth shifted its weight and nearly sat upon a pack of scraggly-looking dire wolves. They yelped and nipped at the giant's ankles. The beast bellowed with a roar like boulders sheering off a cliff side and kicked one of the wolves into a bonfire. The pitiful creature writhed and screamed and burned to a crisp while the other monsters cackled gleefully and danced around the flames.

I backed away from the mayhem as slowly as I could, hoping to find some cover before they realized their barrier was down.

But my attempt to avoid detection wasn't enough.

A shriek rose up from the horde, and a black-robed crone stumbled forward, her long gray hair hanging in lank ropes about her wizened face. A long, clawed finger with swollen knuckles and mottled skin pointed straight at me.

"There," she hissed. "A spy in our midst!"

A cacophony of shouts and squeals and roars shook the trees of the forest, and even Lord Drakkus might have been proud of me as the camp erupted into chaos.

Chapter 23

The horde surged toward me in a haphazard race to be the first to smash my skull in. I had nowhere to run, nowhere to hide. Blood pounded in my ears, and a hard-edged clarity focussed my vision. I wished I had some kind of cloaking spell like the barrier that had hidden these monsters from me in the first place.

I had touched the iridescent barrier, though. I had felt its strange magic. Maybe I could do something like that if I tried? I reached for the crystalline core of magic in my chest. I imagined my energy flowing through that heart and transforming into a shield of invisibility.

Suddenly, the approaching marauders stopped and looked around in confusion. A volley of arrows launched from somewhere at the back of the group, and I ducked under my buckler to avoid being struck by any of them. But the few that came close hit a wall about two feet above my head and bounced harmlessly away. The horde of monsters roared furiously.

A fat gray goblin squealed and thumped the end of its spear on the ground. "Where'd it go, then?"

It had worked! I inched my way to the left, testing if the spell held while I was moving. No one seemed to notice me. I moved to the right.

"It were just 'ere!" the troll with the boil on its head bellowed. "I seen it wiff me'n own eyes."

There was a gap in wall of lumpy, misshapen bodies gathered around the bonfire. Just on the other side of the flames, the faint green trail of Ruhail's magic glimmered. My heart beat faster in my chest as I locked my gaze on the fastest route around Drakkus's soldiers.

"The hag's playin' tricks on us, she is," said another voice. "Castin' shadows."

There was an uproar of garbled cursing, weapons clattering, and chest thumping as the masses turned their wrath on the crone.

"Fools!" She pointed at me again, and I froze. She said, "Can't you see a barrier spell when it's right in front of you?"

They all turned to look, but their glazed eyes seemed to stare straight though me at the dark trees beyond. They roared again and turned their wrath upon the old woman. She shrieked and covered her head as the trolls and goblins showered her with a barrage of sticks and stones. The crone attempted to protect herself with magic. A sheer greenish-white bubble formed over her head, but it only managed to slow the projectiles not stop them completely.

I watched the attack with bile rising in my throat. She might have been the one to rat on me, but I couldn't just stand by and watch an old woman get beaten to death. And her magic was green, not the corrupted red of Voron Blackthorne's. Perhaps she was still neutral enough to be converted to our side. I swore under my breath and changed my course.

I crept closer to the throng of angry beasts. The pathetic creature in the middle of the fray whimpered and cowered beneath their assault. As I got nearer to her, a stray rock bounced off my invisible shell, but no one seemed to notice. A goblin, leaping up and down in deranged excitement, tripped over his own spear and toppled backward. I cursed and tried to dodge.

Its thin arms pin-wheeled, but when it fell, the little bastard went straight through me like I was a ghost, just like what had happened with Ruhail in the tunnels. I pushed my way through the rest of them and found that none of them could touch me. Occasionally, a weapon would bounce off my shield, but the beasts' bodies passed straight through. I wasn't sure what that meant for my ability to protect the crone, but I had come this far.

A troll lifted a club over its head to deliver her a killing blow, but I leaped forward and covered the old woman with my own body. She looked up at me with terror inscribed in the hard lines etched into her sun-browned skin.

"Idiot!" she hissed, clawing at me as she tried to scramble away. "You'll be killed!"

The ring of trolls and goblins roared with delight as the club came down. The old woman shrieked and tried to pull away from me. I closed my eyes, reached for the core of my magic, and imagined bringing her with me into this secret plane of existence where none of them could touch us.

The club slammed into the dirt between us, as if our bodies weren't there at all. The crone stared, wide-eyed, at the spiked log that would have crushed her skull had I been too late. The beasts bellowed in outrage, and the troll whipped his tusked head back and forth looking for his victim. The boil on his forehead looked ready to erupt with rage.

"How—," the crone stammered. "How did you do that?"

I grabbed her by the arms and hoisted her to her feet. "Less talking, more running. Are you hurt?"

"Just bruised," she said, shaking her head. The long, gray ropes of hair swayed back and forth beneath the dirty black cowl.

"Follow me."

I dragged her through the mob of monsters, nearly choking on the stench, and toward the bonfire. The air held a putrid combination of scents: rotten meat, bodily fluids, and unwashed flesh. Piles of feces had been left indiscriminately about the camp. I dodged around them, not wanted to risk a shit-bath in case my spell stopped working. Fortunately, it seemed to hold and we managed to creep around the main throng of freaks and made it to the other side of the blaze.

I only wished the shield spell could protect me from the smell.

With my back to the fire, I could see the magical green path more clearly than before. It trailed through the darkness toward another glowing patch in the trees. I pointed at the light. "What's over there?"

The crone tugged her arm out of my grasp and narrowed her rheumy eyes me. "Fool. What did you save me for? You nearly got yourself killed!"

"Well, I wasn't going to stand by and watch that mob stone you to death," I said. "What should I have done?"

"I set them upon you first," she said, sneering with a mouthful of blackened teeth. "You should have let me die."

"You're not like them," I said. "You're not corrupted by chaos. Why are you here?"

She backed up in surprise, her eyes darting from side to side. "What do you mean?"

"When you protected yourself," I said. "You used green magic, didn't you?"

She hissed and stumbled backward. I caught her, fearing if she got too far away she would no longer be protected by my spell. She flinched away from my touch as if she thought I would hit her. "He sent you, didn't he?"

"Who?" I said, letting go of her arm. "And please don't run, I don't know how far I can extend this spell. I'm not going to hurt you."

"The general," she said. "The one chosen by Drakkus to lead the war on the forest temple." She shook her head and muttered under her breath. "He has keen eyes that one. I should have known I couldn't fool him."

"Tell me what's going on," I said through gritted teeth. "My friend is in danger, and I need to help her before—"

I cut myself off, not wanting to warn the crone of the impending attach by Queen Venemia and her spider soldiers.

Her red-rimmed eyes narrowed to thin slits, and she peered at me with her head cocked sideways like a curious crow. She sidled toward me, tilting her head farther until I thought her neck might break. "Before what?"

Just because I'd saved her life didn't mean she wasn't going to throw me to the wolves the moment my back was turned. I'd taken a chance, but there was no guarantee I was right about the old woman.

"Listen," I said, placing my hand on the pommel of my sword. "I saved your life because I sensed that you were different from the other creatures in that camp. You didn't ask me to do it, and I'm not asking you to be grateful for it. Maybe you'd rather be dead. If I was wrong, I'm sorry. But I need to know what's over there. My friend is in serious danger."

She grinned at me, suddenly. Her ancient face breaking open like an ugly mask. The expression was hideous, but seemed to be genuine. She said, "So you're the one."

I blinked at her. "Excuse me?"

"Never mind," she said, waving me away with a gnarled hand. "Tell me about your friend. Who are you looking for?"

I narrowed my eyes at the old woman. There was a mischievous glint in her eye that I didn't quite trust, but Ruhail was running out of time and I was running out of options. I could just follow the trail and hope for the best, but I had a better chance of saving her if I knew what I was up against.

"A dryad," I said. "She was abducted and brought here maybe an hour ago. I don't know what they want with her, but I am sure she's still alive."

She nodded her wrinkled head and peered into the forest toward the glow of the campfire. "I saw them. An ogre, a couple of trolls, and the general himself."

"What do they want with her?" I asked. "Do you have any idea what they are doing over there?"

"Old magic." She closed her eyes and breathed in deeply through her nose, shuddering as she exhaled. "Dark magic. You must tread carefully."

I clenched my jaw and spoke through gritted teeth. "Isn't there anything you can tell me? Anything that might help?"

She opened her eyes and stared at me through a film of watery fluid. The red rims around her eyes were irritated, almost infected looking. I stepped back involuntarily. She pressed her lips together into a cracked fissure across her face.

Trembling, she said, "Stop the ritual, and you stop Drakkus from bringing the rest of his army across the veil."

She fell to her knees, screaming as if she was being tortured. I knelt next to her as she writhed on the ground in pain. None of the creatures in the camp seemed to hear her cries. "What's happened," I said. "Are you hurt?"

"Stop him." The woman's twisted fingers gripped my arm like a vice. She was far stronger than she looked. She met my gaze with a desperate fervor. "Stop him and I will be free."

I placed a hand on her back and kept it there until she stopped shaking. When she had recovered I said, "If I go alone, you will not be protected by my spell anymore. Will you be safe?"

"I have my own magic, child," she said. "Different from your own. Different from his. I will be safe for now. If you defeat him, I will find you again. My name is Maggi."

"Thank you, Maggi," I said. I wondered how I should introduce myself, if I trusted her with my real name. I hadn't even gotten used to it myself. I decided to go with the safest option. "I'm Logan Greenwood. I will do my best."

She let out a long, wheezing sound like air being let out of a balloon, and her shoulders shook. It took me a moment to realize she was laughing.

"I know who you are," she said, once she had recovered herself. "I like that pronunciation, though I'm not sure it suits you."

"You know me?" I said, startled.

She shoved me away and sat up on her knees. "Later. If you succeed in defeating Drakkus's general, we will talk. If you don't, there will be no need to. Good luck to you."

"How will you—?" I began to ask how she was going to protect herself, but the strange old woman was disappearing before my eyes. Her mottled black cloak and long, ropey gray hair melded together, and she curled herself up in a ball on the ground.

As I stared, she took on the shape and appearance of an old mossy stone. I reached out to touch her, amazed at the illusion, and found that she had actually become a stone. Even more strangely, I couldn't sense any magic around the illusion at all. No green haze or wispy gray smoke. No smoldering red. Nothing.

Maybe the old crone had her own 'old magic.'

I left her there, still as a stone, and none of the creatures in the camp paid any mind to the new boulder in their midst. I only hoped no ogres or giants decided to pick the old woman up and use her in a catapult. Perhaps her magic could protect her from that, too.

I shook my head and followed the path into the woods. I noticed the riff-raff in the camp seemed to be avoiding the narrow, beaten trail through the trees. Though I couldn't see any magic yet, the glow of the camp fire through the forest had an ominous feel. Shadows moved and swirled through the darkness. I hoped my cloaking spell would allow me to get close enough to whatever was going on that I could make a plan before attacking.

But the farther along the path I got, the more I sensed something was wrong.

The trees loomed above me like spectral sentinels, and the path darkened. Other than the bloody light of the strange moon, and the orange flickering of the bonfire, the forest had been consumed by darkness.

The shifting shadows weren't shadows at all, but a nebulous pitch-black fog oozing through the trees. Blood throbbed in my ears as I ran faster toward the light, my heart beat against my ribs like an animal trapped in a cage. Black magic. Old magic. Whatever ritual Voron and the werewolf general were planning, it had already begun.

If I didn't stop them, they would open a doorway between Drakkus's realm and the Ring Wood and the temple would be overrun by the minions of chaos.

Even our alliance with the Arachana wouldn't help us then.

Chapter 24

A shout rang out from the camp behind me. I was afraid the old woman had been found. I cursed under my breath and kept running down the path toward the heart of darkness in the woods. I couldn't go back for her now; it was too late. She would have to fend for herself.

More shouts followed, accompanied by animal roars and the clanging of metal. Then another sound joined the fray, the terror-inducing shrieks and clicking of Queen Venemia's enormous spiders.

Relief flooded through me as I ran. My plan actually seemed to be working. Venemia would lead the charge against Drakkus's infantry, and could help to protect the temple. Clearly, they hadn't been expecting us to strike while the Chaos Lord's ugly soldiers sat around twiddling their thumbs and arguing amongst themselves as they awaited their general's orders. We had caught them unawares and unprepared.

The general had hidden the full extent of the soldiers amassed outside the temple using the shielding spell, perhaps to lull the Priestess and her elf guards into a false sense of security. I could only assume he had been waiting for a path to open between the chaos realm and the Ring Wood before launching the full assault.

If I could interrupt the ritual, Drakkus's invasion would fail before it even started.

Encouraged, I continued along the path. The sounds of fighting escalated behind me, but I couldn't see anything through the thick, black fog of ancient magic. Even the green shimmer of Ruhail's trail was lost in the pitch. I had to believe she was still alive, though. I had to believe I could save her.

The flames of the bonfire were my only visible marker as I moved through the woods. As I got closer, I saw shapes moving around the fire. Hunched, lumpen things that were probably trolls, and a thin, robed shape with a staff that had to be Voron.

Priestess Kalia had said she'd never heard of anyone being able to see magic before, so I felt reasonably confident that Voron and his minions wouldn't be able to see me. But as the spell didn't seem to mask scent—at least, it didn't stop the stench of trolls and goblins from assaulting my nostrils—I would have to be cautious if the werewolf was around.

When I was close enough to hear muttered voices, coming from the clearing ahead, I stepped off the path and into the thick, soupy black fog between the trees. The magic swirled around my shielded form as if I had an invisible eggshell protecting me. It bounced away from me just like the stones and weapons had. I wondered if the black fog would hurt me in some way, if Voron had put up defensive spells to protect him while he engaged in this ritual.

I tried to creep close enough to hear what the voices were saying or to see what was happening. The voices were low and garbled, like whoever was talking had a mouthful of rocks. I guessed that would be the trolls, and they likely didn't have anything all that useful to say. I hadn't seen any evidence of the ogre yet, and this worried me. Perhaps the torn earth and broken trees it left in its wake were hidden by the black fog.

A howl rose up from the clearing that sent chills of dread down my spine. It was nothing like the wolves I knew from Colorado, or even the dire wolves I'd heard when Drakkus's soldiers first started to harry the priestess's borders. It must have been the werewolf, Drakkus's general. Rage bubbled through my veins that I had allowed Ruhail to be captured by this monster again.

This time, I would finish the beast.

I pushed through a wall of desiccated shrubs, grateful that my shielding spell allowed me to pass through them like a ghost. I crouched between the thorny brambles and peered into the clearing, preparing for the worst. But my heart was in my throat when I surveyed the scene before me.

A raging bonfire, flames leaping twelve or more feet in the air, burned in the middle of the clearing. In front of the fire, a huge slab-stone table sat like an ancient altar, covered in an assortment of arcane objects. A shard of crystal glowing with an eerie red light, dusty tomes covered in cryptic writing, black candles puddling with wax, and a vial of green liquid that smoked and bubbled like something from a witch's cauldron in a kids' cartoon, were all set out like the ingredients for an experiment.

An opening in the tree canopy allowed the strange orange moonlight to filter down from the sky and onto the table where a lens, like a big magnifying glass in an ornate golden frame, concentrated the light into a red beam that glowed like a laser. The werewolf stood behind the table with a book in its hands that I immediately recognized as the Book of Elders that belonged to Priestess Kalia.

Wherever the traitor Voron was, it was clear that he had taught Drakkus's general how to use the ancient spells inside. The werewolf held the enormous book in one clawed hand and pored over the book with saliva slavering from its jaws. Where was Voron anyway?

I glanced around the clearing. Behind the bonfire, lying there like a mountain of bumpy, discoloured flesh, was the ogre. A river of blood flowed from the fat rolls of its neck and pooled around its body, creating a black lake on the far side of the open space. The flames of the bonfire flickered on the surface of the still, black liquid, which looked more like an oil slick than a blood stain.

A pile of deep green fabric had been left next to the fire and the gnarled, blackened remains of Voron's staff were visible within the flames. Triumph rose in my chest. The traitor had been betrayed by the Lord of Chaos after all! A flash of disappointment that I wouldn't be the one to end the treacherous elf surged through my mind, but I shook it off. As long as he was dead, I wasn't going to complain about how it happened.

One less thing for me to worry about. That left saving Ruhail, and slaying the werewolf.

But where was she?

Black magic swirled around the werewolf as it chanted in a guttural language I couldn't understand. Unlike the ancient words in the little blue book Kalia had showed me, my power didn't seem to translate spoken words. Fortunately the creature seemed too distracted to notice my scent, if it could smell me. The smoke from the fire blew toward me, too, so I had the advantage of being downwind. I crept closer and prayed the winds wouldn't shift, that the werewolf wouldn't notice me until it was too late.

The beast's black eyes began to glow around the edges like magma beneath a crust of lava rock. The magic inside him seemed ready to erupt like a volcano. Voron's eyes had once held the same burning magic, though, and it hadn't saved him. The werewolf wasn't invincible.

It set the Book of Elders down on the table and picked up the glowing red stone—perhaps it was the spirit crystal from the top of Voron's staff—and the vial of bubbling green liquid. The black candles guttered in a breeze I couldn't feel in my protected space, but my heart leaped into my throat as I worried that Drakkus's general would soon know I was there. Though it still hadn't noticed the sounds of battle coming from the other encampment. The beast was either sufficiently fixated on the ritual, or it believed opening the door into the chaos realm would win the war either way.

The wolf-man snarled and dropped the crystal into the vial, causing the liquid to transform from toxic green to blood red.

"Now!" it said, panting slightly. It poured the fluid into its gaping jaws and licked its lips. "Bring her to me now!"

There was a commotion from the bushes opposite me, on the other side of the clearing, and two trolls emerged dragging Ruhail between them. She screamed when she saw the werewolf and fought like demon to get away from her captors, but the trolls held her tight. Without her staff, she was powerless against them.

"What you want us to do wiff 'er?" one of the ugly bastards said with a grunt. It had two broken tusks and skin the color of bread mold.

The werewolf pointed to the ground before the table with a long, clawed finger. "Leave her there. I will hold her."

The trolls dumped Ruhail unceremoniously in the dirt. Tendrils of black magic snaked out from the trees and wrapped around her limbs. She screamed and writhed against her bonds, and my heart tore to listen to her. But I couldn't risk revealing myself yet. Not until I knew the general's plan. The second troll, shorter and fatter with a stringy black braid running down the center of his otherwise bald, spotted scalp, crouched next to the dryad and sniffed her.

"Too bad, innit?" The troll's wide nostrils quivered. "I 'ad plans for dis one."

Ruhail's green eyes bulged as she fought to get away from the leering creature. The tattered remains of her dress suggested the trolls had been already pawing at her. I gripped the hilt of my sword and crept closer to the beasts with bile burning in the back of my throat. Fuck waiting for the plan, I was going to murder them all.

"What about dem 'lil bouncy ones?" the other troll asked, putting its meaty fists on its hips and glaring at the werewolf with a pair of runny, yellow eyes. "You still want dem ones?"

Others like Ruhail? Bouncy ones? My throat constricted as I realized what the ugly bastard might be referring to.

"I don't need the nymphs anymore," the werewolf said. It waved the trolls away impatiently. "The dryad is much more powerful. Do with them as you will."

The troll grinned down at its compatriot from between its broken tusks then shoved it to the ground and scrambled out of the clearing snorting with laughter. The pot-bellied troll rolled around on the ground, trying to get its feet underneath it, then lumbered after the other cursing loudly.

The werewolf watched the trolls leave with its eyes narrowed. Ruhail screamed and strained against the thickening swirls of black magic as if they burned her skin.

"Shut up!" the werewolf snarled. It hunched over the table with its clawed fingers scraping the stone table top. The red behind its black eyes flashed dangerously. "You've already had more time than you deserve, you silly little bitch. If you hadn't run away from me last time, this would already be over and done with and we wouldn't have to bother with this foolish battle."

I crept around the edge of the clearing, wondering if I should intervene with the general's ritual first or try to save the nymphs first. I hadn't liked the looks on the trolls' faces as they ran down the path. I didn't like to think of what they might do to the captured nymphs. But I had promised to protect Ruhail and I couldn't just leave her.

The dryad tried to speak, but a coil of black smoke twisted around her neck and snaked down her throat when she opened her mouth. Her eyes went wide, and she tore at the magical ropes, gagging like she was being suffocated. The ropes dissolved under her touch and reappeared the moment her fingers moved, as if they were holding her from another realm.

"I would have killed you quickly and painlessly," the werewolf said. It crept slowly out from behind the table, its shaggy black shoulders hunched and twisted as if its transformation wasn't quite complete. "But now you shall suffer for the humiliation you have put me through. Do you know what it is like to have to tell the Lord of Chaos that you have failed him? You will. You will feel every second of this ritual and I will revel in your pain."

It dragged its left leg, limping as it approached Ruhail. A festering red wound marred the matted black fur of its haunches from where I'd struck him with the sword of Grenwyld. I was gratified to see that Kalia was right, the magic was still working and the wound had not healed at all since I'd dealt the blow.

But between the beast's legs, the evidence of its excitement at having the captive dryad sent a tremor of disgust through my body. I froze, halfway between Ruhail and the path the trolls had taken toward the nymphs. The sounds of battle raged on beyond the edge of the clearing, and I hoped against hope that Venemia and her soldiers were decimating Drakkus's troops. Because I was going to stop this ritual from happening, even if it killed me. And I had to do it quickly if I was going to have a chance to save the nymphs as well.

A shrill cry tore from the bushes in the direction the trolls had gone and shook me in my very bones. There was no more time for thinking and planning. It was time to fight.

The werewolf dropped to its forelegs and crept toward Ruhail like a jackal taunting an injured gazelle. The snarl on its muzzle had become a kind of sadistic grin, exposing its long, knife-like canines. I circled behind it, mirroring its movements, with my sword clenched in my hand and my shield gripped close to my body. As soon as I struck the beast, I was certain the magic shielding me would evaporate, so I had to make my first strike count.

The screams from the next glade over became more frantic, and I was surprised to hear a pained yowl from one of the trolls as well. Were the nymphs fighting back? Hope surged through me. If they could just hold the trolls off a little longer, I could save Ruhail and the nymphs.

I was close enough to smell the oily stink of its fur and the sickly-sweet stink of its infected leg. I just needed an opening. The werewolf raised its right forepaw, its muscle bunched to strike the dryad. My eyes locked onto an opening between its arm and its ribs. Without hesitation I lunged forward with my blade and thrust the sword deep into the werewolf's chest.

But my blade went right through the beast as if I was a ghost. It slashed down at Ruhail and raked her with its curved claws, leaving thin gashes across her pale flesh and tearing the last of her clothes from her body. Panic seized me. I swiped at the werewolf again and again, but nothing happened. The blade passed straight through the beast and its captive.

Chapter 25

The black magic bindings tugged at Ruhail's limbs, pinning her arms to the ground and spreading her legs before the beast like an offering. Rage pulsed through my body. I was forced to watch helplessly as the thing dipped its head between her thighs and inhaled deeply.

"Are you afraid, dryad?" It snarled and nipped at the inside of her thigh, leaving a slash of blood. "You smell afraid. And... maybe even a little... excited?"

She tried to scream again, but the sound was choked off by the ropes she should couldn't even see. I tried to imagine destroying the shielding spell the way I had destroyed the one surrounding the camp, but fear and anger made it impossible to focus my thoughts. What was I going to do? I slashed at the beast over and over again, willing the sword to find purchase, but the creature lowered its body over her writhing form as if I wasn't even there.

I was in the other realm, only seeing what was happening to Ruhail without being able to affect it. Like Ruhail's fingers had scraped uselessly through the magical bindings, I couldn't touch the werewolf or Ruhail.

But maybe I could cut the bindings.

I gritted my teeth and stabbed my sword through the form of the werewolf and, just like the monster wasn't there, the blade came through the other side with ease. I swept the blade over Ruhail's throat and arms, and dragged it down over her legs.

The coils of black magic wriggled like tormented worms as if trying to escape the kiss of my blade. Some fell away.

I ignored the heaving shoulders of the beast as it hunched over the dryad, completely unaware of me, and I slashed my blade over the remaining tendrils of magic like I was carving flesh from the monster's bones. My chest tightened with rage as I poured all my energy into destroying Ruhail's bonds.

This time, the worms of magic writhed and hissed, disintegrating beneath my sword. Ruhail screamed, and my heart leaped into my throat. Had I cut her? The dryad curled her legs up against her chest protectively. The beast faltered over her, its eyes darting down at its victim in confusion as she was freed of the magical chains. Ruhail's scream twisted into a cry of rage and suddenly she kicked out with both feet, catching the werewolf in the chest. The beast reeled backward.

I jumped back at the same time, reaching behind my shoulder to grab the gnarled wooden walking stick that hid the dryad's powers. As the werewolf stumbled to its knees, panic and confusion squirming behind its eyes, I threw the camouflaged staff toward Ruhail. I didn't know if the staff would make it out of the bubble I was stuck in or not, but I knew with her power unleashed, Drakkus's general wouldn't stand a chance against us.

Ruhail had scrambled into a crouch, her piercing green eyes locked on the werewolf. The werewolf recovered from its shock and met her on all fours, hackles raised. Beneath her curves and pale, delicate-looking flesh, muscles bunched and tensed as the dryad prepared to fight.

When the staff flew toward her, her left hand lashed out as if to defend herself against a blow. Then, like her body sensed the magical implement before her mind did, she caught it and swung it around her head. An arc of green light exploded from the staff—which transformed the moment she touched it—and knocked the werewolf sideways.

It flew off-balance and landed on its injured hip with a yelp and rolled backward, directly into my legs.

Unlike the last time I'd tried to hit the thing, this time it connected with the solid thud of flesh and bone.

Caught off-guard, I fell like a sack of bricks.

The beast clawed frantically at the ground to get away from me, terror and disorientation filming its black and red eyes. It stared at me like I was the nightmarish hound, rather than the other way around, and swiped erratically at me with its clawed foreleg.

I braced my knee against the bare forest floor and turned my shoulder. The blow ricocheted off my buckler, and the werewolf howled in rage.

"Loghann," the dryad cried out. "The potion obscures the beast's vision. He does not know what is of this world, and what it of the realm of chaos. Strike him down now!"

I swung my sword at the monster, missing by mere inches, but it bought me just enough time to get to my feet and ready myself for its next attack. The werewolf made a desperate lunge toward me, gnashing its teeth and swinging its arms, but it didn't seem to really know where I was. I sidestepped the clumsy attack, brought my sword up, and swept down with all my strength.

The hard crystal of power within my chest hummed inside me as I moved and a painful jolt shot up my arm as I struck the monster down. When my blade connected with its corrupted flesh, an explosion of white light burst into the clearing.

The energy of the blow knocked me backward, and I blinked blindly in the aftermath of the flare. When my eyes cleared, all I could see at first was a quivering mass of black hair writhing on the ground. But as I watched, the convulsing pile revealed patches of sallow skin, and thin, stringy limbs. An elven head, severed from the beast's body, stared up at me.

It was the head of Voron Blackthorne.

"I guess that explains the limp," I said. I slung my shield on my back and bent down to pick the traitorous elf's head up by a length of greasy black hair. "Not to mention the claw marks in his study."

"Put that thing down, Loghann. " Ruhail stared at me with a look of awe and disgust on her face. "And where did you come from? I thought I was..."

She turned away from me, her shoulders shuddering. She pressed her forehead against her staff, and a swirl of green magic enveloped her. When it dissipated, the dryad was cloaked in a pale-green, hooded robe that hid every inch of her body including her face.

My heart ached. I wished I could go to her, but I had to make sure that Voron was truly dead. Sure, I'd chopped the guy's head off. But I wouldn't put it past Drakkus to be able to bring his minions back from the dead.

"Do you think it's safe to leave him here?" I said. "We have to go after those trolls. I think they have nymphs captured somewhere and—"

"Oh no," Ruhail gasped, spinning back to face me with her wide eyes staring out beneath the hood in a panic. "The ritual Voron was performing requires the sacrifice of a spirit of pure order. He must have captured them after I escaped with you the first time, intending for them to take my place. We have to save them!"

A swishing noise drew my attention away from the dryad and there was a wet thud at my feet. A hideous troll's head gaped sightlessly up at me, with two broken tusks protruding from its jaw. With another thud, another face joined the grotesque masquerade.

I looked up just as Queen Venemia strode into the clearing, her shiny black armor glistening in the light of the fire, with two naked wood-nymphs leaping at her sides. Their ridiculously voluptuous bodies were naked, except for the streaks of blood they wore like war paint.

"A gift for you, Loghann Grenwyld," one of them said. The two grinned like lunatics at the severed heads at my feet.

I raised an eyebrow at Ruhail. "Are you sure these nymphs of yours haven't already been corrupted?"

The nymphs locked arms with one another and danced a wild dance in circles around Venemia.

"A couple more curios for your collection," the spider queen said in her soft, sultry voice, and she licked her red lips hungrily. "I am pleased to see we have similar... tastes."

She stared at the dripping head of Voron Blackthorne hanging from my fingers.

"It's not usually my style," I said. "But under the circumstances, it seemed the safest thing to do. Thank you for your help."

The queen stretched her arms high over her head and shuddered, her lips parted to reveal her fangs. "It is a pleasure. It had been far too long since I have tasted the fruits of war."

I kicked the shoulder of Voron's headless, naked body to the side. Ruhail winced and kept her gaze averted. A shard of red spirit crystal swirling with black magic was fused to the middle of his chest. I pressed the point of my sword against the dead elf's sallow-skinned chest and pushed it beneath the stone. Using the sword blade as a lever, I pried the evil-looking artifact out of Voron's body.

The crystal shard flared bright red for a moment, faded to a dull gray color, and then became clear again.

"Do you think it's safe to touch that?" I asked.

Ruhail took a deep breath and strode across the clearing toward me. She avoided looking at the severed heads, and crouched down next to the spirit crystal with her staff clutched in her hand. Green, glimmering mist showered down upon the shard, and she reached out a pale hand from within the folds of her cloak. She picked it up and turned it over.

"It is safe," she said. "But it would not hurt to burn it with the bodies."

"Will Kalia need to see the evidence?" I asked. "Or should we deal with it now?"

"The sooner the better, I think," Ruhail said. She tossed the crystal shard into the flames where it burst in a flare of blood-red smoke. "We should destroy all the artifacts gathered for this monstrous ritual."

I shrugged and heaved Voron's head by its hair into the middle of the bonfire. I bent down and did the same to the two troll's heads. Then I cleaned my sword and sheathed it before dragging the rest of the traitorous elf's remains onto the pyre. It wasn't until I saw his flesh blackening and crackling on his bones that I allowed myself to feel a moment of triumph at his defeat.

"Loghann," Ruhail said. "You still didn't tell me how you got here."

"I was here with you from the moment the trolls brought you into this clearing." I wiped my hands on my thighs and finally took the dryad in my arms. She yielded to me instantly, her head resting in the crook of my shoulder. "I found a way to hide myself between realms, like what happened in the cave. I only wish I could have told you and eased your fear."

"I'm so glad you came," she said. "What he was planning..."

She shuddered. Then she pushed herself away from me and turned to face the spider queen.

"I am honored to meet you Queen Venemia," she said with a bow. "I thank you for your help in rescuing my sisters."

"You are most welcome, Spirit of the Forest," the queen replied with her own bow. "I do not forget my place within this realm."

Ruhail stiffened against my side and shook her head. "I am but a servant of the Spirit. And I will repay my debt to you as such."

The spider queen smiled again, her red lips stretching so wide across her pale face that it looked painful. Her glossy black eyes widened and she cocked her head.

"Perhaps now you are but a servant of the Spirit," she said. "But I am old enough to recall that ritual. Had the elf succeeded in his corruption of your flesh, the Spirit of the Forest would have been crushed. Is that not so?"

Ruhail nodded slowly. "He was going to sacrifice himself and me in order to open the door between our realms. A creature of pure chaos defiling a creature of pure order in such a way... it would certainly have killed us both. But in the moment of our destruction, the door would have opened. The forest realm would surely have fallen."

A chill passed over my flesh, and I pulled Ruhail closer to me. I wrapped her in my arms and kissed the top of her head. "Thankfully it didn't."

I was grateful she had been spared the violation and death that Voron had planned for her, but the thought of Drakkus and his hordes invading and defiling this realm made my stomach twist in knots.

"We aren't finished here, though," I said, straightening up suddenly. "We have to join the fight at the temple."

Queen Venemia surprised me by bursting out in a trill of laughter that sent an instinctive terror through my bones, the way I might feel looking over my shoulder and seeing a mountain lion stalking me.

"The fight was over the moment my soldiers arrived. You were right to seek my help, Loghann," she said, striding across the clearing with her black armor gleaming in the firelight. A strand of white hair fell down from her spiked helmet and a part of me longed to wrap it around my fingers and pull her toward me.

The more logical part of my brain screamed internally and fought the urge to flee. She dragged a pointed fingernail down my sword arm, sending a feeling like a thousand tiny spiders crawling across my flesh.

"Few have braved asking favors of the Arachana," she said. "We do not grant them lightly. But if you are interested in future... partnerships... I might be convinced to cooperate again."

"I will remember." My voice came out tight, but I managed to keep it from trembling. I had no doubt that if I took the spider queen up on her suggestion before I was ready, that she would gleefully make me pay for my hubris. Still, I couldn't deny my attraction to the ferocious woman. Once I had come fully into my own power, conquering Queen Venemia might be exactly the kind of challenge I was looking for.

She smiled at me like she knew exactly what I was thinking.

Then she turned to Ruhail and bowed low, fixing the dryad with her glossy black-eyed gaze. "Forget your debt, child. I will take my payment in the blood of Drakkus's minions. There shall be plenty to spare. Speaking of which, I must join my soldiers in their victory feast."

"Won't you come with us to the temple?" Ruhail asked. She leaned against me as if she wanted to back away from the spider queen but didn't want to appear rude.

"No," Queen Venemia said. "I have other things to attend to. Give my regards to the priestess." She flashed me a slightly evil grin. "Leave the clean up to us."

A swirl of white fog swept into the clearing and when it dissipated the formidable woman was gone. The nymphs gaped at the spot where she had been standing, their over-sized breasts heaving with excitement.

"Maybe we should go with her," the blond one said. She raked her fingers through her tangled hair and smeared troll blood on her forehead. "I had no idea violence could be so exhilarating! Almost as good as sex."

The one with short, messy brown hair pursed her blow-up-doll lips and put her hands on her hips. "She could have asked if we wanted to come."

The naked nymphs sent a surge of arousal through me that I had managed to hold off in the presence of Queen Venemia. But with Voron defeated and the battle winding down, other primal urges were beginning to replace the need to fight.

I pulled Ruhail in to me and kissed the side of her neck, revelling in the sweet herbal scent of her skin. "Do all creatures of order have a vicious streak?"

"They're nymphs." The dryad shrugged and leaned into my embrace. "They follow their passions. Being a creature of order doesn't necessarily mean a being 'good' in a moral sense. They are bound by certain rules that prevent them from being actively destructive in their passions, but..."

"There's no rule that says they can't enjoy defending themselves?"

"You did request their help," she said.

"And you did promise them something in exchange for that help, didn't you?"

"...Ye-esss..." She drew out the word uncertainly.

The Lord of Chaos had been thwarted, for now, but I knew our victory would be short lived. The humming power in my chest told me that Drakkus was growing stronger despite this defeat, as if there was some kind of connection between the two of us. Until I took the scepter of power and became Emperor of the Five Realms, Drakkus would continue to grow in strength and to strike at our weak points.

Which meant I had to do everything I could to grow in power until then.

"Speaking of rules," I said. "I believe I saved your life again. Which means—"

She turned and pressed a finger to my lips. Then she drew down the pale green hood and stared up at me with her bright emerald eyes. Her auburn hair fell in rich waves around her beautiful face. She pressed her full lips against mine. When she pulled away, she said, "I am bonded to you again."

"That's what I thought," I said, pulling away. "Too bad. I guess my plans for you will have to wait until you return the favor."

"What!?" Ruhail shrieked. Her cheeks burned as red as the flames of the bonfire. "You can't just... I never wanted you to... We've already..."

"I cannot in good conscience take you the way I want to take you while you are bonded to me," I said, grinning at the dryad's distress. "But I will let you watch while I demonstrate on these two."

She spluttered angrily as I waved the nymphs toward me. They eagerly bounced across the clearing, the flames dancing over their naked bodies with a kind of Bacchanalian magic.

Blood throbbed in my cock as the blond nymph shoved Ruhail out of the way and pressed her bare breasts against my armored chest.

"Does that mean you want to play?" she said, staring up at me with startlingly yellow eyes.

Her brunette friend squeezed in next to her and slipped her little fingers into the top of my pants. "Why didn't you say so?"

"Why don't you two come back to the temple with us and get cleaned up," I said, lifting the blond nymph's heavy breasts up to my face and biting one of her nipples gently. "I believe I have a promise to make good on."

Ruhail stomped her foot. "I can't believe you!"

I grinned at the dryad over my new prize. "You are the one who made the promise. How many nymphs did you say there were?"

"Ugh!" She turned and strode off through the forest toward the temple.

I wrapped my arms around the nymphs' waists and followed her.

Chapter 26

When Ruhail, the nymphs, and I arrived at the temple, my high spirits dissipated. The beautiful gardens of the temple grounds had been crushed into a pulpy, muddy mess. The ornate bridges had been burned. The walls of the temple were seared with streaks of soot and blood. Ruhail and the nymphs huddled close to me as we made our way through the ruins, the stench of smoke and death burning all around us. We may have won this battle, but we didn't do so without loss.

Still, word of our victory against Drakkus's army spread through the Ring Wood like wildfire. Many creatures who had hidden themselves during the conflict came out to help clean up the messes made by the hordes of trolls, goblins, ogres, and dire wolves. Queen Venemia made good on her promise to clean up the battlefield. She and her soldiers bound up and dragged off the bodies of Drakkus's slain minions, and helped the survivors meet their fate as well.

Maggi, the old crone, helped the spider queen to suss out other pockets of hidden chaos warriors that had been secreted about the perimeter of the temple grounds. Screeches of glee could be heard throughout the forest as the Arachana hunted down their fleeing prey. Soon, the trees around the temple were filled with the glittering green mist of healing magic as nymphs, dryads, and green witches soothed the wounds of the Spirit of the Forest.

As much as I had teased Ruhail about repaying her promise to the nymphs, I struggled to regain my post-battle enthusiasm for play time. We were quiet as we walked through the empty stone corridors of the temple, making our way toward the priestess's pavilion. Our footsteps echoed around us like whispers from beyond the grave. Even the nymphs weren't giggling anymore. The back of my throat ached like I was holding back a scream and dread seeped in on me from all sides.

Priestess Kalia had been working to defend the temple against Voron's magical onslaught and, for the first time, I realized she may not have been up to the task. Even Iymbryl, when I had stopped to talk to her, hadn't seen the priestess since the fighting began.

When we passed through the stone archway into the lush gardens of the interior courtyard, I breathed a sigh of relief. Here, at least, the temple remained unscathed. I hoped Kalia would be safe too. The sweet floral scent of pink blossoms hanging from the trees, and the steady roar of the waterfall behind the temple, gave the pavilion a serene, dreamlike quality after the hard realities of the battle-field outside.

But as we climbed the stairs to the top of the pavilion, and the dais came into view, my heart leaped into my throat. The priestess lay on her back, her golden hair spilling over the raised platform. Her tawny complexion was wan and wasted, her closed eyes sunken.

"Kalia!" I shouted, rushing toward her. I knelt next to the priestess and lifted her head onto my lap. Her skin was cool and clammy, but she was breathing. "She's alive. We have to do something."

Ruhail placed her hands on the priestess's cheeks. "Her magical reserves are overdrawn. She's probably in shock."

"Will she be alright?" The blond nymph asked, her strange yellow eyes wide with worry.

"I have never seen someone so drained of their essence," Ruhail said, tears streaming down her face. "We have to find a way to bring her spirit back to her body. She's gone too far to get back on her own."

"What do you mean?" My voice shook. "Where is her spirit?"

Ruhail shook her head. "She must have attempted to repair the protection spells from the spirit realm. But even a priestess should not attempt such a thing alone. It is too easy to get lost, wandering with the Spirit of the Forest."

"We can help." The messy-haired brunette nymph climbed up on the dais next to Kalia, and snuggled her naked limbs in against the priestess's side. "Come, Sunni."

I held Kalia's head while the nymphs pressed themselves against her body, like she was suffering from hypothermia. Ruhail gripped her staff tightly in one pale hand, chanted something under her breath as she showered the priestess with the soft green glow of her healing magic.

Instinctively, I reached into the core of my own power and willed the priestess to wake. Voron was dead, Drakkus had been thwarted, the temple saved. I refused to lose Kalia when we had gained so much. My own magic, invisible to the others, appeared to me as a blinding blue-white light. Fine coils of power erupted from my fingertips, wrapping themselves around the priestess like jolts of electricity spreading across a stormy sky. My magic mingled with Ruhail's to create a kind of cocoon around the ailing priestess. I didn't know how I was doing it, exactly, but I felt some of my own power transferring into Kalia's body, urging her back to life.

We stayed like that for what seemed like hours. The nymphs fell asleep, curled up against Kalia's sides. Ruhail's eyelids began to droop. I felt like I'd run a marathon and been turned around at the finish line to do it all again, but I kept pushing out energy into Kalia from the invisible source inside me.

Ruhail collapsed, her body falling across Kalia's. Her shoulders shook as she wept. "I can't do any more. She is lost, Loghann. We can't help her."

Tears stung my eyes. My joints began to ache and my limbs shook with exhaustion, but I refused to give up. What good was all this power if I couldn't save Kalia after all she'd done for me? Why would I want to be emperor of a world so unjust? I would save the priestess or I would die trying; I refused to accept anything else.

The strands of burning white magic seared my fingers like fire now as I drew on deeper and deeper wells of power within myself. I sensed the hardened crystal core of strength within me, that part of myself that only awakened since I arrived in this world. It pulsed violently in my chest like it was about to shatter.

Good, I thought. Let it break. Let me give Kalia the power she transferred to me, and all of mine as well. This world needs her more than it needs me.

"Loghann, no!" Ruhail's voice came to me as if from another world, it sounded so far way. "You have to stop. You're going to hurt yourself!"

But I didn't stop. I closed my eyes and reached deep inside for every last shred of magic I could sense and I pushed it out of myself and into the priestess. It was like shoving against a brick wall, but I sensed it shifting.

Suddenly, it was as if the wall disappeared and I was flying over the edge of a cliff, with my own body hurtling away from me. Cool mists swirled around me as I fell, the black shape of me receding into the distance like a shadow. I could see nothing but the mist, feel nothing but the stomach-dropping sensation of freefall. Fear pounded through my veins. Where was I? What had I done?

Then it was over. I found myself standing in a lush, mossy glade in an ancient forest. A massive tree, like many different trunks wrapped together into one prehistoric-looking specimen, stood at the center of the clearing. Pale tendrils of mist swirled around the base of the tree and in between the shadowy trunks of the surrounding forest. And Kalia, draped in swaths of sheer purple fabric, lay at the roots. She looked like she was sleeping.

I ran to her and grabbed her by the shoulders, screaming, "Kalia, wake up!"

"Loghann?" she opened her strange, violet eyes dreamily and smiled at me. "There you are. I've been looking everywhere for you!"

"What are you doing here?" I said, my voice shaking with relief. "You have to come back with me. Back to—" I looked around us. "Where are we, anyway?"

"We are in the Heart of the Forest," she said and caressed my cheek. "The Spirit has been healed, but I couldn't find my way back without you. It seemed so far away."

"Your body is back in the pavilion," I said. "We thought you were dying. Come back with me."

"You did it, Loghann." She smiled softly, her eyes sparkling up at me. As she sat up the fabric she was wrapped in fell away, baring a smooth, tanned shoulder. "You saved the temple. Your plan worked."

"You held off their advances," I said. "You kept them away until I could bring help. We did it together."

Kalia pushed herself up onto her knees, and let the rest of her robes fall away. She placed her hands against my chest and pushed me backward. I was surprised to feel her cool skin against my own bare flesh. When I looked down, I saw that I was completely naked. She said, "Only priestesses of the forest realm have ever been to this place. I never thought you would come, but here you are."

I fell back on my hands as she crawled over my legs and settled herself into my lap. My body instantly responded to her presence, and she reached down to grip my shaft in her little hand. I groaned as she squeezed.

"We should get back," I said, without conviction. "The others will be worried."

She pushed me down onto the moss and pressed her hot mouth against the side of my neck. My arms and shoulders seemed to sink into the earth and when I tried to move them, I found I couldn't. She bit the skin on my chest gently and rolled her tongue around each of my nipples sending shivers of pleasure over my body.

"I submitted to you, Loghann," she said. "Here, you will submit to me."

As her mouth moved farther and farther down my torso, I found myself unwilling to protest. Every kiss from her lips sent tremors of pleasure through my skin, like every nerve in my body was connected to the throbbing erection between my legs. The feeling of her firm little breasts pressing against my cock as she lapped at my skin was enough to drive me insane with lust. Not being able to move heightened the sensation. Her hard nipples touched my thighs as she lowered her full lips over the head of my cock, sucking teasingly at the tip as she stroked me with her hand.

I gritted my teeth and closed my eyes as she dragged the tip of her tongue up and down my shaft. She dug her fingernails into my thighs and dragged them over my skin as she licked at my balls. The heat of her tongue and the cold misty air of the glade created a discordant sensation that kept all of my nerves on edge. I wanted to grab her and force myself into her throat, but I couldn't move. I groaned in frustration.

When I opened my eyes again, the priestess was straddling my hips with her thick tawny thighs spread wide. She stroked my shaft with her hand and rubbed the tip of my cock against the warm, wet lips between her legs. I longed to thrust up and take her as I had before, but she teased me infuriatingly. She pinched one of her nipples between her fingers as she rubbed my cock against her clit and moaned.

The tease was working on both of us. She rocked her hips faster as she slid over my shaft, slathering me in her juices. The nipples of her firm little breasts were so tight with excitement that they looked painful. I knew if I said anything she'd just make me wait longer, so I watched as she pleasured herself with my body and imagined spraying my cum all over her belly and tits. Pressure mounted at the base of my spine as she moaned louder.

She gripped my shaft and held me still, lowering her pussy over the tip of my cock. "Oh, Loghann..."

"Fuck, Kalia," I said, suddenly unable to stay quiet. "You're killing me."

"I have to go slow," she whimpered, bouncing up and down on the tip and driving me crazy. "You're too big."

"Play with yourself," I said. "It will help."

She pressed a finger to my lips. "You submit to me."

But she slipped her fingers between her legs and drew the wetness over her lips and rubbed at her clit as she lowered herself even farther onto my cock.

Her pussy was unbelievably tight. The pressure of her inner walls squeezing my shaft was maddening. When she shifted up and down to help ease me inside of her, she went so slowly I wanted to scream.

But her cheeks were getting flushed and her chest was heaving as she rubbed her little clit and rocked her hips, and the slow build had my heart hammering like the most frantic fucking session.

Finally she got all of me inside her, and she sat with her round ass pressed against my thighs and her bare lips spread impossibly around the thickness of my cock. She rocked her hips while her fingers stroked at the center of pleasure between her legs. She began to bounce up and down.

Had I been able to move I would have grabbed her hips and fucked her until she screamed. But I couldn't. So I just watched as she used my body like a toy, focusing on the sensation of her muscles squeezing against me as she rode faster and faster. Her blond hair fell around her shoulders and her gorgeous purple eyes rolled back in her head as she lost herself in pleasure. My own pleasure mounted with hers.

Kalia's fingers rubbed harder, and she tossed her head back and moaned. Her entire body shook as the orgasm took hold of her, and watching her cum was like a dam breaking. A gush of hot wetness from her pussy surged over my cock and my body tensed as I exploded inside her. She kept moaning and rocking, her clenching muscles milking every last drop from me.

But when she reached down to pull my shaft out of her pussy, another burst of cum sprayed up, splashing her belling and her little tits with a stream of pearly white semen.

"Not done," I grunted.

The priestess hovered above me with my cum dripping down the insides of her thighs.

"I'll help," she said and scooted her bottom back so that she could lick up every drop that had spilled out of her. When she was done cleaning my belly and thighs, she sank her mouth onto my cock. She sucked and swirled her tongue as she bobbed her golden-haired head up and down, watching me with her piercing violet eyes. A second wave of orgasm rose up within me. I cried out as it broke, and I unleashed another burst of cum into her throat.

She moaned with pleasure. I could feel her throat muscles tightening as she swallowed without backing off my cock.

Finally, when I was spent, the mossy earth released me and Kalia collapsed into my arms. We lay naked in the glade, sleeping, for what seemed like hours before the priestess stirred and said, "It is time to go back. Are you ready?"

"Do we have to?" I said, rolling over on my side. I nuzzled at her neck and breathed in the sweet, earthy scent of her skin and the surrounding woods. "I could stay here with you forever."

"I would like that very much." She giggled as my stubbled chin tickled her. "But there is more for you in the world than just this. Time passes more slowly here. If we go back now, they will hardly know you've gone anywhere."

I pushed myself up into a sitting position and pulled the priestess into my lap. She leaned against my chest and I wrapped my arms around her narrow shoulders.

"We tried to revive you for hours before I found my way here," I said. "You must have been stuck here for ages."

"It feels like years, Loghann," she said with a sigh. "I want to go home."

I kissed her one last time as the mists of the glade swirled, enveloping us in the cool, white fog.

"Then let's go," I said.

The threads of magic that had pulled me into this mysterious glade tugged me back, and we drifted, hand in hand, back toward the real world.

Chapter 27

Kalia and I came back to our bodies with a start, like waking from one of those falling dreams. Ruhail and the nymphs stared at us in confusion. Iymbryl and the old witch, Maggi, stood behind them with concern on their faces.

The crone cackled and clapped her wizened hands together. "You see! I told you he went travelling. Looks like he found the priestess, too!"

"Impossible," Ruhail said, her usually pale face a deathly shade of white.

"Not that impossible, I guess." I shrugged my shoulders and stretched my arms, feeling like I'd been sitting in the same cramped position for too long. "I did find her. What happened, exactly?"

"Loghann, you were dead," Ruhail said. She pushed her auburn hair away from her face and stared at me with her bright green eyes filled with tears. "I felt your spirit leave your body. Your heart stopped. I thought I was going to die too."

"I'm sorry." I pulled the dryad into my arms, where she sobbed and trembled. "I didn't mean for that to happen. But I'm okay and so are you. So is Kalia. We're all safe."

Kalia sat up and rubbed Ruhail's back. "The Spirit of the Forest and the temple are safe too. We did it. We saved the Ring Wood."

The naked nymphs, still streaked with troll blood, jumped into the air, dancing a spritely if slightly obscene dance around the priestess's pavilion. The blond nymph grabbed her friend and hugged her, squashing their enormous breasts together. "We saved the Ring Wood, Rosa!"

I was wearing pants and leather armor again and watching the bubble-bodied females bouncing and rubbing themselves against one another made my confining clothing extremely uncomfortable. Now that I knew everyone was safe, I didn't think a play date with the sultry nymphs was a bad idea at all.

"What happened?" Kalia asked. "Tell me everything that happened after you left."

I managed to tear my eyes from the distracting duo and Ruhail and I told our story, though I had to leave out some parts thanks to the prophecy I couldn't share. As I spoke, Maggi's watery eyes bored into me, and her wrinkled lips spread into a crazed, toothless grin.

"I knew you were the one," she said. "My sister spoke of you in bits and pieces, though she never revealed what she knew."

"Your sister?" I asked. Then I remembered the vision my mother had shown me, of the old woman dead at the foot of my cradle after delivering her prophecy. "You're one of the Fae?"

She nodded her head gleefully and clapped her hands again. "It's true, it's true! Drakkus captured me by playing an ancient trick, trapped me as I was gazing at my own reflection in an enchanted mirror. I should never have fallen for it, but even I am not immune to my beauty."

She said this without any hint of sarcasm or irony, and I wrinkled my brow at the old woman.

She winked at me and continued. "When the Lord of Chaos dragged me out of the northern isles to this forsaken realm, I was transformed of course. We cannot appear as in our true, immortal forms outside of the land of the fae folk. It is our curse, and why we never leave the northern isles unless compelled to do so by a vision, as my sister was."

"So you know who I am," I said. "Did you tell Drakkus about me?"

Maggi's wrinkled face puckered in a frown. "I spoke around the truth as much as I was able. He knew of you, though not specifically who you are. I fear you may have revealed yourself to him in your battle against his general, though. He was in the chaos realm, watching the ritual as surely as you were from this realm. No, I did not tell him. But he knows you."

"What are we going to do?" Ruhail said, her voice cracking with emotion. "Drakkus will gather his forces and attack again. How many times can we defeat him?"

"He will not attack the forest realm again," Priestess Kalia said. She stood from the dais and strode across the pavilion to embrace Iymbryl. The elf guard's rigid posture sank into her priestess's arms. Kalia removed her helmet and let the blond elf's pale hair fall free over her golden armor. "You have all fought valiantly, and Queen Venemia has disposed of Drakkus's minions remaining in this realm. With Voron slain, and the Book of Elders safe... where is the book?"

My heart clenched with panic, and I cursed loudly. I had forgotten the book on the slab-stone table. But Ruhail stood and walked toward the priestess.

"Here," she said, and withdrew the book from some hidden compartment of her pale green robes. She gave me a sly look. "I took it when you were busy ogling the nymphs."

"How did you hide that in there?" I said. "You weren't carrying it."

The dryad shrugged and grinned. "Magic."

"Thank you," Priestess Kalia said, taking the book from Ruhail and wrapping her arms around it tightly. "With Voron slain, the book safe, and the protective spells surrounding the temple repaired, we will be safe from future assaults."

"How can you be sure?" Iymbryl shook off her relief at seeing the priestess safe and straightened her spine. "They've been infiltrating our realm for years. We must remain vigilant."

"We will," Kalia said, nodding. A fierce light blazed in her purple eyes. "I've found the areas Voron weakened throughout the realm. His meddling allowed the Lord of Chaos to take advantage of the blood moons, and leak his minions into the Ring Wood. As I walked with the Spirit of the Forest, I healed those wounds. We are safe, but..."

"But what?" Tension gripped my shoulders and I realized I had been holding my breath.

"But Drakkus has sown discord in all the realms." Maggi's ancient voice croaked and she shook her head sadly. "The forest realm is safe, for now, but he will move on to other realms. Your fight is not yet over, young prince."

Tears brimmed in Kalia's eyes. "It's true. I must send you away, Loghann. You must visit my sisters in the other realms."

"I don't want to leave," I said. "There is so much to do here to put things right."

"The Azurian Sea is not far," Kalia said. "Cordelia, the priestess of the ocean temple, will want to speak with you about what happened here. You must convince her of who you are."

Iymbryl tossed her pale blond hair over her shoulder and gave me a scornful look. "I will take care of the priestess and the temple. You've done enough damage."

"No." Kalia wrapped an arm around the elf guard's waist. "I am sending you to aid Loghann. He needs you more than I do."

Iymbryl paled with anger. "What?!"

"I don't need her," I scoffed.

"What about me?" Ruhail said. "I want to come with you too. I've travelled the realms, I can be of help."

"You will go with him," Kalia said, giving Iymbryl a stern look. "That's an order. Just be grateful that I am not ordering you to submit to him as you do me."

Iymbryl ground her teeth together loudly.

"Well, there is still the matter of our bet," I said. "I might have you submitting to me after all..."

She curled her lip in a snarl. "It goes both ways, boy soldier."

"Enough," Kalia said. "Iymbryl and Ruhail will accompany you at least until you meet with Cordelia. From there, I will let you decide who your companions are. But Iymbryl must go. She will vouch for you as my personal guard. Ruhail, I cannot thank you enough for volunteering. Your help will be invaluable."

I swallowed my pride. "I'm sure you know best, priestess. I am loathe to leave you so soon, but the safety of the realms is more important than anything. When will we leave?"

"As soon as possible," she said. "I'm sorry, Loghann. Go to the baths, we will prepare a small victory dinner while you bathe. Tonight you will sleep in my arms. And tomorrow you must go."

I felt immensely tired at the thought of it, but I nodded my head.

"If that is what you wish."

I turned to go, the weight of my responsibilities to the realm laying heavily on my shoulders. Only days ago, I had been a purposeless entrepreneur in Denver, battling against the crippling self-doubt and abandonment by my parents. Now, I was in a fantasy realm, surrounded by beautiful women, with two parents who gave their lives to protect me, and I faced another scale of battles entirely.

But that powerful core inside me thrummed with energy, washing away my fears. This was the right path. I could feel it with every fiber of my being. I was ready for the trials ahead.

"Uh, Loghann?" Ruhail's voice called out. "Aren't you forgetting something?"

I turned and raised my eyebrows at her. "What's that?"

She smacked the blond nymph's ample bottom. Sunni squealed.

"Yay! It's bath time!" Rosa grabbed her curvy friend and the two bounded toward me. "Let's play 'taken by the trolls!'"

They ran down the stairs and into the garden. I grinned over my shoulder at the dryad. "Well," I said. "Aren't you coming?"

She stomped her foot and pouted slightly. "Not if you insist on keeping me at arms-length because of this stupid life bond."

"Come on, Ruhail," I beckoned to her. The dryad rolled her eyes and slowly crossed the pavilion to me. I wrapped my arm around her waist and waved at the others.

Iymbryl scowled and Kalia waved with a smile on her face.

Maggi cackled again. "I knew he was the one!"

As Ruhail and I descended the stairs, I looked out at the golden rays of sunlight spilling down into the luscious temple gardens and breathed a sigh of contentment. I didn't know what tomorrow held, but for the first time in my life I knew I didn't want to be anywhere else in the world.

Or the universe for that matter.

"What are you smiling about?" Ruhail asked, taking my hand and staring dreamily into my eyes.

I squeezed her against my side and kissed her forehead.

"I was wondering," I said, "How many nymphs I have time to play with before we have to leave to-morrow."

"Ugh!" She slapped my arm and shoved me away.

I scooped her up over my shoulder. She kicked her legs and screamed, smacking my back with her hands. But her screaming turned to laughter as I ran through the garden, following the shrieks and squeals of the playful nymphs where they lounged on the rocks beneath the waterfall.

"Loghann Grenwyld," the dryad giggled. "You are impossible!"

I didn't bother to argue with her. I just tossed her into the water and began removing my armor.

There were many hours before sunrise, and I in-tended to enjoy them.

To be continued in
Elemental Empire 2...

Author's Note

Thank you so much for reading *Elemental Empire*! I hope you enjoyed your time with Logan Greenwood—aka Loghann Grenwyld—and his forays into the wild and enchanting world of the Empire of the Five Realms.

If you'd like to read the deleted scene of Loghann's play time with the nymphs you can sign up for my VIP Readers content. I will have at least one deleted scene and one NSFW artwork done for each book for my VIP Readers only. Don't miss out!

I plan to write a book for each of the five realms for this series, provided readers are happy with it and want more adventures. Please be sure to drop a review so I know I am, like Loghann, on the right path.

If you like my stuff, consider sharing a review in your favorite reading groups, too. I am, admittedly, a nobody in the HaremLit scene, and this is the only way I can hope to compete (I wish!) against the big names in the genre. Every little bit of visibility helps!

A big thanks to the admin teams over at Harem Lit and Harem Lit Readers on Facebook for their awesome reader groups, too. If you're not a member yet, you should definitely come have a peek at what's going on.

If you'd like to be notified when the next book drops, be sure to follow me on Amazon too. That way, if I get sent to the naughty books dungeon you'll still be able to find my stuff. You can also connect with me via these channels:

Email: contact@peternorthauthor.com
Facebook: www.facebook.com/peternorthbooks
Website: www.peternorthauthor.com

Thank you for taking a chance and supporting a brand new author. I couldn't do this without you!

Nymphs, naiads, and sirens... oh, my!

The adventure continues...
Summer 2022

Made in the USA
Coppell, TX
27 October 2022